Miles

by
Adam Henry Carriere

MW01536586

DISCLAIMER

A brief word to the ether-bots, lawyers, and aggrieved passed participants:

I'm told it is advisable to point out the story you're about to read is conspicuously a work of fiction. The furthest, most indistinct similitude between the imagined characters of this story and real persons, whether man or woman, living or dead, is the sheerest mishap of happenstance and in no way intended. To say it plain, no such persons as these ever walked God's green earth. Likewise, the occasions, affairs, and scenes of the story are similarly imagined, and exist nowhere but in air, ether, and one's own mind.

Adam Henry Carrière
Nevada, 2016

I

Men at some time are masters of their fates:
The fault is not in our stars,
But in ourselves, that we are underlings.
Julius Caesar

I stood there staring, and remembered.

We used to be able to feel the cold November wind through the closed window of our classroom. The panes were thin, and the wood around them old and rotting. The ugly radiator below the sill never kept up with the unwanted ventilation. The thin, leafless branches of the dark grey courtyard tree tapped and scratched against the window and side of our school building, an imposing, gothic horror of a place, surrounded by a prestigious and exclusive lakefront university, of which it was a nominal part. The entire Youth Pilot Institute facility had that wonderful air of benign decay so many of us confuse with elegance. In the hot and sticky Chicago summer, my school looked and felt like a mislaid Cambridge, while in the bitter winter, it could have been a proud embassy to a Hapsburg or Romanov court. The rainy spring brought images of the blossom around the Sorbonne, while in the toxic fragrance of a colorfully muted autumn, my favorite season, our school impressed you as a haunting remnant of our civilization's better days.

My fellow students had been a mixed lot: male and female, black, brown, yellow and white, Catholic and Protestant, Jew and Muslim, atheist and agnostic, Chicagoan and suburbanite. However, we shared two important similarities: we were all bright enough to be accepted into the place, and had families that could afford the Youth Pilot Institute's extortionate tuition, qualify for some remission, or have a ride on one of the Institute's famously lousy teams like I did.

Even though the Institute had no definitive dress code, we all dressed stylishly and well, hoping to blend in better with the energetic, high-brow college-types who buzzed back and forth through the school grounds during their class day, occasionally putting in grudging internship hours with us, as well. The lower grade kids looked like yuppies from Lilliput, while the bulk of the Institute's fashion independence came from the middle graders, who were at that age where a good deal of their individuality was derived from how they dressed. Rarely could you tell the difference between us upper graders and the collegians too many of us tried to emulate, except for a handful of misfits like me. I was in a "high-class hippie, low-class outdoorsman" phase in those heady days of my Junior year, rife with jeans, various combinations of t-shirts, sweaters, and flannel shirts, a brown suede fringed jacket if it was above freezing, a thick Navy pea coat liberated from my Dad if it wasn't, and hiking shoes, whose steel-tipped toes usefully served as concealed weapons, though I never had occasion to use them as such.

Our curriculum emphasized a classical, liberal arts education, delivered in a college seminar manner. It was all very progressive, to the point of being chic, but it actually made spending every weeknight in a pile of books, breaking your ass to be a scholar, seem fun. Our teachers were the font of this. Like the students, our "adult resources" represented virtually every demographic niche, from the tough old battle-axes that had forgotten more about geometry than an aeronautics engineer was ever likely to learn, to the middle-aged, ex-campus radicals cum social engineers who couldn't do anything else except teach. We also had our fair share of stereotypical schoolmarm history freaks, grandfatherly language dominies, and hyper-talented liberal arts maestros with fresh ink on their doctorates that scared everyone else on the staff because of their brains, degrees, and youth.

Nicolaus Matthias Székelyvon Straußenburg was one of these.

Just as there was no dress code, there was also no set way to refer to our teachers, except for the crazed and permanently menopausal Mrs. Jinak, who was known throughout the Institute as "The Psycho Bitch". One could be an invariably dull 'mister', like Mister Greene; or an aging 'professor' who ought to be at Yale or Stanford, but, like Professor Fleming, chose to write the texts they use there instead; or a military rank, for those middle-aged, ex-armed forces officers about to begin their decline, like Captain Selby; or 'doctor', for the conspiratorial ex-government scientists like Doctor Clemens, Ph.D. in biochemistry from the University of Porton, so we would maliciously gossip. As for the awfully young von Straußenburg? Well, our short, lemon-faced Principal Connelly (always a terse 'sir' to his face, but 'old boy' when he was out of earshot) snarled Nicolaus Matthias, harshly enunciated to emphasize his (implicitly unimpressive) heritage. Students who had the good fortune to attend his music classes just called him Nicolasha. He had only joined the faculty in that autumn of my eleventh year, but had quickly become everyone's favorite, including mine.

Nicolasha's parents came from the dwindling strains of both Saxon German and Hungarian in Communist Romania, violinists with their State Opera who had defected with their teenage son, already a prodigious cellist, when their company toured the eastern United States. The family was well-received by the close-knit arts community in Washington, D.C., and taken under the wing of another defector from the Soviet Union, a famous cellist who had become musical director and chief conductor for the National Symphony Orchestra. He saw to it that the Straußenburgs were taken aboard the NSO as soon as possible, and that young Nicolasha received the best music instruction available - namely, himself. As one of the only students of, arguably, the world's finest cellist, Nicolasha was blessed with unmatched instruction and attention, but cursed with the very high expectations that came with such an honor. His public debut, playing a Prokofiev concerto written for the elder cello master himself, was strangled in the grip of stage fright, producing a form and function disaster, an embarrassment to his parents, and a blow to his beloved mentor. So unnerved was Nicolasha that he retreated to Georgetown University, where he earned all three degree levels in music history and instruction on academic scholarship, but never played in front of an audience again. We student types were exceptions to this. Even then, it was never the cello.

I guess Nicolasha never watched the news or read anything in the papers about child molesters, or the sad, very American spectacle of gossip, charges, lawyers, reporters, lawsuits, book and movie deals, talk show visits, and general strife that accompany such stories (regardless if they be true or not), because he was the warmest and most openly affectionate teacher any of us have ever had, and didn't seem to give a damn to what anyone else would or could think. Everyone got a kind hand on their shoulder, a gentle rub of the hair, a fond touch on the arm, a kindly grin, or an affectionate bear hug, a hug as big as old Siebenbürgen (or Erdély, or now as way back then, Transylvania – Nicolasha had a mouthful of names, so it seemed natural where he came from did, too). Sometimes you got hugged alone, and sometimes you shared the hug with four others, but it was always done with a wide smile and a gregarious laugh, and was a full and tight hug, not one of those cheesy hugs relatives give each other. The only people who were safe from Nicolasha were his fellow teachers, who didn't talk much to him (and he didn't talk much to back), and the Principal, who saved all his hugs for his seven adopted children at home. Everyone giggled and blushed when they became the object of Nicolasha's beaming attention, but a lot of us were sustained by the glow he brought to the hallowed halls and classrooms of the Youth Pilot Institute. I know I was.

My class had music history for last period, around two-thirty p.m. It was always a wonderful way to end our long, dreary day. You could feel the change in atmosphere just by walking in the classroom, which had pictures and posters of all the great classical composers surrounding a map of Europe on the wall opposite our leaky windows, and was littered with virtually every musical instrument and tool you could imagine, including a stand-up piano that Nicolasha usually sat on when he lectured (and leapt off of to make a point). He could efficiently demonstrate a few notes on most of them, but really swept into our hearts when he would seize our sole violin to perform whole stanzas of a particular piece or composer. Nicolasha seemed to know volumes about the masters and all their works, from Handel all the way to the 20th Century composers, which we could tell were Nicolasha's real favorites.

Nicolasha and I became friends on that particularly raw autumn afternoon, a day I can remember like it was yesterday, and not entire years ago. The dingy grey sky was covered in a familiar November cloud blanket and was filled with a sharp wind, blowing the leftover leaves along the bleak sidewalks and hardening lawns. We had been grilled in an oral quiz by Professor Tanaka, our Asian History teacher, and just finished an essay test in Italian from Signore Abbado - this was how our teachers liked to finish things up before a holiday. No matter what Nicolasha had planned, it would be a relief. As we filed into the room, he smiled at each of us in turn from atop the piano, violin in hand. I took my usual seat in the first desk nearest the door and readied my music notebook in the customary silence of the room.

We were a well-behaved class, unusual, I suppose, since most of us were deep in the post-puberty adolescent blues, but it was easy to see why: we loved Nicolasha and everything about his class, we were usually shagged from our typical study routine by the time we got there, and none of us were very friendly with each other. We were all too diverse and out-of-water, as it was, to really become close. Our intellect and parental income tax brackets may have brought us there, but our disassociated neighborhoods (and suburbs) kept us from being much more than acquaintances. A lot of times it felt like we were in training to become our parents. Maybe that was part of our bond with Nicolasha. He made us feel like this big, warm family, at one with the music we listened so closely to.

It also occurred to me that Nicolaus Matthias Székelyvon Straußenburg was a little out-of-water with the rest of the world, and the only thing that kept him from completely separating from the outside was his passion for music.

Nicolasha's idea of a test was to tell us all about a composer, play little bits and pieces from his body of work on the record player or right there in class with an appropriate instrument, and then, have us listen to a different full-length composition and write a descriptive essay about whatever images, thoughts, or feelings the music inspired in us. This beat the hell out of reading and re-reading your textbook and notes for a couple of hours the night before, and trying to spit it all out the next day.

Nicolasha had spent the last few days telling us about Dmitri Shostakovich, and, boy, what a chord those lectures struck in me. I especially liked the newer guys, like Bela Bartok, Paul Hindemith, Richard Strauss, and Benjamin Britten, because there was just so much more oomph in their stuff for me. But Shostakovich? He was the best of all. Talk about <u>big</u> music. You could *hear* the tank battle taking place, right there in the middle of the Eighth Symphony! Some downright silly stuff, too, like any of his Ballet Suites, probably the real source for all that great, goofy music in the Warner Brothers cartoons. Nicolasha said that if orchestral music had a fifth gear, Shostakovich was it.

Thus did I make not one but two friends from east of Vienna that autumn.

We all got ready to write as Nicolasha shut the classroom door and turned on the phonograph. The *Age of Gold* Suite emerged. The Introduction, its nervous, playful woodwinds chased by the string section, warned off by the urgent crash of the percussives, leading into a sneaky, childlike march that ends with a militaristic waltz. I saw many of the other guys begin to write, attracted to the hint of martial fervor in the beat. Then the Adagio softly began, a pastoral, longing melody carried by a flute against the strings. I later read this was scored as a seduction scene between a devilish Western ballerina and a good-hearted Red Army soldier. Hm.

Nicolasha's wide, light blue eyes caught mine staring at his face, a full-bodied, closely-shaved face with unkempt, unsettled dark blond hair and the thin nose, jaw bone, and eyebrows of strong family lines that had been softened by a softer lifestyle than that enjoyed by those ancestors who had contributed to his gene pool. His eyes plunged into mine with undisguised melancholy as he put the violin to his cheek, closely accompanying the record's soloist to the hypnotic gypsy stanza that was enriched by the orchestra behind it, flowing onward until the background players ceased and the solo violins of the recording and Nicolasha played in flawless unison for a few magical seconds, twisting the notes downward until the clarinets, strings, and flutes rejoined them. My teacher left off there with a self-effacing shrug and another glance toward me. I was embarrassed, and quickly started writing.

The famous xylophone Polka followed, attracting many of the girls to their notebooks, and finally, the proud, peasant Dance, a tense, raucous spin that really has to be a ball for a musician to play. But my mind was still on the violin solo in the Adagio. I heard such sadness and longing there, something I could identify with at that point in my little life. Nicolasha's eyes seemed so far away. Did he see his parents? His boyhood friends still inside ghastly Ceausescu's Romania? His old home in Sibiu?

Home. Now there was a real joke for me. It had been a joke for a few years by then, but really turned into a laugh-a-minute that autumn. My home was a distinctly unmusical one in those halcyon Carter days, in many respects. I was bored to tears with the gooey, synthesized mush Top-40 music had become, and was proud of being the only member of my class that had neither seen "Saturday Night Fever", nor bought its soundtrack. All of a sudden, here came this young bear of a teacher, a real-life *human* teacher, completely in love with all these dead composers who got talked about and played with openly expressed love, love which flowed right into all of us. And that was it for me. I had become a regular listener to a small, "mom & pop" classical radio station, and went out and bought almost every record Nicolasha played in class, much to the chagrin of my Dad, who had evidently come to the conclusion that a Brink's armored car might actually go to the cemetery with him when he died, because he resented my acquisitiveness, or the impermanent happiness the music gave me, I couldn't tell.

Our eyes met again, and I knew. Nicolasha saw all of this, and let me see something inside of him, whatever it was. I was eight years younger than he was, yet he trusted me, which I thought was pretty cool.

The final bell rang. The rest of my classmates threw in their papers and charged out the door to begin the much-anticipated Turkey Day weekend. I had put the finishing touches on my last sentence and handed it to Nicolasha, who stood near me in the doorway, wishing his students an enjoyable Thanksgiving, a happy holiday, a safe weekend, and a good evening for good measure. I gathered my books and put on my Dad's old pea coat while Nicolasha followed suit with his papers and the KGB-style black leather trench he had worn since the cold weather began, probably the only piece of clothing he owned that was worth more than twenty bucks.

(Nicolasha had two suit jackets to his name, one grey and the other brown, both tweed and fallen on hard times, as well as a couple of identical pairs of tight blue jeans, white button-down shirts, and a few lackluster knit ties, all in earth tones. He never wore a belt, or any other jewelry, and had a single pair of black loafers worn with a series of grey wool socks, all in desperate need of replacement. What did he do with his salary, I used to wonder, gamble?)

"You played that solo really well, *Freiherr* von Straußenburg."

He swatted my butt with a sheaf of papers. "You're the only one who calls me that."

"And pronounces it correctly," I added with a grin.

"It is one of my favorite Shostakovich melodies. I could not resist." He tucked the violin case under his arm and waited for me to exit before him.

"It sure is sad, though. Are you thinking of home when you listen to it?" I peered at the album cover in Nicolasha's brown leather tote.

"Home?" He handed me the record.

"You know, Siebenbürgen," noting the album number in my mind.

"Nobody calls it that anymore."

We walked down the cavernous, nearly empty hallway, past a couple of lower graders, who got patted on their backs and shoulders while they bundled up at their lockers. He remained silent until we got outside, where a few parents waited in their idling cars for their kids. The sky was already beginning to darken, and the cold lake wind hit us hard on the face.

"It certainly feels like Siebenbürgen in the winter today!" His rich, pleasant voice had only a tiny trace of accent. I went to give the album back to him, but he held up an unlined hand. "You can have that, if you would like. I have a different reading at home."

I smiled happily. "Are you sure? This is really cool. Thanks, Nicolasha."

He put his free arm around my shoulders and gave me a gentle cuddle. "Happy Thanksgiving." My eyes closed with a smile as I leaned into his embrace.

I thanked him again and ran off to catch my southbound commuter train. Up on the thick wooden beams of the platform, I watched Nicolasha walk slowly towards the lake, and waved at him when he turned around to glance at something. A silver double-decked electric train rolled to a halt in front of me. I couldn't see if he waved back.

II

A surfeit of the sweetest things
The deepest loathing to the stomach brings.
A Midsummer Night's Dream

The turkey was dry and tepid. The cabbage was strained poorly, the mashed potatoes weren't mashed very well, the stuffing had too much celery in it, and nobody looked twice at the lima beans, not even my mother, who prepared the meal. A com-pletely inconsequential football game between two teams who were already out of the playoffs droned on in the background. Every light in the living room, kitchen, and family room was on, yet, the small dining room in which we struggled through the Thanks-giving meal seemed ill-lit. Certainly, my spirits were.

I think my family was cursed.

My mom, Frederika, was a tall, well-proportioned woman with thick, dramatic brown hair. A real hard case, some cop might have said. As passionate as she was hard, the kind of passion that let the heart and the soul control a life that would otherwise have been regimented and accomplished, passion that remains an anomaly for a pure-bred Hessian.

Her parents gave up a small foundry and the rest of their family in Hesse after Hitler took over. The rest of their relatives died during the war. They moved into a small apartment above a bakery in Roseland, the largely Catholic, multi-ethnic neighborhood on the far south side of Chicago. Her father went to work at the nearby steel mills, and her mother worked in the bakery downstairs. Mom was born a year after that, right there in the bakery. She grew up to be a strong-willed, bright woman, raised by the hard-working women of the bakery. Grandfather died in an accident at the mill when she was ten, but they were able to make it through on the last of their savings and the kindness of the bakery women.

OK. When Mom was downstairs one morning, she heard the women gossiping about one of their neighbors, a Polish laborer with two young boys. The laborer had gotten blind drunk the night before, which had been his wedding anniversary. Mom was intrigued. He was despondent over his wife's death to tuberculosis earlier that year, and confided to the bartender that his younger boy, Simon, wasn't really his, but rather the illegiti-mate son of his sister from Cracow, who fell in love with a young German Jew refugee. They both died during the war, too. He had been visiting Poland weeks before the invasion, and she gave him her baby to take back to America. My Mom went to school with Alex and Simon, and had a crush on both of them. They were inseparable, but polar opposites: Simon was gregarious and visceral, tall for his age and wiry, with trim, curly brown hair and eyes, while Alex was a shy, artistic, private child, somewhat short and plain-looking. Their bond was baseball, and they attended almost every White Sox game together, first with their father, and then alone, as soon as they were old enough to take the street car to the park.

Simon and Alex came to the bakery one rainy afternoon. The White Sox were playing in Cleveland, and the ladies had the game on the radio. They came to buy some bread for dinner that night, but really wanted to hear the game. So, business being slow, the old ladies, Frederika, Simon, and Alex huddled around and listened with glee as the Pale Hose crushed the Tribe, 10 to 2. The whole time, Simon and Frederika's eyes were never far from each other. Before leaving, he asked my mom if she would like to come home and have dinner with them. My grandmother waved her off with a smile.

15

Mom and Dad pretty much fell in love that night.

High school went by quickly for both of them: they excelled in their studies, both competed in sports, and went to a lot of White Sox games with Alex, who really didn't have any other friends and had a tough time getting along with his hard-working father. Alex liked painting and drawing, which weren't very reputable pursuits to anyone who lived in Roseland, and was a sharp contrast to Simon, whose sterling academic record and athletic accomplishments had gained the notice of the local congressman, a big-hearted Machine hack named Kasza, who also attended too many White Sox games. Alex's father (and Simon's guardian uncle) worked for the honorable gentleman's ward organization from time to time, and Kasza liked the idea of promoting a fellow Pole to one of the national military academies. However, the glow of Simon and Frederika's romance dominated everyone during what always sounded to me to be a warm, happy time for both families.

Until our curse made another appearance.

As they all geared up for graduation week, one night, a massive fire swept through the corner bakery, and killed both Frederika's mother and Simon's uncle, who became trapped in the upstairs apartment. The entire neighborhood grieved for Alex, Simon, and Frederika, who spent the rest of that horrible night crying in opposite corners of Palmer Park.

Their adult lives began there. Alex blew off the cap and gown ceremonies and took a train to New York and fell in with the Beatnik art scene in Greenwich Village, where he made a name for himself as a painter some Madison Avenue types dug. Simon and Frederika decided to marry, but Simon wanted to wait until he finished college. He was overruled by the Machine pol, who virtually bribed him into marrying beforehand. So they did, at Holy Rosary, a small turn-of-the-century Catholic place of worship near the ruins of the bakery.

Simon graduated from Annapolis in 1962, just in time for the next big bad shindig in the jungle. I was born a year after that. Mom and Dad went back to the old neighborhood to baptize me. Uncle Alex was my Godfather. His second wife was my Godmother. I don't even remember her name, and I'm not sure Uncle Alex does, either. I saw very little of my dad in my early childhood, since he was a young officer with the Pacific fleet. Mom refused to accept life on some drab military base from day one, so I did most of my growing up in a large Roseland bungalow "loaned" to us by the now-retired Congressman Kasza. Mom enrolled in and struggled to finish nursing school at night while she worked at the local bank during the day. Dad got around to resigning his Navy commission in 1970, came back and moved in with us, and went into law school at Northwestern a few months later.

I swear, my parents were closer when Dad was in country, writing letters back and forth almost every day, than when he finally came home.

Both of them came from families broken apart by some tragedy or another. They raised themselves while others worked or became distant memories. Their ultimate tragedy was that they became the kind of invisible parents to their only child that fate had cruelly given to them in their youth.

Dad was a smashing success as a brave officer and then as a lawyer, a right corporate torpedo nearing in on a six-figure income, a beautiful wife, a beautiful little boy, and a beautiful track house in the suburbs, an upper-class burg where a lot of the exiles from Roseland ended up after the neighborhood changed a few years ago. And now he had our beautiful life ruin, sitting alongside him at Thanksgiving dinner, to add to his list of accomplishments.

Mom's natural tenacity found a home in her nursing career. She wasn't content to check pulses and stick needles in the asses of sick children. No. In less than a year, she was not only assigned to, but running, the night shift at a large inner city Chicago hospital's emergency room like she was a *Kriegsmarine* admiral. I guess you need someone like that dealing with gunshot wounds and diseases of the poor. I just didn't like the cold, driven, Cybernaut mom she became (to spite my absentee Dad, I often believed).

They were in the trenches, and had been there once Dad's stud lawyer career was matched by Mom's stud nursing career. They were always driven to bigger and better things, the American Dream gone bonkers - work, damn you, work! Make more money! Buy more better shit more often! Be better than everyone else, and you can have a piece of this rotten apple pie culture (like a virus culture, from a lab that should have been blown to smithereens in an air strike a long time ago).

I know they saw themselves in my cherubic features, my light sand eyes and small ears and full lips and long fingers, my test scores, my home runs, and my growing, terrible loneliness. I was twice the athlete and the intellect my parents ever dreamed of being, but half the child. My parents may have been alive, I was having dinner with them, but they sure didn't feel that way, to me. When I was little, I had every toy and gadget on the market bought for me at Christmas, which was cool, I guess, and I won't lie that all the birthday parties at Comiskey Park with my baseball buddies were the best days any kid like me could ever want, but I had this lawyer who I had to call up for an appointment to see as my Dad, and this Emergency Room chieftain who could handle twenty traumas, an overworked staff and green interns with a shrug, come home and be a crack suburbanite social butterfly while she ignored my silences and closed doors and late baseball nights off with the aplomb of a true, upwardly-mobile busy-body. I'd have given every single one of my things for either of them to show up one night when I played ball with the local guys, and maybe even thrown in a few of my Opening Day visits for a joint parental appearance, since the White Sox usually lost their home opener, anyway. You know, just to prove to everyone I had some parents, too.

On the rare, latter-day occasions they had put in an appearance together, it was only by accident. Like a car accident. It wasn't at any of my games, that's for sure. Maybe that's why I had stopped playing so much, that junior year. You always knew when they were within striking distance of each other, because you could cut the tension in the room with a butter knife. The only saving grace to the whole meal was my Mom's homemade bread, a recipe given to her by one of the bakery ladies. It certainly wasn't my feeble attempt to pretend either of them felt like parents anymore.

"One of my teachers gave me this really cool album yesterday. Would you like to hear it?"

"You mean I won't hear it tonight, when I'm trying to sleep?" Dad even looked at me when he spoke. Wow. I stared back into his eyes. They used to be clear and sharp. Now they were just haggard and angry.

"Maybe later, baby. Let's finish eating first." Why? You don't look like you want to, either, Mom.

"I'm finished now." My voice slipped. It was harsh and abrupt. I looked downward at my lap. All I could hear was a fork hitting a plate and the football game far in the distance of the family room.

"So am I, with that sullen attitude of yours."

"Let it go, Simon. We're all tired right now."

"Tired of what, Rika? You said you were tired of waiting for me to get home. Well, I'm home, honey. Can't I be tired of something, too?"

"No, Simon. Just let the whole Godforsaken thing go. You're not in front of a jury that's impressed by you, so ease up on the dramatics *and* my china."

I pushed my chair backwards and went to leave the room. My Dad's tight hand grabbed my shirt sleeve and pulled me back down. I kept looking at my lap. He wouldn't let go.

"I'll tell you what I'm tired of, Rika. I'm tired of my son always walking away and closing some damned door behind him. I'm tired of getting home just in time for him to go out. And I'm really dead fucking tired of coming home and feeling like I went through some vortex and ended up back at work!"

I pulled my arm out of his grip and stared at him with wide eyes. I felt empty inside, even though I was stuffed with homemade bread and milk. Mom glared at Dad like he was suddenly some alien life form. My bottom lip began to quaver. I had heard them do battle at night, the yelling and swearing, the occasional broken knick-knack, and the silent meals the next day. I heard it coming. I'd felt it coming, but, when it finally came, the barren Thanksgiving night we all stared at each other in despair, hurt, and anger, I felt afraid and alone with the two people who used to cuddle me to sleep between them in bed.

Mom's eyes began to fill with tears of sorrow. Was that her only response? "I'm tired, too, Dad. I'm tired of both of you."

His hand slapped hard across my face. It sounded like a rifle shot. The corner of my lip split on my front teeth. I let out a single, soft cry as I landed on the thick shag carpet at the base of the dinner table. He never used to touch me when I was little, never, no matter how much of a brat I was. But since my teenaged voice changed and Mom and Dad became East and West Berlin, evidently my remarks and responses stopped being cute and started cutting closer to the bone, and getting me slapped a lot. I guess I had become used to it.

With as much dignity as I could muster, I stood up and walked out of the room, ignoring the verbal explosions erupting behind me.

III

My mind is troubled, like a fountain stirred;
And I myself see not the bottom of it.
Troilius and Cressida

I spent the rest of the night in my bedroom. My desk lamp and the dial of my stereo receiver were the only sources of light. I switched on the classical station, turning the volume loud enough so I couldn't hear anything else, knocks on the door, phone rings, or my own empty thoughts. They had just started broadcasting a performance of Mozart's *Le Nozze de Figaro*, a sweet, exquisite opera whose joy really magnified how shitty I felt. I had put on a thick sweater over my dress shirt, a pair of thermal socks, and an old pair of Dad's hiking boots, and kept my pea coat, black wool scarf, leather gloves, and surplus Army beret at the edge of my bed, in case I got thrown out of the house, or decided to leave. I laid on top of the covers of my new king-size bed, a birthday present from last year I pretty much hated, and buried my head in four pillows, trying not to cry, which was hard, and made the tears that eventually came that much more painful.

*

I could feel winter coming and Nicolasha's arms around me, squeezing me against his cold leather coat, my lips touching a snowflake on his lapel, tears running down my face, and his soft voice whispering a Siebenbürgenlied into my ear, rocking me back and forth as we stood together at the edge of the large, rocky steps that led downward to the icy waves of Lake Michigan, his hands slowly rubbing my back.

I woke up with a start, my eyes fixed on the green glow of the stereo receiver. My face and pillow were damp with sweat. I peered out of my bedroom's large window at our vast and empty backyard. I could see the corner of one of the village's dainty little parks beyond it. The sky was black and starless. I stumbled over to the receiver and turned it down to a mere roar. It was four a.m., and the deep-voiced announcer read a brief news update while I took off all of my clothes and crawled back into the womb beneath the quilt, blanket, and bed sheet. My God, the station then started playing *The Age of Gold* Suite.

Well, it looked like dear old Mom and Dad were going to hear Nicolasha's record, after all.

I heard every note of the Suite, but I wasn't listening. All I could think about was leaving school yesterday, and how it felt to have Nicolasha's arm draped over my shoulders. I pictured Nicolasha tucking me into bed and kissing me on both cheeks, like my Dad used to, holding my face in his warm hands as his body pressed against mine. I struggled to keep my own hands outside of the covers and away from my waist, trying to blot the image out of my mind. I turned over to lay on my stomach and my erection. It took me a long time to fall asleep again, and, by the time I did, it was almost light.

*

While walking through the frost-covered park to the train station, I passed a young couple making out on a wooden bench. I remembered she went to the local public high school. She was pretty, too, with short black hair and a full chest that pressed out from her tight leather jacket. I didn't recognize the football jock. He was a beefy red-head with freckles all over the back of his neck. He didn't look very bright. She sat on his lap with her hands deep inside of his lettermen jacket, while he held her waist with one hand and rubbed her legs with the other. I heard a funny mixture of moaning and soft laughter between the sucking sounds of their lips.

His eyes shifted to meet mine. I slipped on a small patch of ice and landed painfully on my knees. They stopped kissing for a moment, their faces red from the cold and wet with saliva, staring at me as if I was a clumsy kindergartener. I hurried to my feet and ran to the platform, too embarrassed to look back.

Peeking from around the corner of the platform stairway, I stared miserably at them, kissing each other like a Soviet nuclear attack was imminent. I begged for a train to pull in and take me away from them.

IV

I never heard so musical a discord,
such sweet thunder
A Midsummer Night's Dream

"Count Dracula and His Vampire Bride."

A couple of dozen intrepid moviegoers and I emerged from the faded and threadbare single-screen cinema near the heart of Hyde Park's business district into the cold and cloudless Friday afternoon. Most of my fellow horror film connoisseurs were unoccupied students like me, enjoying the free day before the gear-grinding stretch leading up to Christmas break. Despite a tatty budget and outrageous re-title job done by the film's third distributor (it was once "The Satanic Rites of Dracula", the final installment of Hammer Films' wonderful series starring Christopher Lee and Peter Cushing), we all had a good time listening to the British actors confuse the film with a new West End performance of *Edward II*, and watching sexy vampire girls get staked between their bobbing tits.

The temperature couldn't have been any higher than twenty degrees. The air was thin and sharp, making the exhaust fumes from the passing cars and the rush-hour buses that much worse. The sun was bright, but was already moving to the other side of the apartments and trees that separated Hyde Park from its desperately poor neighbors to the west. I began to wander in the direction of the train station, even though I sure didn't feel like leaving the city anytime soon. I had considered going downtown and seeing some film, *any* film, in one of the remaining movie palaces left in the Loop, but the thought of doing battle with the hordes of "opening day" Christmas shoppers kept me from going any further north than the odd, integrated neighborhood of the

Pilot Institute. And now, having seen the Dracula film and digested a hardy breakfast of unbuttered popcorn, a plain hot dog, and a large Coke, it was time to go home.

And the hordes didn't sound so bad, right then.

A warm hand reached over the back of my neck and squeezed gently. I stood still, imagining some hulking, deranged Vietnam vet wanting to kill some silly white kid from the suburbs. Nicolasha peeked around my shoulder with a dimpled smile, his right arm dropping across my shoulders as I recognized him and relaxed. I involuntarily wrapped my arm closest to him around his waist and returned his smile with a pretty bright one of my own, before blushing and drawing a few inches away, like everybody around us was suspicious of something.

"I would have thought commuting to school five days a week would be quite enough for anyone. Do not tell me you wanted to see the Dracula film that badly!" Nicolasha stayed close at my side as we walked to the stoplight together while my eyes stared at the train station across the street, as if its terminus were Treblinka.

Nicolasha patted my shoulder, drawing me back to him. "So? How did you like the film?"

"I love all those Hammer Films! That was a pretty odd one, though, like an episode of *The Avengers* with a few vampires thrown in." His nose and ears were red from the chill, and his hair was its usual mess. His face looked so kind and happy, sticking out from the plump woolen scarf wrapped around his neck. "I'm glad I saw it, all the same."

"So am I. At University, we all used to stay up to watch them on late-night TV. I like the Frankenstein movies best."

I laughed. "Besides, stuff like that never plays out where I live, and I wanted to get out of the house." My teacher noticed the slight change of tone and expression as I mentioned home. His eyes looked sadly into mine. I think he understood-... some-thing.

"Are you enjoying this very Siebenbürgian weather?"

"It's OK." I looked at my Dad's hand-me-down Omega watch, a neat golden job with a worn but elegant brown leather band that was a souvenir from my rather quiet fourteenth birthday. The boxcars would be arriving in a few minutes. I avoided Nicolasha's baby-blue eyes, but not the feel of his hands on my shoulders.

"I can tell something is bothering you, little friend." 'Friend'? Damn. I had never thought of Nicolasha as a friend. I guess my only other friends were the guys I played pick-up ball with during the summer (nobody on the school team were the 'making friends' type). We hung out after our games, and I got invited to all their houses for barbecues and sleepovers and birthdays, but when we finished playing, I mostly just went home. Damn. "Would you like to go someplace and talk about it? The lake is just there. Or perhaps over some warm tea?"

Two pedestrians hustled past us into the street, cutting off a station wagon in the middle of a turn. I shook my head and glared at the pavement. "I don't usually talk about stuff like that, with anybody." I suddenly felt very empty again. It never occurred to me to talk to anyone about how I felt. It always seemed safer to keep it in and wait for my thoughts to go away.

"I know what you mean. That is why I listen to so much music," Nicolasha sighed. "It is much easier than trying to say all the things I want to say, and the music never talks back or argues. It just listens to my heart, and makes me feel better. After all, it is hard to find somebody who you want to talk to, and wants to listen, at the same time."

"No shit." I watched my train roll to a halt on the platform up ahead, looking packed, as usual. Oh, well, I mused, there would always be the next one. "I guess that's what parents are supposed to be for." Or the next one after that.

"And yours are not?"

"I don't know. I've never tried to find out." Well, you know, booking months in advance for a heart-to-heart can really be hard for a sixteen-year-old, even an intelligent one like I used to think I was. What would I have said, anyway? Ask my Dad what he thought a good dad was? Or why I didn't think he was a very good one, nowadays? Ask my Mom how to love people? Or why I wasn't sure she could answer that question anymore? To hell with that. I'd rather have just gone to bed, maybe cried a little bit, and hoped I forget everything by the next morning. I felt like I wanted to cry right then, too, damn it.

Nicolasha wrapped an arm inside of mine and turned us around, heading back toward the city dusk. The creepy orange street lights had switched on. I missed the plain white ones the city used to have. He pointed to a small storefront a block down from the movie theater. "They have an excellent used record selection in there. Let me buy you something to cheer you up."

"Get out of here, Nicolasha. My Dad buys me off with a big allowance, and I don't get most of the music you really seem to like, Ligeti for one. I mean, I love the stuff, but it's all pretty sad, you know?"

Nicolasha put his lips close to my ear. I could feel the warmth of his breath near my neck. My legs practically locked where I stood. "Life cannot always be like a Strauss waltz, little friend." He tried to smile me out of the dirty look I didn't really mean to give him.

"It shouldn't always be like the *Trauermusik*, either."

"No," he admitted, acknowledging my reference to a past lecture on Hindemith with a respectful glance. Nicolasha kept our arms together as we trotted across the street to the store, whose large front window was safely locked behind decaying riot bars and was filled with posters of mostly dead jazz and rock musicians. A scruffy ex-hippie store clerk winked at us as we headed to the back of the densely stocked shop, where the massive rows of classical recordings awaited us. My eyes gleamed. There was the rest of my fifty-dollar holiday allowance, I concluded with a thin smile.

Nicolasha stood beside me as I rifled through the stacks of records, nodding at works or readings he thought were good enough to buy. We each ended up carrying a large box filled with my purchases out onto the dark street, where it had gotten even colder. I was flushed with the odd thrill of spending a lot of money on things I knew I would love and my parents would hate. Hell, I wouldn't have time to listen to half of these by the end of the weekend!

(I saw Nicolasha checking out a boxed recording of Massenet's *Thais* and snuck it into my haul without his notice. He would appreciate that, I thought.)

"I do not think you will be able to take all these home with you, little friend." Oh, man, I hadn't even thought about that. I could see myself, lugging the boxes out onto the platform in my old neighborhood to change trains and getting jumped over my thin supply of Al Green. "I can give you a ride home, if you would like."

A gust of Arctic wind hit us, almost blowing my beret off of my head. To hell with the train, I thought. "That would be great. Thanks, Nicolasha." I didn't know he even had a car. I hoped it was in better shape than his wardrobe.

*

Nicolasha led the way to a clean, attractive block, lined with thin trees and a collection of vintage, World War One-era dwellings. Despite the bulk of my record haul, we walked quickly, driven on by the frightful wind chill in the air. He stopped at an imposing three-flat walk-up that would fit right into any of the Hammer films I've seen. "Here is my flat. It often reminds me of my old home."

A silver Volvo sedan that looked brand new was parked in front of the granite-faced building. Nicolasha set his box onto the edge of the Volvo's bumper, opened the trunk, and put the records into the tidy compartment. I did the same. He wrapped a heavy blanket over the boxes and slammed the trunk shut.

"Cool car."

Nicolasha smiled proudly. "My mother and father gave it to me when I earned my doctorate. It is my first car, so I treat it like a baby." He gestured to the passenger door. "Are you ready to go, little friend?"

"Can I use your bathroom first?" My breakfast Coke had become painful, and I suddenly wanted to know what his apartment looked like.

Nicolasha slapped his forehead gently. "I am sorry for being so rude. I should have invited you in. Please." He practically ran up the porch stairs to hold the front door open for me. The entryway was small and dark, lined in aging pine. There were three brass mailboxes on the wall. The staircase, set against the side of the wall, was even darker than the vestibule. Nicolasha unlocked the door to his first-floor apartment, switched on a light, and beckoned me in.

He took off his black loafers and set them beside the door. "The bath is in there," pointing to the half-open door in the middle of the narrow hallway. "I will make some tea to warm us up." I smiled at my teacher as he headed to the kitchen and I pulled off my cold hiking shoes.

The room was spotless, even though the bathroom fixtures showed the age of the building. Everything was done in bulging, white porcelain. The bathtub was gigantic and stood on four legs, like the one in our old Roseland apartment. The light switch was at the end of a thick, fabric-covered wire that hung from the middle of the high ceiling. The chilly floor was made up of hundreds of tiny white and black square tiles. Good Lord, Nicolasha had a bottle of Mr. Bubble near the tub. Did Soviet Romania produce a rival equivalent, I trifled? What did they call it? Comrade Bubblevitch?

I was embarrassed by the harsh echo my pee made.

I passed through the plain dining room to join Nicolasha at a small coffee table set against the wall of the kitchen, just in front of the apartment's back door. He poured the hot tea from a stainless steel pot into a pair of small, clear glasses with ornate copper bases and finger-holders. The kitchen was small but fluorescently bright. The gas stove, sink, cupboard, and refrigerator all looked fairly antique. I couldn't help but think of one of the bakery ladies, Antonia, and the constant warmth of her little apartment near the train tracks. She always had me and my Mom over for huge Sunday dinners, wonderful dinners, when Dad was still off in the Navy, defending democracy or some stupid thing.

Nicolasha spooned some honey into our glasses. "This will take the chill out of you." The tea was delicious. He pulled a small loaf of black rye bread and a block of dark orange cheese from the oven and cut them in half. A wave of contented warmth swept over me. "I am sorry I cannot offer you dinner, little friend, but I usually eat out on the weekend, and do not go to the store until Sunday night."

"It can't be any worse than my Mom's turkey." Nicolasha laughed. I took a bite of the rich, salty bread and the sharp cheese. Where was the schnapps? "They're great." I finished my glass of tea in one gulp. My teacher smiled and served up another for me. "Where do you get bread like this?"

"Three old brothers from Brody have a delicatessen over on 55th Street. They bake it fresh for me when I come in, which they enjoy doing, because we gossip in bad Hungarian."

We finished our bread, cheese, and pot of tea without further discussion, alternating our eyes between the food and each other.

*

Nicolasha retreated to his bedroom to make a phone call while I checked out his small living room. A few history and music books lined the top of an unused fireplace, surrounded by hundreds, if not thousands, of records, neatly filed on wide shelves cut directly into the wall. An easy chair, reading lamp, and end table pointed outward from the corner of the apartment's picture window to my right. There was no TV, which explained a lot about Nicolasha. What looked like an expensive stereo system, including a reel-to-reel tape machine, lay to my left. I sat underneath a broad, discolored mirror on a worn-out and uncomfort-able beige couch, with another end table and lamp pressed to its left armrest.

I tried to listen into Nicolasha's conversation without success, but noticed a drawer at the base of the couch's end table. Below a swamp of bills, cancelled checks, and letters, I discovered a photo album. I opened the cover and stared downwards at an 8x10 black and white portrait of my Nicolasha. His hair was in its usual chaotic state. His eyes and face looked directly into the camera, and at me. Half of his nose was cut off in a shadow, and his smile was wide and happy, his dimpled cheeks pulled upwards, showing a neat line of upper teeth. His body was turned, facing sideways from the camera. His left arm was wrapped over his lower abdo-men, his hand rested flat on his stomach, pulling the white, sleeveless t-shirt away from his exposed breast. A tangle of hair was visible in the upper corner of his arm. His left leg was raised, like he was about to take a large step, disappearing beyond the frame right before the knee, while the bottom of the picture ended just below *Freiherr*von Straußenburg's pert, bare buttocks.

I slammed the album shut and shoved it inside the bundle of my pea coat as my teacher hung up the phone. I closed the drawer and hurried back over to the record shelves before Nicolasha came into the room.

"I am sorry to keep you waiting, little friend. I was supposed to visit a friend this evening, and I wanted to let them know I would be late. Are you ready to go?" No, I growled to myself, I want to sleep over tonight. He walked up to me and placed a hand on my shoulder. I nodded, trying very hard not to show any reaction to my own thoughts. "Do you like my record collection?" Yes, Nicolasha, I do. My smile said that. It's almost as impressive as you in that t-shirt. The sinking feeling in my throat and chest and the warmth below my belt said that.

"It's really fantastic! Now I know where all your money goes!" He beamed, in an exact replica of his smile in the picture. And I was trapped there, somewhere in the shadows behind the photo of Nicolasha's naked body. I didn't want to go home.

"We better go. It is getting late."

I didn't want to, damn it.

V

This bodes some strange eruption to our state.
Hamlet

It wasn't surprising that the Volvo's radio was tuned to the mom and pop classical channel. We reached the southbound expressway as the station began playing a pair of gentle, almost pastoral horn concerti by Richard Strauss, which I thought sounded like they were written by Mozart or Schubert. The music kept Nicolasha company. My mind was on my lap, where the photo album was wrapped inside of my coat, and the biggest, longest, most painful erection I ever had smashed against the fabric of my underwear and jeans.

It faded the moment I saw Dad's white Stingray in our driveway.

Dad walked out into the endless cold to greet us. Huh. Nicolasha introduced himself, explaining how we ran into each other outside of the movie theater, my record store shopping bonanza, and our walk back to his flat. The entire sequence inside of his apartment was neatly omitted. Dad smiled at me and turned on his considerable professional charm, thanking Nicolasha for his kindness and inviting him in for a drink. I couldn't tell if it was one of his perfect lawyer performance smiles or a real one. Of course my young teacher swallowed the bait, and they went off together as I was left to unpack the records and carry them up to my room.

Mom had already left for the hospital.

I nearly panicked when the photo album slid out of my coat and landed on the carpet in front of my bedroom door. I spun around to see if either Dad or Nicolasha were near the stairs, which, thank God, they weren't, and hid the album in my school bag before swinging it under my bed.

I took the recording of *Thais* from one of the boxes and headed downstairs, where Nicolasha was being suitably impressed by my Dad's house tour and his free blended malt scotch. I held the record set behind my back as they approached from the kitchen hallway.

(You know, they actually seemed to complement each other? There wasn't much comparison between their respective Mitteleuropean features, Dad with his indistinct, heavy-lidded peasant face, and Nicolasha with his thin, fancier family lines, or in their build or appearance, Dad still in combat fitness, Nicolasha soft and slight, Dad only a bit older. What was it, then? I looked closely at them both. Despite the grins and chatter and all, my Dad looked a little mean, like an ex-sailor who had seen some action he couldn't un-see. Nicolasha looked kindhearted and suitably impressed by his welcome and the show house, sensing Dad's mettle, youthful where Dad was seasoned, the privations of his childhood mostly forgotten. I couldn't put a finger on what I was feeling, seeing them together for the first time. It was weird.)

"I was just showing Nicolaus around." Dad smiled at me again. Huh! He seemed to approve of my teacher. Who knows? Maybe it was the scotch.

"Your home is very, very nice, sir." Nicolasha raised his glass toward my paternal unit and finished the ghastly drink.

"Can I get you another, for the road?" He reached for the glass, an expensive crystal with Northwestern's crest frosted on the side, the only glass Dad took his poison in. Not everybody got a drink in one of those.

"I would actually love to, sir, but I am already late meeting someone downtown." In this cold, it would have to be another Siebenbürger, I thought.

"Can I give you some money for gas, for your trouble?" Dad's tone was too damn nice. Suddenly, I realized I was being girded up for something.

"Oh, no, sir, that's very kind, but it was my pleasure."

"Please. I insist."

Nicolasha bowed his head reluctantly. Dad grinned and headed back into the kitchen, where his wallet was usually tossed. I hesitated, wanting to give Nicolasha the record and get a hug back when Dad returned with a scowl on his face, his natural look, if you asked me.

"I must have left my billfold upstairs."

"Please don't bother, sir."

Waving him off, Dad bounced up the stairs and down the long hallway to his bedroom, away from us. Nicolasha turned and winked at me, touching my cheek and smiling lips with a mock fist. I took the opera out from behind me and handed it to him. Surprise, *Freiherr*. His mouth and eyes opened a bit as he stared at the flamboyant, over-decorated belly dancer on the box cover, swallowing audibly in his astonishment.

"What's the matter, Nicolasha? Doesn't anybody ever buy you a gift?" He looked like he wanted to say something, but nothing came out. "That's for being a great teacher, and a friend, too." I giggled quietly as I held my arms open. Nicolasha practically jumped into them. I rested my face sideways across his chest, while his cheek touched my hair, his arms and the opera pressing against my back. He kissed the top of my head and gave me a last squeeze.

"Here it is," Dad called out from his room. We took an immediately step back from each other. Nicolasha glanced nervously between me and the staircase, shifting on his feet. He looked so afraid and so alone, all of a sudden, like he was about to be locked outside in the cold for a year.

I wanted to leave with him. I wanted to go back and see the Hammer film again. I wanted to sit next to Nicolasha. I wanted to listen to all of his records, and sit in his lap.

Hell, I wanted to take a Comrade Bubblevitch bubble bath with him.

I reached forward and took my teacher's arms in my hands, holding him still as I leaned forward and put my lips on his for a soundless, full clock second, followed by a silence so deadening it would make the falling snow sound like a Shostakovitch symphony.

"My kind of woman." Dad smiled at the belly dancer, nudging the wide-eyed Nicolasha in the side as he handed him a twenty-dollar bill. "I don't think I've ever heard that one before. Have you, son?"

"Nope. *Freiherr* von Straußenburg will have to lend it to me after he's had a listen." I smiled at him, my voice and gaze strangely confident in Dad's presence, as if I had just proved something to somebody.

"My God, is that your proper title?"

"I think it was extinct before my father got it." Nicolasha stumbled through the rest of his good-byes and thank-yous and see-you-on-Mondays and careened out of our little big home into the safety of his Volvo. He sped away from us like we were a pair of grumpy commissars.

The front door closed. The house was left as quiet as a crypt. Dad's hand touched my shoulder. I turned around and stared at him impassively, the only real defense I had left.

"I'm sorry about last night." He didn't look me in the eyes, the coward.

"So am I."

"Your mother and I...we've run out of answers. It's all gone wrong, son."

"No, *it* hasn't. *You* both have." My voice was soft and level, quite an achievement, I thought, considering how I felt at that particular moment.

He finally looked back at me, his eyes bloodshot and wet. "I've decided to take a job with some outfit in New York. I'll be moving there just after Christmas. Your mother wants to stay here, in the house. It's up to you where you'd like to go."

I knew where I wanted to go. I wanted to go out, far out.

*

There were no lights on in the room except for the fireplace, which blazed away. I huddled myself into the corner of our over-stuffed couch with my arms around my knees, staring out at the cold, blue picture of our moonlit yard. I hadn't heard my drunken father stumble about upstairs for a while.

I kept picking up the phone to call Nicolasha, but kept hanging up halfway through his number. I wasn't sure what I wanted to say. It felt like he was my only friend in the world. Anyhow, I didn't know if that was what I really wanted to say. I wasn't sure how that felt, either.

My mind began to blur, flashing back throughout my life, remembering all of the things me, Dad, and Mom used to do together, when we were still a sort of family, careful to omit about two years worth of meals at home.

Like my first helicopter ride over Cape Hatteras. It was a flimsy Bell 25; Plexiglas bubble, bench seat, and engine. This was the way to see the spectacular Outer Banks scenery. Mom was petrified, but I loved it, especially when the ex-Marine pilot veered the bird to the right, leaning me over the rough sea below.

Or being "absent" from school whenever the new James Bond film opened at the Woods Theater downtown. 1971 came to mind. We loved "Diamonds Are Forever" so much, Mom took me with to buy her first brand new car, a fire-engine red Mustang Mach 1, just like the one in the movie. It was the coolest car anyone's mom drove. But 007 only came every other year, while my beloved White Sox were an annual "he has a slight fever" event.

My favorite "fever" was 1973. We were getting killed by the Oakland A's (again), but we all were having a good time, because our entire row was taken by the old Congressman's friends and cronies. Mom set fire to a senile Cub fan's pennant (which hopefully taught him to stay on the North Side where he belonged), and Dad got thrown out of the park after tossing his beer at some guy's head when the silly ass stood up for the Oakland seventh.

And then there was our Road Trip from Hell (no family should be without one) to Rock City and Lookout Mountain in Chattanooga, Tennessee. Despite rainstorms, Ford Motor Company water pump engineering, and cartographic illiteracy by Daddy dearest, I enjoyed all the Civil War stuff, but not as much as charging across a steel suspension bridge to shake up my terrified Mom and Dad.

Of course, there were all the times the young couple from next door to our Roseland bungalow, Scott and Roberta, would take me off of Mom's hands to go to the drive-in to watch classic Hammer, Amicus, and AIP horror movie double features from the roof of their old Impala two-door. Scott lived off of the sort of food they served at the concession stand, and would overstock the car with dry hot dogs, soft Raisinettes, tasteless popcorn, rock-hard frozen Heath bars, badly carbonated cola, and out-of-date Dolly Madison fruit pies throughout the movies, which weren't nearly as chilling as the Halsted Drive-In's bathrooms, next to the projection booth.

There was going tubing down Wisconsin's Apple River with a bunch of Dad's weekend-warrior buddies from law school. We had separate tubes for the sandwich basket, and for the Point beer and Tahitian Treat coolers, the gooey Canada Dry fruit punch I was addicted to for a few years. Most everyone got sunburned to death, but me and this young stoner (that Dad hated) who took up law to figure out how to break it (Dad's description) were the only ones with enough balls, or stupidity, to sail through the rapids at the end. I was actually pretty scared, but I was determined to show up all the future shysters, even if I did almost drown myself in the process.

Of course, I'll always remember my collection phase, when it seemed like I collected collections. We went hunting for sea shells in Miami, man-o-wars be damned, and took pictures next to every spacecraft at Cape Kennedy. We scoured the undusted corners of the country in search of small breweries and beer cans. I had to have every Hot Wheels, Johnny Lightning, Matchbox, Dinky, Corgi, and Solido car ever produced. Then I moved on to matchbooks, just so Dad had to spring for dinner at every high-class restaurant downtown.

I drove Mom and Dad nuts one summer, demanding to see the White Sox play at every American League team's home park. They saw me so little, they agreed to split the difference and take me to see the whole American League visit the Sox at home. Most of the games were at night, all the better to see our scoreboard explode when the White Sox rustled up a home run. We sat at third base side upper deck railing seats provided to us by old Congressman Kasza, who became the grandfather I never had in those days, lavish and affectionate, sizing up every player and every pitch and every swing as we sat next to each other with our eyes locked toward home and our arms crossed over the railing.

Papu would let me run from aisle to aisle at Bargain Town on my birthday, picking out whatever I wanted, until the cart was full. He got off easy the year I went for Tonka trucks. He got hit pretty hard the year I discovered board games.

He would take me and Mom and Dad for weekend trips up to the Playboy Club in Lake Geneva. Mom liked to go horseback riding, while Dad studied in the lounge. I still wonder if it had anything to do with all the illuminated pictures of Playmates behind the bar. Papu always went fishing, winter or summer, rain or shine, while I hung out in the indoor pool. One time, Dad and Papu bought me a leopard-print silk bathing suit and had two young bunnies cuddle up to me on top of the game room's pool table for a picture that never fails to gall my buddies or Uncle Alex.

I know I cried more than anyone else at the funeral home when Papu died a few years back. I was too distraught to go to the funeral. I wish he was still here.

A couple of winters ago, when the sniping started, I got shipped off to Uncle Alex's Minnesota farm for Christmas. I hated it at first, because Uncle Alex had moved from LSD to bags of weed by then. One morning, two older teenagers saw me ice fishing from across the lake. They rode over on their snowmobiles, introduced themselves, and invited me to go sledding with them. We went out every day for a month after that, tearing the lake and the nearby golf course to shreds, before coming back to spend the evening playing with Unc's pinball machine while he tripped out in the privacy of his bedroom.

I was sent back the following summer, as things continued to get worse with the parental units. This time, I didn't mind. Unc was dried out, had sold a painting, and decided to spend a lot of his money on me, that is, whenever I wasn't playing baseball with Kevin, Joel, and the rest of their friends, all of whom were pretty nice to me, considering I was barely fourteen and they were all pushing eighteen. You know how the age caste thing works with kids.

It was even fun running away from Dad and getting lost on Danger Island on my first trip to Disneyland. I cried a little bit when I misplaced my stuffed Shere Khan Bengal tiger. For us six-year-old tykes, "The Jungle Book" was the big movie that year.

Our yearly pilgrimages to the Adler Planetarium (to make sure Jupiter was still there) and Marshall Field's (to see their massive Christmas tree, pick out beautiful new tree ornaments, and to have lunch at the Walnut Room) were staples to me.

I broke down. I began to cry for my lost family, hard and loud, and cried myself to sleep on the couch, still in my clothes, weakened with shame for having cried in the first place.

*

I woke up later that morning, feeling like I hadn't slept at all. A few embers remained in the fireplace. The harsh, pale sunlight I associated with winter poured into the living room. It looked like another cloudless, and, no doubt, bitterly cold day.

I peeked into the garage. Mom's station wagon was there. I checked the driveway, confirming Dad's Stingray was not. Perhaps sacrificing your family on Saturdays was the price you had to pay for a six-figure income.

It was every bit as cold as I figured it would be.

Soundlessly, I climbed upstairs, made sure Mom's bedroom door was closed, and headed to my own room, locking the door behind me. Kneeling down at my bed, I pulled out my school bag and opened the leather album to the first photograph of my teacher and stared at it for many minutes, with my hand pulling at my jeans to give my erection some room. I stripped to my t-shirt and socks, and turned to look at myself in the dresser mirror. I wrapped my arm around my lower abdomen and perched my left foot on my desk chair, mimicking Nicolasha's pose. My upper thighs were more muscular than his.

I sat down on the floor with my back against the side of my bed, took off my t-shirt and socks, and leafed through the rest of the album, the immediate chill over my body roundly ignored. If I was groggy before, I was wide awake by then. There were five more black and white photos of Nicolasha. Clearly, the pictures were the work of a professional: both the lighting and focus were soft, and the composition chillingly distant. I began rubbing one hand over myself while turning the pages of the album with the other. My feelings flailed from stimulation and desire to sadness and confusion. This was my teacher, for God's sake, facing the camera with a bizarre smile, wrapping the front of his dago-t over his fingers to show the camera his crotch; naked and standing straight, a hand on a hip, looking at the cameraman with a hint of impatience; laying on a blanket and the edge of a bean-bag, partially erect with his legs spread out and arms folded over his head, staring off into the distance; sitting on a bar stool with his hands on the inside of his thighs, his face covered with the utter boredom of a commuter; and the fifth, another detached, absent glare, his arms crossed behind his neck, his knees raised toward his face, exposing the bottom of his rear end and balls.

Who the hell took these, anyway?

My breaths became shorter. I began to tense up. I flipped to the next page and stared down at two color pictures of my teacher. The first was taken from behind him. He was wearing a dark blue denim jacket with a tall collar, with his thick hair wet and ragged, like he had just gotten out of the shower. Again, he was staring into the distance, this time, affording "the audience" an incredible profile shot, his unlined, pale face set against the dominant shadows in back of him, his sky-blue eyes and full lips plain and uninterested. His perfectly shaped rear was accented by the position of his legs, which were spread outward, braced like he was about to lunge forward with a sword. The lighting revealed a hint of a soft tan on his bare legs and face, which told me these hadn't been taken before school began, since

Nicolasha sported no trace of sun when we first walked into his classroom.

But it was the last photograph made me take pause. I picked up the album in both my hands, staring closely at Nicolasha's peasant features, one side of his face obscured by a shadow, his thin, bare chest exposed from breast to breast inside the denim jacket, his fingers resting on the edge of the jacket and his hips, and his thickly-skinned penis pointing downward between his legs. But I was drawn into Nicolasha's heartsick expression, and away from my own stimulation. What was he thinking as the camera went off? What was he feeling, deep inside of his heart, where he told us all true music flowed in and out of?

Anyone would find this body in this pose an object of desire and beauty. What I couldn't imagine was that this was Nicolasha, my beloved *Freiherr*, the young, caring teacher from Siebenbürgen who brought so much warmth and so many feelings to all of us at school. I just couldn't accept what I was looking at. I had burned every inch of his face and body into my mind, flown reconnaissance over him every day in class, pictured us holding hands and hugging while I took my morning shower, dreamed about seeing him perform with the Chicago Symphony, but...this?

In all of these pictures, he was standing there almost naked, staring at something nobody else could see, ready to have sex with whomever, smiling at a joke nobody else could hear, but he wasn't really there. Nicolaus Matthias Székelyvon Straußenburg was off someplace else, perhaps back at home in Sibiu, or being held in someone's loving arms, or wandering between the chords and stanzas in some overture, maybe.

Look at that last picture - he was challenging the rest of the world to look and stare at his bare, young body, to try and touch him, to reach through his eyes and into his soul. And he was sad, either because he knew no one could, or was afraid no one would.

I was suddenly cold. I returned the album to my school bag and buried it beneath my other books and papers. I slipped back into my t-shirt and socks, found some long johns, my maroon University of Chicago sweat pants and hooded sweatshirt, and a down ski vest so I could go jogging for the next couple of years.

VI

His heart and hand both open and both free
For what he has he gives, what he thinks he shows
Troilus and Cressida

You know you've had an awful weekend when you're happy to get back to school.

My family spent the rest of the holiday weekend staying in our rooms and alternating our visits to the kitchen so we wouldn't run into each other. I almost sat down at the dinner table with my grand dinner of peanut butter, bacon, and jelly sandwiches before Mom came downstairs to start a pot of strong black coffee. I left when she began slamming the cabinets, noticing we were out of sugar.

I didn't listen to any of my new records.

I got an **A-** on my Italian exam, and **96%** on the Asian History test, so I was confident I did just as well with my music essay, even though I had butterflies about seeing Nicolasha again, with or without his clothes on. I tried staying focused on what was being said in my classes, but I couldn't keep from daydreaming about the album of photographs I was carrying around with me, or agonizing about how I was going to return them.

Was there such a thing as a wet daydream, I wondered?

I stalled at a water fountain, watching Nicolasha confer with Principal Connelly while my classmates walked past them into the music room. The old boy had an over-dressed (and rather short) new student with him, ridiculous in a double-breasted blue jacket, yellow tie, starchy white dress shirt, grey slacks, blue argyle socks, and tan suede saddle shoes. He even had a traditional raincoat draped over his arm, which looked like my Dad's Burberry. What, no morning coat?

The shoes were cool, anyway.

He was perfectly groomed, his parted black hair swept off to one side of his bright, anxious baby face, complete with thick eyebrows, somewhat feminine dark eyes, and tiny pink lips, which were sculpted like a child's. I self-consciously glanced down at my dull ski sweater, turtleneck, jeans, and hiking shoes. The Principal saw me and held his hand out, indicating the classroom door to me like it was a five-star grand hotel. I was the only student left in the hall.

The new arrival looked sheepishly at me as I walked toward him, sizing up his flawless, 'Young Republican from Hell' Halloween costume. We glanced at each other with mock disregard. Nicolasha patted me on the back as we went in. I took my front corner seat. The little senator sat in the empty desk to my left, folding his raincoat into a neat pile and putting it on his lap. He sensed half of the room was staring at him, and shifted uncomfortably in his seat.

"Good afternoon, friends. As you all have noticed, we have a new student who has just transferred in. Principal Connelly has asked me to introduce you to Felix Cromwell, and for you to welcome him to our family." Nicolasha smiled warmly at Felix, who gave a friendly little wave to each side of the room. I was not the only one whose eyes widened at this Felix character's silly gesture. Maybe I should have reached over and messed up his tidily groomed hair, but I was afraid he might stand up and punch me in the knee.

"As for your essays, they were quite creative and very well written. I would like to read a few of them, if you do not mind." Nicolasha sat down on his desk, next to the school phonograph. Our eyes met for a moment.

I pictured him crossing his arms over his head and pulling his jeans down as he began to read this rather odd, stream-of-consciousness poem about Soviet leprechauns dancing in a corn field made out of rifles, and then played the introductory Allegro from the *Age of Gold* which Farrah based it on. She was always out in the bleachers.

(I liked the recording Nicolasha gave me better than this one.)

He skipped to this riotous song, a collection of rapid-fire words and phrases that our teacher struggled to enunciate in coordinated time with the Suite's Polka that Zane conjured it up to. Of course, that's pretty much how Zane talked when he cornered some poor idiot into a conversation with him.

Nicolasha then spent almost ten minutes reading an incredibly rich and detailed portrait of a chaotic night at the circus. Kim had composed a nearly perfect accompaniment to the Suite's Dance. She looked around her desk casually, but I could see that gleam of triumph in her pale green eyes. The whole time, Felix sat there smiling, openly impressed by what he was hearing.

Nicolasha reached for another essay. His eyes linked up with mine, and I began to wish I had missed my train that morning.

"Picture a very large and empty courtyard, a field of cobblestones. Far in the distance, the field is lined by dark, unoccupied, but fabulous old palaces. The firmament above is a sunset mixture of orange clouds and blotches of deep blue sky peeking out from the thick cumulus veil. The courtyard is littered with music

stands that face in every direction and surround a tall monument topped by an archangel reaching up to the spectacular heavens. A cold wind flips the blood red pages on the stands. Suddenly, a ragged young boy, dressed in beggar's clothes, dances onto the courtyard, holding a wood-carved toy violin to his coal-smudged cheek, playing the instrument from the crimson sheets of music. The archangel's arms move gently in rhythm to the unseen orchestra that wells up from the unlit palaces, accompanying the boy until he cannot keep up and drops exhausted to the damp, hard cobblestones. The red pages are swept off of the music stands in a savage blast of wind, a scarlet tornado that pulls the toy violin out of the boy's dirty hand and across the courtyard. The archangel sees this and floats down from the monument, hovering over the sobbing child and taking him in its stone arms back to the top of the monument, where another violin appears, and the boy begins to play, even while his body and his clothes turn grey and then to stone."

I was so embarrassed, I could have died, right there in my desk.

I could feel Kim's glare burning itself through my back. Nicolasha played the recording of the suite's Adagio, sweeping his arms back and forth, conducting the piece with erotic precision. Felix now looked at me with wide eyes. "That was really beautiful," he whispered. "It's even better than the music." He reached out to shake my hand. His grip was warm and firm, even if his hands were a little on the small side.

"You should hear Nicolasha play it live."

"Who's that?"

I pointed my thumb toward our teacher as he brought the selection to a close. From the look on Felix's face, he had never referred to a teacher by their first name in his life. Until Nicolasha came into our lives, the rest of us hadn't, either.

Our music teacher handed back the essays and assigned a chapter on Prokofiev in our text for homework. He waved us out of the room, even though it was almost ten minutes before the final bell was due to ring. For his consideration, Nicolasha was nearly run over by escaping students. I used the ensuing chaos to slip out of the room before he could call out after me.

*

I bolted down the stairs and collided into the locked half of the Pilot Institute's north door, which led into the labyrinth of brooding, gothic buildings found at that end of the University, a fine place to lose anyone tailing me. I was interrupted by Felix, who slid down the wooden banister and landed beside me with a happy grin.

"You sure know how to beat feet at the end of a school day."

"I have to go, Felix."

"Let me come with." He took hold of one of my arms, but let go when I glared at him with wide eyes. "I'm sorry. I just want to talk to you for a couple of minutes. Please?"

He had a pretty cute smile, I'll say that. I was torn between blowing him off him and messing up that perfectly parted hair. I heard people entering the staircase from the floor above. He yielded to me as I exited out of the door's open half, and did so with hurt in his eyes. I sighed and waved for him to join me. "Are you ready to go?"

Pulling a plaid scarf tightly around his neck, he smiled again. "Where to, buddy?"

Buddy, huh? I looked at the classical spires around us and suddenly felt adventurous. "We're going to Checkpoint Charlie. That would be the 55th Street IC train station." I pointed northwest, eleven o'clock. "We're in East Berlin now, and have to get these plans away from a dangerous Soviet agent." I held up my leather book bag. "The last one there buys dinner!" We began walking quickly into the nucleus of the acclaimed campus.

Felix was excited, and smiled again. He smiled a lot. "How about the loser has to have the winner over to their house for dinner?" My face fell as I stopped in my tracks, giving Felix a cold look. His hand touched my arm again in apology. "I only have enough change to get home."

I wrapped my arm around Felix, pulling his trench coated shoulders close to me as we continued on. He smiled again. "We're buddies, right?" He nodded quickly. "Good. Then I can trust you." His arm reached around my back. This was pretty cool. "I'm going to get to Checkpoint Charlie first, because I know Berlin better." Don't bet on it, his shaking head said. "But if the Reds get me and you escape, than its dinner on me, OK?" He nodded with another damn smile. Stop it! "Well, Felix, let me tell you, 'home' really blows for me, nowadays. I mean, it really sucks whenever I'm there, so, if I don't want to be there, it wouldn't be fair to subject you or anyone else to a visit, now, would it?"

"Then you better cross the border before I do, pal!" With a friendly slap on the back, Felix pulled away from me and charged up a short, grassy incline between two maroon brick buildings, heading through the common and the nearby dormitories toward the train line.

Wait until he sees the size of the fence which separated that end of campus from the tracks, I thought to myself with a grin. I shot due north, keeping to the hard, discolored grass of the block's front yards for better traction, up to the bustling 55th Street, where I spun around a bus stop and stayed close to the curb as I maneuvered away from a few shoppers before reaching the underpass station. I fumbled for my ticket pass, slapped it into the turnstile, bound up the short wooden steps three at a time, and crashed through the flimsy spring doors that opened up to the long, empty Hyde Park station platform. I trotted further down, hoping to catch a glimpse of Felix struggling around the fence.

"Drop the bag, you son of a bitch!"

Felix rolled out from under the edge of platform to the gravel carpet beside the inside rail, his hands cupped, holding an imaginary pistol at me. I dropped my bag and dove down, stomach first, to the opposite side of the deck, taking cover behind a large, two-sided metal bench. I held my own illusory handgun, a simple Colt .45 automatic, it had to be, and peered around the base of the seating area, ready to unload the gun into the little creep.

Felix fired three times from behind my back. Shit! I jerked my back and cried out, before slumping to my death against the bench. I lay completely still, waiting until I heard my short buddy climb up from the tracks. How the hell did he get under the platform? I looked up at Felix's grinning little face, and then at his blood-stained leg. The right knee of his dress slacks had been torn open, and, apparently, so had his knee. He helped me to my feet and patted me on the arm. "You should see what it looks like under there." We sat close together on the bench.

"No thanks. Are you OK?" I brushed his hands off of his lap and looked at the bloody horizontal gash running across the top of his kneecap. "What was it? Nothing rusty, I hope!"

Felix's smile was forced, this time. "I think it was a bottle. Damn."

I shook my head and reached for my school bag, pulling a souvenir bottle of cheap Smirnoff vodka out as I propped an elbow over his leg to get a better angle. "I can think of a lot of things I'd rather do with this than pour it down your leg, Felix, but since we're buddies and all that, I'll make an exception, just this once."

Felix seized the bottle out of my hands. "Give me a sip, first." He took a little swig, made a dirty look, and handed it back to me. I had one, too, before leaning over to pour a few drops across the entire gash. Felix moaned painfully. "God, that stings."

"Not as much as a tetanus shot would." I bounced my fist on his thigh a few times before throwing the empty bottle onto the tracks. His moan felt like it was caught in my ears. The buzz of the neighborhood was a little quieter than usual, as if the world had suddenly decided to be quiet and catch its breath for a moment. I could feel the late afternoon sun on my face, and wondered if Nicolasha had gone straight home, or might be watching us from the street below. The wind was pretty calm. I assumed it was Chicago's way of telling me a particularly fearsome winter was on its way. In fact, it was something I was too unfamiliar with to recognize.

"So why does home suck so bad for you, nowadays?"

I began eyeing the old bank across the street and exhaled tiredly. "It's a long and boring story, Felix."

He patted me on the back again. You know, I thought, I've been touched more this month than I had for the last three, maybe five years? "That's what friends are supposed to be for."

My face and voice were blank. "I thought we were just buddies."

"Well, I'd like to be friends, too. Wouldn't you?"

Sure I would, Felix. I'm just not very good at it, that's all. Ask the guys I used to play ball with. "I'm really kind of a loner."

"So am I. We can be loners together, you know." He nudged me in the arm and held out his hand. I took it and we smiled at each other for a couple of seconds before the gleaming double-deck train rolled up to a halt on the northbound side of the platform.

Felix stood, trying to cover up the pain I could see he was in. He waved at the graying, impatient conductor who stepped from the train doors as a few passengers got off. All stops at 55th Street lasted for a few minutes. Felix wrapped an arm inside of mine. I tried not to blush. "Why don't you come home with me?"

Could I stay there? "It's a school night, Felix!"

"Oh, big deal. I didn't pick up my books because I wanted to catch you before you left, so I can't do any homework. My mother is cooking a big dinner tonight, we'll eat, you can tell me all about school, and I can study one thing while you do another. My building has a pool, so we can take a dip afterwards, sleep, and come back here tomorrow morning. This way you won't have to go home, and we loners can keep each other company."

Do you like classical music? "Where am I going to sleep?"

"I've got a bunk bed. When I was a kid I was afraid of floors in the dark, ha. Now I just like being up in the air. But you can be on top if you want."

The conductor looked at the large, round pocket watch attached to his vest by a silver chain, and stepped back into the belly of the train car, waiting for us to make a decision. Felix held up a one-more-minute finger.

Now, let's see. Dad didn't usually roll home until at least eight. Mom was already off teaching, and had to be at the hospital by eleven. I debated whether either of them would notice if I didn't come home. Now there was a stupid question! "Wouldn't you rather wait until Friday, when we can stay up later?"

"We can do it Friday, too."

"What about your parents? I don't want to impose on them."

Felix walked me onto the train by the arm as the conductor closed the sliding metal doors shut behind us. "They love company. Besides, I won the race, so shut up and pick out where you'd like to sit."

VII

There is no evil angel but love.
Love's Labor's Lost

Felix Cromwell lived in a rust-colored skyscraper near Wacker Drive, one that looked more like an office building than an apartment complex. I always figured a condo or flat in the Loop would be big, luxurious, and expensive, but Felix's current home wasn't very big - two bedrooms, a bath for each, a large living-dining area combo, a kitchen, and a tiny vanity bath. Hell, my Dad's bedroom was that big. Even if the apartment had a great view of the Chicago River, the Wrigley Building, and the Merchandise Mart, it couldn't cost much. Furnishing-wise, Felix's parents went in for the modern, Scandinavian look, which I'd hardly call luxurious. Any furniture that makes the hardwood floor seem appealing wasn't luxurious. No. What made the Cromwell apartment special was the Cromwell family.

Felix's hyper-ingratiating chit-chat ("What kind of sports, movies, books, music, clothes, travel, people, etc. etc. etc. do you like?") and manner (smile, nudge, pat, smile, laugh, touch, smile, hold, and so on) had been driving me nuts from the minute we got on the train until we walked into the apartment and I was greeted with the rich aroma of broiling steaks, and a very warm welcome from Felix's good-looking mom, who was happy to abandon dinner to give her only child a hug and his new friend a very unexpected kiss.

"I'm Arlene, the person responsible for the little guy." Her face was deeply tanned, soft and friendly. The large curls of her dark blond hair were thrown back with abandon. She wore a fuzzy red turtleneck, tight blue jeans, and snakeskin cowboy boots rather well. Her smile was wide and sincere, and was already making me feel very comfortable.

"It's good to meet you, Mrs. Cromwell." We shook hands.

"Call me Arlene or I won't let you stay for dinner."

Felix shifted on his feet and cleared his throat as Arlene's eyes zeroed in on his torn slacks and bloody leg. Her glare could have stopped a tank division in its tracks. "Can he stay over tonight, too, Ma?"

She looked at the gash, seemingly satisfied it was nothing dramatic, and then detected the faint smell of cheap American vodka. The glare moved in my direction. "I couldn't think of anything else to use, Mrs. Crom - Arlene."

Felix blushed. Arlene peered at me with the patented you-can't-fool-me look known to all mothers. I shrugged my shoulders and tried my innocent look, unsuccessfully. "Do you always bring vodka to school?" She propped one of her hands on a hip. No, I thought, I'm usually just equipped for little things like broken hearts and sexual confusion. Poisonous leg wounds and making friends are new to me.

"Just on days they hand back some exams." All right, don't laugh. "No, ma'am."

"Do you have any more?"

A veritable distillery at home, but it's my Dad's. "No, ma'am."

"Do you smoke pot?"

If I started, I'd put Timothy Leary to shame. "No, ma'am."

Arlene reached for a large cutting knife and held the tip of it to the edge of my throat. James giggled quietly in the background. I think Felix was embarrassed. "Don't fuck with an armed Jewish mother." I shook my head. "Good. No booze, no drugs, and no noise after we go to bed."

"Yes, ma'am."

She nodded and returned to the huge salad she was preparing. "We'll be eating in about an hour. Felix, get your friend set up, and change out of that suit, for Heaven's sake." She rolled her eyes at me. "I told him to dress like a normal human being this morning, but, no, I'm only the mother, what the hell do I know?"

A mother with a sense of humor. What a novelty!

"Ma, you're the one who told me the Institute was part of the university, and everyone who went there was a rich brain! I just wanted to fit in!" Felix pointed at me. "I didn't think they went in for the ski lodge look!" No, there's more heat in a ski lodge, pal.

"At least your friend doesn't look like an overdressed car salesman, dear."

We retreated to Felix's bedroom.

*

While telling me about his folks and their last home in Cleveland, Felix got out of his church, er, temple threads. Seeing him in his shorts got me very hard, very quickly. He had a soft build and broad shoulders, which I thought was the suit jacket talking. His arms, legs, chest, and back were all bare but he had a thin pencil of black curls that led down from his belly-button into his tight white briefs that looked like they had been unwrapped that morning. They highlighted his bubble-butt and fit to bust crotch. Now I knew where Felix's height genes ended up.

I watched him clean and dress his leg in the bathroom from the reflection on the door mirror. He picked out a worn-out pair of jeans, a black sweatshirt, and white gym socks from his over-stuffed closet. The room was sparsely decorated. Felix had a shelf of toys and gadgets over a small writing desk and an elaborate telescope, which was positioned near the wide picture window that faced the S-Curve on Lake Shore Drive and the murky sight of Lake Michigan. There was a framed Air France poster of Paris over the desk and an assortment of framed postcards depicting large sailboats at sea on its top shelf, waiting to be hung. Felix sat next to me at the edge of stiff bottom bunk. "I hope there isn't a lot of homework tonight."

"No, thank God, only about an hour's worth. I'll tell you about all the teachers and stuff over dinner. Your parents would probably like to hear it, anyway."

"Great."

"And then what?" I have a suggestion.

"We can go swimming. There's a huge pool and health club in the basement. You'll love it."

No, that's not what I was thinking of. "I don't think one of your suits will fit me." But I'll do without one if you will.

"No. I'll get one of my Dad's. He isn't much bigger than you are."

"Sounds fine." Felix did not move to get up. I nudged him gently with an elbow. "Well? Let's eat, buddy."

"Thanks for coming over tonight." Felix looked down at his lap, pretty much where I was trying not to look.

I tried not to sound as painfully grateful as I suddenly felt I was to be there, with Felix. "Well, thanks for inviting me."

Someone came in the front door. Arlene called out for us from the kitchen. I gulped loudly before reaching across Felix's chest pushing him softly back onto the bed, leaving my arm draped across him as I leaned backwards and settled on an elbow, my forced blank face close to his.

Felix hid his confusion with a half-smile. "What's up, bro?"

'Bro'? Man, did I like the sound of that! "Tell me what you're thinking about, Felix." Quick, before I blurt out what I'm thinking about!

Felix's eyes closed for a moment. "You never told me why you don't like going home anymore."

"Because every time I think about it, it hurts so much I want to cry," I sighed. Felix reached up and squeezed my arm once, but looked at the bedroom's closed door instead of at me. This can't be what was on his mind, I thought. "It's not that I don't want to tell you, though, or talk to you about anything else." Felix finally turned back to face me and squeezed my arm once more. Now, finally, our eyes met. They swallowed the other's whole. Nobody had ever looked at me like that before. "I just want you to go first."

We each smiled, but almost as quickly, I felt Felix drift away again. What did he think was on the other side of that door? I turned his face toward mine, my fingertips tingling with the contact. I camouflaged the lump in my throat by looking at my watch, supposedly to urge Felix on. He nibbled on his lip before replying. "We move around a lot. Dad has a lot of money. Well, it's all from

Grandma, really. But he goes from one project to the next, and we have to pick up and go with him. Just like that, sometimes." He snapped his fingers harshly.

"It sounds like a lot of fun."

Felix tried to smile, but couldn't. He shook his head doubtfully. "Sometimes, I guess. It's one thing when you're little, because you can make friends anywhere. You know? You just walk up to another kid and say, 'Will you be my friend?', but that gets a lot harder when you get older."

"Wow. You're a whole sixteen!"

"I'm serious. I've got friends in back in Cleveland, and cousins and friends all over Florida and New York City. My favorite aunt lives in Vermont. But I don't have any friends here with me, now, except you, and I may be gone by Hanukkah, uh, Christmas."

I glanced away from Felix, toward the city lights outside his bedroom window. All those people doing whatever they did, the wind blowing, the waves on the lake, the stars, if you could see the damned things with all the glare from the buildings, it all seemed so distant. It was just us lying there together, and, at a time in my life that resembled one giant bumper car ride without the rubber bumpers, it felt like a million dollars.

"Will you promise me something?"

I looked back at my friend and nodded once. He sat up and I did too, moving a few inches closer until we touched, from our shoulders to our stocking feet. "Only if you promise me something back."

"Okay." Felix took a deep breath and folded his hands together, as if he was unsure whether to beg or pray or something while he asked. "We're friends. At least, I think we're friends." 'Friends'. Wow. I put my arm on his shoulders, like Nicolasha taught me to, like Papu used to when I was younger and didn't cry so much, like Mom and Dad did...a long time ago. "We might be friends for years. Maybe even for the rest of our lives."

"It depends on what you get me for Christmas."

Felix laughed, or, rather, exhaled in a short breath, like he might have started crying, if he didn't think he'd ruin dinner or have his mother throw a knife at him. "But when I leave..."

"*If* you leave..."

Felix's lowered head shook slowly. "*When* I leave, whenever I do, promise me we'll spend my whole last weekend down here together, just doing everything, all over the city, and when the weekend ends, we won't say anything. We'll hug each other until someone makes fun of us. And then we'll walk away, but stay friends, for as long as we can. Okay? It's a promise?"

I didn't know what to say or how to feel at that particular moment of my life. It was like I had touched something outside of me I didn't even know existed, and was being touched, too, and had no idea what to do about it, other than to want to feel that way for as long as I could. So I pretended it was all a little joke, as if we were in some idiot school play or something. "What if I don't like the way you give hugs?"

Felix gave me a hard stare. "You promise?"

I returned his look meanly. "Hey, I spent all last weekend crying, like I was six, totally helpless, with no one there. I hate feeling like that, and I keep doing it, more and more, and I don't want to. But I probably will, maybe even with you."

"What do you mean, feel that way or cry? You won't be helpless if I'm around. And I don't care if you cry in front of me. No one ever has before, but I won't mind. Boys can cry, too. Hell, I might start if you do!"

I exhaled hard, pulling my arm from Felix's shoulders. "My whole life is turning upside down." I could feel the edge of tears welling in my empty stomach. I clenched my jaw and tried to ignore it. "Don't make fun of me or laugh if I do." Arlene's rather insistent voice from down the hallway broke the silence between us. "You promise?"

"I promise."

I got up and took Felix's hands in mine, pulling him up from the bed. He blushed, but smiled, too. I wanted to keep holding his hands, but he snapped us both out of our preoccupation and stretched to put his arm on my shoulders as he led me out of the room to a dinner that smelled fabulous. "You better call your parents when we're done eating."

I'd rather have put on a sock with a tarantula inside.

*

Jason Cromwell welcomed me to his dinner table with a fearsome handshake and slap on the arm. Even as I took my seat between him and Felix, I could feel Jason's sharp eyes sizing me up. He was about six feet tall, graying, maybe a few years older than Arlene, and seemed quite fit. He shared his wife's unusual November tan. I didn't know it was that sunny in Cleveland. Like his wife, his clothes sported a western touch: snakeskin belt with a wide silver buckle, jeans, fancy boots, and a denim shirt with silver collar edges. A pair of mom-and-pop Jewish cowboys Oy-haw!

We began with a fantastic Caesar's salad and very fresh banana muffins, and headed directly into the steak, filet you could cut with a fork, nicely broiled in thin peppercorn au jus. Felix and I exchanged amused glances when Arlene and Jason hummed along to a soft country & western ballad playing on the nearby cathedral radio. I expected a polite, velvet-gloved interrogation from Jason at any minute, you know, the new friend's first visit routine, but we finished dinner in relative silence, Johnny Cash's "Home of the Blues" notwithstanding.

"What a fabulous meal. Thank you for having me."

"I'd have to die, waiting for one of my sons to give me a compli-ment like that." Arlene dipped her fingers into her water glass and flicked a few drops into Felix's face, who responded by picking up his entire glass, threatening to wing it at his mom.

Felix cleared the plates from the table as Jason sat back and lit a large, dark cigar. "Do you guys have much homework?"

"We'll be done by nine, Dad."

"Then get to it, so you can go swimming before they close." We began to leave the room. "Did you let your parents know you're spending the night?"

"No, sir, I hadn't. I will right now." Ugh.

Felix touched my arm. "You can call from my room, buddy." Arlene and Jason sent us off with big country smiles. I'd rather have made that call from somewhere out in that countryside.

*

Eight rings to get a "Hello?"

"Hi."

"Where the hell are you?"

"Downtown. A friend of mine from school invited me to spend the night. Is that OK?"

Pause. "Well, it's too late to be taking the train home, so there isn't much point in giving you permission."

"I have all my school stuff. We're doing our homework together."

"You could have called hours ago. You'd better, next time."

"Fine."

"I don't need that tone of voice from you, son. Save it for your teachers. I'll leave a note for your mother. Make sure you come straight home tomorrow."

"I will."

"By the way, that teacher of yours, Nicolaus? He called."

My second pause.

"Did he leave a message?"

"He likes the opera you gave him."

Click.

I stared at the phone on Felix's desk until he squeezed my shoulder from behind. My face was blank as he handed me a white terrycloth robe, oversized towel, and a yellow nylon bathing suit.

"Which one did you talk to?" The scotched one, I think.

"My Dad."

"Was he pissed?"

"He's been like that for years."

*

We finished our calculus without too much panic, our dull sociology with a sigh of relief, and the chapter on Prokofiev rather quickly, all before eight-thirty. We didn't switch off using my books. We did it together, sitting next to each other on Felix's bed, something I had never done before, but thought I'd like to do again.

It was a nice feeling, being so close to someone for so long.

(I'd hid the photo album in a separate pouch of my bag when Felix took a pee break.)

"Are you ready to go swimming, pal?"

"I've been ready since dinner."

"Me, too!"

Felix was naked before I began to pull my clothes off. He threw a sock at my face when he caught me watching him. He slipped on a pair of red floral Hawaiian print shorts, and waited for me to try on his dad's suit, which was a little baggy on my frame. "We look like we've been shopping at the Salvation Army."

Arlene and Jason's bedroom door was closed as we passed by. The apartment was dark, except for the television set and the skyline beyond the window. We rode down in the elevator with an old woman, who was bundled up for a cold night's stroll and looked at us oddly, standing there in a couple of bathrobes and bare feet. She seemed relieved to exit at the lobby, while we continued to the building's second basement.

Walking into the health club, we were instantly overwhelmed by a powerful chlorine odor from the pool. A cute blond girl in snug green shorts and a white sweatshirt with the club's emblem on the left breast waved us past the reception desk after recognizing Felix. She smiled at me as I followed my friend into the men's locker room, where we left our robes and towels, and acknowledged two thoroughly exhausted racquetball players who staggered in behind us.

The pool area was large but deserted, and somewhat claustrophobic, with a low ceiling, dark blue walls, and fairly dim lighting. In fact, there were more lights inside the rectangular pool itself than there were in the warm, musty room. It certainly had an atmosphere about it. We stood at the edge of the deep end. "Pretty cool, isn't it, buddy?"

"You're right. I love it."

"Good. The last one to the other side has to strip in the elevator!"

I stared at Felix incredulously, and he winked at me. Before he could react, I pulled Felix' shorts halfway down to his knees and pushed him in the water before diving in and racing to the opposite side. I heard Felix begin his pursuit behind me and increased my speed, coming to a halt at the shallow end two full lengths ahead of him. I jumped up and sat on the smooth concrete edge, my legs hanging in the clear water. Felix stroked up to my feet and spun around underwater, hurling back toward the deep end with a push from the wall of the pool. Damn! I sprang to my feet and shot back into the water, a few feet behind him. I nearly caught him as Felix reached the other side.

We draped our arms over the pool's edge, out of breath. "I won! I won! I won! Na na, na NA na!" Felix stuck his tongue out at me before I decided to dunk him into shutting up. He climbed up the back of my legs and wrapped his arms around my waist from behind, pulling me off the edge into the chlorinated depths. We wrestled underwater, trying to get a better hold on each other's twisting body before stopping to get some air.

"I'm sick of losing races to you, Felix!"

"Hey, that's what you get for underestimating us little guys!"

"Hm. Modest *and* aggressive."

"You'll never beat me in any water sport - swimming, diving, water skiing, sailing, whatever!"

"Too bad you almost killed yourself getting out of East Berlin today." I splashed him in the face.

"I'm pretty proud of that!"

"Proud of what? Crawling under a train platform?"

"No, putz, being good in the water." He splashed me back. "Ever since I was two, we've spent the holidays at my Grandma's place down in Fort Myers."

"Did you ever learn how to play ball?"

"A little bit. I catch better than I throw, and run a <u>lot</u> better than I hit. Dad thinks I'm a natural shortstop, but I don't really play enough to be much good."

"You just don't want anyone calling you 'shortstop'."

"Well, that, too." We exchanged smiles. "So what are you good at?"

"Hitting." And keeping my hands off of you, Felix.

"Do you play in a league or anything?" I shook my head regretfully.

"You should, if you're good at it."

"I hate groups." I don't think I could handle having twenty three friends all at once.

Before Felix could encourage me further, the young receptionist trotted out from the ladies' locker room with an armful of towels. She pointed at a clock on the wall. "We're closing in a few minutes, guys."

Felix nodded and climbed out of the pool, eyeing her carefully as she straightened up the chairs and switched off the underwater lights. The dark pool seemed scary, all of a sudden. Felix offered his hand and helped me from the water. "Isn't she cute?"

"You should have pushed her in with me," I lied.

*

We peeled off our suits and hurried into the shower. Felix unnerved me when he chose the showerhead facing mine, chatting happily about having won a swim meet back in Cleveland while he rubbed hot water over his body and I nodded and smiled and kept my eyes locked on him, forcing myself to listen

71

With our wet suits wrapped in our towels, we headed back upstairs. As soon as the elevator door closed, Felix pointed at me. "Take off your robe." Oh my God. "You lost the race, buddy. Remember?"

"I beat you to the shallow side," I stammered.

"After you pulled my trunks down, cheating bastard." Felix must have sensed my growing panic. He smiled devilishly. "I beat you round-trip, though."

The tiny elevator bell sounded and we reached our floor, thank God. "Too late, shortstop!" I gave Felix the finger and ran out down the hall, trying to keep my borrowed terrycloth robe out of his hands. We stopped at the foot of the apartment door and I wrestled the laughing Felix to the burgundy carpet. I began tickling him into submission, my hands reaching into his loosening robe, poking and pinching and pulling every inch of his soft, hairless chest, stomach, back, abdomen, and neck. Felix begged me to stop through his hysterical laughter, completely immobilized by my assault.

As soon as I saw it, I placed my hand around his thick erection for a moment and held it there, a moment we were both still and silent. "No," Felix whispered. I squeezed upward once, slowly, as Felix put his hand over mine. "Please don't." I let go and stood up, tightly closing the borrowed robe around my shaking body. Felix's face was flushed as he slipped back into his, his eyes pointed downwards.

My throat was dry and tight. I could barely breathe, afraid to imagine what would come next. Felix began to open the apartment door, but turned to look at me, instead. Our faces were filled with an odd mixture of apprehension and wonder, staring at each other as if for the first time. He hesitated, trying to collect his thoughts. I would have said something first, if I wasn't too petrified to collect a few thoughts of my own.

"I'm sorry." Felix said it like he was afraid I might punch him to the floor, or turn around and walk out into the night.

"So am I." I tried to smile, and my friend tried to smile back.

*

I felt strangely reassured, listening to Felix lock the bedroom door behind us. He did not turn on the lights. My jeans, t-shirt, underwear, and socks were neatly folded at the foot of the lower bunk, beside an extra comforter and pillow. The clothes were freshly washed. The corner of the room was illuminated by the metallic glow of the high-rise hotel outside the bedroom window. Felix stood beside me.

"Did my Mom wash your clothes? She's really cool that way." I nodded in the dark, suddenly wanting to tell Felix about my visiting Nicolasha's house last weekend, about the fights with my Dad, about the divorce, about the photo album, about everything, but all that came out was a babyish little sob that made me feel like a clown. Then a few tears dropped down my cheeks, damn it. I guess I was going to end up crying all this week, now. Felix's arm was around my shoulders in an instant, the hallway carpet scene swept off into some forgotten corner. "What's the matter, buddy? Please don't cry." Oh, well, that sure helped. Now I really began to cry, despite trying hard not to. Felix folded me into his arms, snuggled his face against the base of my neck as his hands delicately rubbed my back, and waited for me to cry myself out with patience.

And I thought I was embarrassed in class today. I took a deep breath and stepped out of Felix's arms into the full view of his toothy smile. "I've never cried in front of anyone else, before now."

Felix's hands squeezed the side of my arms. His voice was a tender whisper, holding the assurance of someone who already knew the answer to the question he was about to ask. "Is it as bad as crying alone?" I shook my head silently and glanced away. Felix squeezed my arms again. "Does that mean we're real pals, now?"

I looked back at Felix and held a hand out, oh so formally. "How about buddies?"

"I like friends, better." Felix took my hand in both of his and pressed tightly.

"To hell with it. Let's be best friends." This time, Felix looked like he was wobbling with some unspoken emotion. I thought he'd like that. We hugged each other tight for a long time. I was too bushed to notice or care if I'd popped a bone between us. If I did, Felix wasn't saying.

"We better get some sleep, buddy."

"I like friend, better." I messed up Felix's hair and gave him a tiny push as he climbed to the top bunk. I put my clothes on the floor and slipped out of the robe and under the comforter before I realized what I was doing, or noticed Felix looking upside-down at me from above.

"Do you sleep in the raw at home?"

Oops. A burning blush raised my body temperature. "Sorry."

"Don't be. It just shows you feel at home here, which is fine by me." I heard Felix setting a tinny alarm clock.

Then his robe dropped to the hardwood floor beside me. "You know, I've never done this?" It was all I could do not to cry out. "Good night, Hitman."

'Hitman'? Cool! "Goodnight, shortstop."

VIII

Sit by my side and let the world slip.
We shall never be younger.
The Taming of the Shrew

The next four weeks that led up to Christmas passed me by like a montage in a movie, a bunch of little scenes and shots edited together with particularly poignant soundtrack music to indicate a great deal of activity shown in minimum screen time. In other words, the time was spent happily, unlike those lonely, miserable chapters in our lives that plod along in real, *War and Peace* time.

Felix and I started becoming each other's first best friend. We met at 7:30 every morning for juice and the freshest bialys at the deli on 55th Street, bought huge sandwiches for lunch before going to classes together, lunch together, and homework at the University library together before taking our respective trains home. I stayed over at the Cromwell's every Friday and Saturday night, and treated the family to an adventuresome series of guided walking tours of the Loop and Gold Coast while they treated me to their warmth and acceptance, and quite a few free meals. I got the better end of the deal.

We talked ourselves to sleep on those weekend nights. We talked about every blasted thing that had ever occurred in our sixteen-year-old lives, good and bad, but never mentioned our first night together, the looming dissolution of my family, or what Felix obviously felt was the impending, "I'm sorry, son, but we're leaving Chicago" speech from Jason.

We never mentioned girls or girlfriends, either. Arlene asked us once over dinner if there were any cute girls in our class. Felix replied with unusual tartness that most of them were geeks, and the ones that weren't certainly wouldn't go out with anyone they thought might be gone the following month. I remained silent. So did Jason. It was our only meal together that reminded me of dining with my family. We didn't give each other a hug before going to sleep that night.

(We called each other 'shortstop' and 'Hitman' whenever we were alone, together.)

On the collapsing home front, Mom and Dad simply ceased to exist as a unit. I'll give Dad credit, though. When I got back home on Sundays, we watched football games together and went to the country club for dinner, where I de-briefed him on what I had done with the Cromwells that weekend. He tried hard to be pleasant, which had to be a real strain on him, sometimes. It's not like those were pleasant days for any of us, or for me, at least when I wasn't with Felix or his folks. I think he was trying to keep his distance, knowing I wouldn't be moving with him to New York City because of how close Felix and I had become.

When creating some distance between yourself and your son becomes the best way to remain pleasant, it's safe to say the salad days are over.

Mom let her life in the emergency room and the suburban career woman social ghetto take over the driver's seat. You see, if she weren't so busy, she might have had to take a look at her life, or her husband, or even her son. And that wouldn't do, now, would it? Actually, I'm pretty sure she had had that up-close-and-personal look-see, subconsciously, anyway, and that's why she was trying so hard to pretend everything was fine. I'll bet the rest of those over-coiffured, under-emotioned hags didn't have a shred of suspicion Mom and Dad had ever raised their voices at each other, much less thrown things with intent.

At first, I kind of resented Nicolasha carrying on as if I was just another one of his students, one who hadn't been to his home away from home, one who hadn't seen his photo album (did he even realize it wasn't in his end-table drawer?), or one who didn't have dreams about him. But then I came to realize he was afraid, just like Mom and Dad were, of actually living what they felt.

Is this what being an adult was all about? Living what someone said you're supposed to feel, or you imagined you had to feel, instead of what you wanted to feel? To hell with that.

Of course, I refused to accept Nicolasha wasn't feeling something about me. But I thought I knew what he was afraid of. It was the same fear I felt after I touched Felix in the hallway, after I put my lips on Nicolasha's, after I stared into the photo album and...well, you know.

These events are exactly what I mean about living what you feel. I couldn't talk to anyone about it. It ate away at me like an acid. And, of course, it was Christmas.

My mind had seeped into a daze fed by the macabre film I had just seen at the still ornate but fast-fading Chicago Theater, a grim character study of a ventriloquist who loses his mind and becomes a murderer when the personality of his dummy takes over. "Magic," indeed.

At first, I thought I had walked into a street pole. I slipped on a small patch of ice and collided with the large Santa Claus look-a-like before landing on the cold State Street sidewalk with my knees. He was old, haggard, and dissipated all at once, and the chintzy Santa Claus outfit did nothing to conceal these pleasantries from anyone who got close enough to smell the bourbon on the man's strained breath. He started ringing his school bell again, almost directly over me. The harsh, brassy clangs hurt my ears. His bloodshot eyes howled, Ho ho fucking ho.

Rush hour buses, taxis, and people continued their ballet of the dead while I used Santa's red metal collection bucket to climb to my feet. The besotted old gasbag finally looked about to hit me with his bell when a tiny black girl tugged at his loose red flannel pants. Tears were running down her face. "Santa? Where are my mommy and daddy?"

I couldn't tell if he was clearing his throat, or was about to spit a hocker the size of a beer can out towards one of us. "I don't know, little girl. Where did you leave them?"

Her arms wrapped around the imposter's leg. "I didn't. They left me!"

I'll bet he thought the job would be easy money. All he had to do was smile and laugh and ring his Goddamn bell until the passers-by got so irritated they gave up a few cents into the collection bucket. Any wino could do that. His eyes peered out into the crowd and landed on mine.

"Well, let's catch our breath and try to remember. OK?"

He took the little girl off of his leg into his arms, wiping the tear streams from her rounded cheeks. She smiled at him like he really was Santa Claus. He swung the girl away from me and whispered, "What are you waiting for, punk?"

I shook my head and walked off toward the train station with a smile. I was the last person to walk into the boxcar before the doors slid shut behind me and we slowly pulled out of the terminal. On to Theresienstadt!

I guess I was too old to ask Santa Claus anything, but, as the commuter train rolled south through the scarred brick hedgerows of the South Side to the suburban wasteland that lay beyond, I decided to begin asking other, perhaps less important father figurines, about all the aches and pangs inside me I found harder and harder to hide from myself anymore.

*

On the last day before Christmas break, Nicolasha transported his excellent stereo system to school so we could listen to Bach's *Christmas Oratorio* in the fullest audiophonic splendor, short of a live performance. He had also baked dozens of rich, delectable Christmas cookies and brewed gallons of his sweet honey tea, which we devoured with intent while the arias and choruses played forcefully in the background.

It was a Pilot Institute tradition to bring a Christmas gift for each of your teachers, the size of the gift determined by how much you learned from the teacher (or how good your grades were in their class). Nicolasha sat in a silent daze as his desk top was covered with large, prettily wrapped packages. I hoped he got a leg up on a new wardrobe in all those presents.

Felix and I had debated for hours about what to buy for Nicolasha. Since we had no accurate idea of what records he might like (if there were any he didn't already have), we were torn between an expensive, mounted globe from Rand McNally and a slightly worn ebony metronome from a pawn shop over on Van Buren Street. That was, until Arlene came upon a rare book store in Rogers Park that was a trove of musical and literary editions. Felix chose a complete, hardbound score to Prokofiev's *Aleksandr Nevsky*, while the owner, a pipe-smoking, pear-shaped old man in glasses, suggested I opt for an incredible original text of poetry by Yevtushenko (that I really wanted to keep for myself, even if I couldn't read Cyrillic). We congratulated ourselves (with thanks to Arlene), confident in having trumped our classmates.

Felix waited for everyone else to return to their seats before bringing our presents up to Nicolasha, who received them with an appreciative grin. As Felix sat back down, our teacher devastated me with a private, longing gaze, holding his hands over his left breast for a few desperate seconds.

"What's the matter, Hitman?" Felix tapped the edge of my knuckle with his pen. I pulled away from Nicolasha's orbit, only to be met with another one of Felix's kind-hearted smiles. I shook my head and nibbled on a cookie, convinced the safest place for me was somewhere in that oratorio.

*

Nicolasha asked me to stay for a moment as the rest of class left to begin their Christmas vacation. Felix gave me a curious look before I patted him on the shoulder.

"I'll meet you outside, OK?"

"Sure thing. Don't be too long, though. The movie starts pretty soon."

"No problem."

Felix closed the classroom door after waving at both of us. Click. The din of students and teachers and parents occurring beyond the closed door was as remote to us as Iceland. The sudden blizzard of silence stilled us both for many subsequent moments.

Nicolasha took a few hesitant steps toward me, reaching into his tweed jacket for a long, red envelope.

He fingered it nervously as the Bach holiday choral continued to play. I could see it had my name written across it. Clearing my throat with a shy smile, I held out my hand to accept it.

"Please do not open it until you leave. It is a little surprise." Ah ha - airline tickets! He was defecting back to Siebenbürgen and needed someone to help carry his records!

"We're supposed to buy you something, Nicolasha."

"You are special, little friend."

I laughed awkwardly, before Nicolasha pressed the tip of two fingers onto his lips and reached toward me, touching my lips with them in turn. And now I was frozen, right there where I stood. He wrapped his arms completely around mine, pinning them to my side, enveloping me in a true Father Christmas bear hug. Nicolasha kissed my ear and held me in front of him as Felix re-entered the room.

Nicolasha leaned toward my face, whispering. "Please call me over the holiday." How about tonight?

"I will, *Freiherr*." We turned and smiled at Felix, who gestured excitedly for me to come with him. So much for another kiss.

"I can't believe it! Dad's outside. He must have left work early!" A father, leave work early? I didn't believe a word of it. The second coming must be near. I headed to the door with Felix, putting the envelope inside of my pea coat. We snapped our heels together and saluted at our young teacher in playful precision (something we practiced on Jason and Arlene after seeing "The Man Who Would Be King" a few weeks ago) before we made our getaway through the hallways of the Institute. "How come Mr. Nicolaus doesn't give me a hug like that?"

"I've known him longer."

I glanced over my shoulder, feeling like an awful lot of me was still back there in Nicolasha's arms.

*

The ride downtown was hilarious. Jason made us sit together with him in the front seat of his elephantine Lincoln Continental, probably to make sure we didn't miss a single note of his *Elvis Sings Christmas* 8-track tape. In the middle of South Shore Drive, he wrapped his right arm around our shoulders and cradled us both in a savage arm lock while weaving from lane to lane, pretending we were being chased by a car full of assassins. He ordered Felix into the back seat, and refrigerated the car by rolling down and locking the power windows - until the two of us mooned someone. Neither of us was sure Jason was serious, until he slowed down and let a few cars actually pass us, looking for the right target. I laughed and knelt down on the seat with my rear end touching the top of the window sill, urging Felix to follow my lead, which he did just as his father yelled out, spotting an elderly couple in a king-size Cadillac to our right. Jason maneuvered his car beside the old folks, who were treated to a festive view of our bare asses for a few chilling seconds.

We almost drove clear over a tiny Datsun hurrying into a valuable parking space outside the show, let Jason buy the popcorn, Twizzlers (Jason's choice), and Coke - no hot dogs, dammit - and sat in the first row of the Carnegie's "upper deck" (my choice) and laughed ourselves silly watching "The Blues Brothers". Arlene met us for a pig-out pan pizza dinner at Geno's, before Jason offered to buy each of us an album at a nearby record store. Arlene picked out an old collection of torch songs by Frank Sinatra, while Jason found another Elvis Presley Christmas album, I was sorry to see. We lone wolves headed straight to the classical section: Felix took a recording of Prokofiev's *Peter and the Wolf* with Sean Connery narrating ("Those woods are filled with wolves. Do you know anything about wolves? Dangerous lot, wolves.") while I chose Bartók's Romanian Dances, which I'd never heard before.

We drove back to the apartment and agreed to listen to each of the records in the morning. I got an unexpected goodnight kiss from both of Felix's parents before they retired to their bathroom to take a long shower together. Felix asked if I wanted to stay up and watch "It's A Wonderful Life," perhaps my least favorite film of all time, before hitting the sack. I said I was tired, a white lie told just to get us locked away for the night.

Felix stood at the foot of the bunk and reached under where the two beds came together. "Help me with this, buddy." I took the other side and let Felix guide his top bunk directly beside mine. "Right here is cool."

"I'm afraid to ask what you're up to, shortstop." But not as afraid as I was about what was going through my mind like a fever.

"Trust me, Hitman."

The gleaming silver lights from the adjacent hotel flowed over both beds now. Satisfied with our new sleeping arrangements, Felix walked me by the arm to his desk, where he pulled a heavy manila business envelope out from the clutter. He held it up in front of him with a sober look. "This is from all of us."

"Jesus, Felix! You know your presents are at my house. Let's wait until you guys drop me off Sunday, and we can open them all together."

"No. I want to share this with you now."

I had no idea what could be in the envelope, remembering the one Nicolasha gave me earlier, still stuffed in my coat. I wondered if that was why we visited the record store. Gift certificates? That would be really cool. I slid my finger in the seam and pulled out an inexpensive card depicting a cute village scene filled with little kids playing in the snow and a short greeting embossed in gold and written in Cyrillic. I shook my head with a chuckle and opened the card, astounded into silence by the sight of an Eastern Airlines ticket to Fort Myers, Florida.

"We leave late Sunday night. You leave early Wednesday morning." Wham. The sinker hit the catcher's glove, and I was standing there with the bat on my shoulder. "We'll take the sailboat out every morning, play ball all day, and hang out at the beach until we go to bed." I must have looked pretty stupid, staring at the ticket with my mouth hanging open. "If you think your parents won't let you go, fuck 'em. Don't say anything, and just get to the airport. Ma says we can deal with it when we come back."

I have a solution. Let's not come back.

I tossed the card and ticket onto the desk and wrapped my arm around Felix's shoulders. He smiled and put an arm around my back. We stood there together, suddenly feeling the other one saying "Hey, you're my best friend, I love you!" without having to break down and say it out loud. This was all very new to me. Felix reached up and kissed me on the nose. "Happy Hanukah, Hitman." Jesus. I pulled Felix into my arms and held him there for a few quiet seconds before I bent down and lifted him off of the floor from his waist, slinging him over my shoulder. His hands reached down my body, pulling my shirt and the elastic band of my shorts out from my jeans. I pressed my fingers into Felix' legs, triggering his tickling mechanism. We burst out laughing as I began to stagger and we fell onto the beds.

*

We laid close to each other, separated by the edge of the mattresses, our respective blankets, and the underwear we both left on that night. We went to sleep almost immediately after our pillow fight, but I was awake again, anxiously staring at the unfocused dark of the ceiling with my hands folded behind my head on the pillow. My mind was filled with warm images of Florida's Gulf Coast, while my heart was filled with emotion, thinking about Felix and his family.

I'd never been sailing. In fact, the only kinds of vehicles I usually liked were the ones with engines. Maybe Jason would teach me how to sail. I hoped we could find enough people to get a ball game going. Was Fort Myers close to Sarasota? Wonder if any Sox guys were down there yet? I couldn't wait to lie on the beach and talk all night until we saw the sun rise. Hopefully, the Gulf wouldn't be too cold to skinny-dip in. I tried to not get hard just thinking about it. I'll bet Felix' grandpar-ents were really cool. I was glad the Cromwells weren't religious. I could barely stand all my Catholic stuff by then, much less some other name-brand God stuff. If the Jewish holy days were half as depressing as their folk music...oy!

The next two weeks would be great, being a part of a real, live family. That was my idea of a Christmas present.

Felix faced me as he slept on his side, one arm under his pillow, the other hanging loose across his chest. I moved closer to him and touched his loose hand, which closed ever so slightly on my fingers. "You're my best friend, Felix." And my first, I then realized. He moved a little bit. "I love you."

There. I said it.

I ran the back of my hand over his cheek very lightly. Felix began to stir and slid over onto his stomach, dropping his loose hand beside my bare shoulder. He moaned softly into his pillow.

"I hope we're friends forever, shortstop."

"Me, too, Hitman."

I considered slapping him silly with my pillow, but his warm hand closed over my shoulder, and I went back to sleep with a smile on my face.

IX

A little more than kin,
and less than kind!
Hamlet

Outsiders used to have a hard time keeping track of our family tree, but I didn't, since most of the branches have long since been pruned by the tall, hooded guy with the scythe. With the singular exception of Uncle Alex, the branches that were left would make some fine kindling wood.

I specifically refer to the trio of carrion, also known as A) Dad's stepmother / aunt's sisters, B) Uncle Alex's mom's sisters, and C) my great vulture aunts, great when they sent me five or ten dollars on my birthday, vultures the rest of the time. The proper word hasn't been invented to describe these predators when we would spend yet another torturous Christmas Eve at one their homes, straddling the tangled, barbed wire of their malicious gossip, innuendos, suggestions, put-downs, cut-downs, and manipulations.

Aunt Dutch was the oldest, a cold, near-psychotic spinster with an oversized bank account amassed by her dead (luckily for him) husband, who spent her free time hatching attitudes with her submissive shrew of a little sister, Aunt Melody, an alcoholic fool whose singular life achievement had been to bear two children with her oblivious bartender husband, Dad's Uncle Albert. Julia was the oldest. She was an over-educated, fast-talking slut, who bounced from companion to companion (always accruing something tangible from the split, like condos, cars, that sort of thing and career to career (stock broker, photographer, tennis pro, teacher, consultant, and who the hell knows what else), while little Matt was an untalented ex-college jock and failed National Hockey League forward, who trailed along behind his sister, landing jobs and insider scams in her peripatetic wake.

Which brings us to the baby hydra, dear Aunt Hilly, a brittle, ruthless personality with a good intellect and a better mean streak, two qualities she used to dominate the emotionally-trodden lives of her husband, George, an inept tradesman, and her once-handsome son, Lawrence, the big fish mayor of the little upscale suburban pond we all fled to from our old neighborhood in the city.

Ah, Christmas Eve. Wake me when it's over.

Our entire day had been strung like piano wire. Dad stayed in his room and continued to pack his clothes and belongings, Mom stayed downstairs and decorated our huge artificial tree, and I entertained the household with a particularly bombastic collection of orchestral greats, carefully selected from my Thanksgiving buying spree. We all ignored the fact that the sun would eventually go down, our vampire relatives would rise from their graves, and we would be off to Aunt Hilly's lair, an oversized, faux-antebellum home for our family's Christmas Eve masque.

I was glad Aunt Hilly drew the short stick that year, though. She was the only good cook I was related to, and had a stern, unyielding air about her that I kind of liked. Oh, she was a vile bitch, through and through, but Aunt Hilly always let me get away with murder when I was a younger brat (something she never did for the rest of her nieces and nephews), while I enjoyed watching the rest of the family scatter like pigeons when she came into a room.

(I think it was my tenth birthday, when I eavesdropped and heard Aunt Hilly tell Uncle George she thought Dad was a bully and a shyster, Mom was a horseshit cook and housekeeper, Uncle Alex was a pretentious, flaky wannabe artist, and I was the only good thing left out of her dead sister's family. Well, Dad still was, Mom always had been, but Uncle Alex wasn't a wannabe anything. That was his problem. I think the real reason Aunt Hilly liked me because I wasn't afraid of her.)

I hadn't seen my Uncle since last year. I wondered if he had hooked up with another wife?

The volume on my stereo was so loud, I could hear it through my bedroom wall, the shower curtain, and the running water. It was kind of like taking a bath offstage at the Concertgebouw, with their Orchestra in full swing. Every time I heard Prelude to Act Three of *Lohengrin*, I pictured Stukas sweeping out of the sky and panzers bursting across the plain. Wow. I pondered those real-life images in terms of my family's blood and couldn't keep from smirking.

Oh, I forgot, Mom, you don't like Wagner.

I dried off in my locked bedroom. Why I locked the door was anyone's guess. I don't remember the last time either of them tried to come in once my music started playing. The record moved on to the Liebestod from *Tristan und Isolde*. Its passion and devastation filled the dark and my thoughts. The damp towel fell to the carpet as I stood in front of the icy window, reaching a hand out to press my fingertips against the frozen glass.

I put on a fresh t-shirt and a black corduroy shirt, thermal socks, long underwear, a new pair of jeans, and my hiking shoes, just in case Uncle Alex wanted to get away from the party and have one of his famous long conversations outside in the cold. We took Mom's Mercury station wagon over to Aunt Hilly's. It was as old as I was. I think she kept it just to aggravate her husband, successfully. Dad did the driving, without turning on the radio or the heat, but that was OK, because Mom's matter-of-fact Season's Greetings was quite enough comforting entertainment for me, thank you. You see, my parents, in the grip of a heightened state of seasonal dementia, decided to announce their divorce to what was left of the family tonight.

I remembered me and Felix sitting very close to each other in the dark back seat of his dad's Lincoln while his parents drove me home the previous day, and how happy I felt just being in the same vehicle with the Cromwells. Well. I guess I must have fallen out of the car and been run over by a train or something and died and went to hell and just didn't realize it yet.

Was she still talking? Were we moving then? I always thought hell would be a lot warmer than the wagon was at that point. I should jump out of the car when we pass over a bridge, I thought. But there weren't any bridges on the way to Aunt Hilly's. If there were, I'm sure Mom or Dad would have set fire to them by now.

Fuck, when did my flight leave?

*

Everyone got their kisses and phony compliments before fanning out into the nest of vipers. Uncle Albert and Uncle George exchanged opinionated misinformation on the college football scene while watching some lesser Bowl game on TV, Aunt Dutch clawed her way through Matthew's outer defenses in her undisguised effort to make him look bad in front of his pale and dumpy fiancée (his third, I was pretty sure), Aunt Melody was drooling her way through a self-justifying homily with Julia's opaque acquiescence, there were some cousins with bad accents who I didn't even know running around being friends with everyone, Uncle Alex hadn't arrived yet (probably sitting in his rent-a-car a block away, smoking a bag) and Aunt Hilly, while conducting the preparation of her ten-course feast like it was the landing at Inch'on, decided to open up two more fronts, attacking Mom ("No time to be a real wife or mother, in between your overpriced social circuit and your save-the-world turn...") and Dad ("And you call yourself a husband, a father, a *man*, letting your family dissolve like a snowball?).

Aunt Hilly didn't believe in divorce, apparently.

"What about your son? Did either of you selfish blockheads ever stop and think what this might do to him? Or what it already may have done?"

A playwright could not have timed it better. I walked into the warm, over-lit kitchen, playing with one of Aunt Hilly's old black cats, just as she began to pose these questions to my ashen-faced and disoriented parents. My unexpected presence gave a palpable justification to Aunt Hilly's sneering assault. "Their son doesn't give a damn, anymore."

"No, and I don't blame you." She dismissed them with the singular act of putting out her cigarette. "Here," she handed me a large bowl of red cabbage and a basket of homemade bread, "help me bring the food in."

*

Uncle Alex barged into the house in the middle of the meal, accompanied by a Veronica, some young woman with short hair, sleepy eyes, no make-up, and perfectly formed lips. She looked more like my older sister than his latest wife. She greeted Mom and Dad as if she knew them (the only moment Dad took a break from glaring furiously at me), and gave me a hug before sitting down on Uncle Alex's lap. She smelt like a pine tree after a rainfall, and was dressed like Morticia Addams. Of course, everyone acted as if they weren't appalled by the latest addition to our gathering, and the desultory conversation hardly missed a beat, until it wound its way to me.

"So, are you still going to that expensive university school your father always complains about, nephew?" Uncle Alex's fur-lined trench coat looked to be worth stealing.

"Uh huh." I took a mouthful of sweet potatoes and stuffing.

"Learn anything interesting for all that litigation money?"

Well, I thought, let's see. I could tell you all about the Manchu Dynasty, or discuss Nietzsche, or fake my way through some geometry, or have a few opinions on Buddhism, or respond *non capisco cos'e che non va* when you asked about my parents, or make you swim in lines from *Much Ado About Nothing*, or even what records to buy if you went on a mad shopping binge, Unc. And a little about Judaism. Oh, yes, and a little about modern photography. I have this album at home. Would you like to see it?

I washed my food down with a sip of tart New York white wine. "I'm learning a lot about classical music." I smiled at Aunt Hilly. I bet she liked Wagner.

"That's it?" Uncle Alex grabbed a drumstick from my plate.

"I'm learning how to make friends, too." My face was blank as I stared back at Dad.

"Good. That's more important than the rest of the crap these schools push, lately." Uncle Alex kissed Veronica. "What are your plans for the next couple of days?"

I shifted uneasily in my seat, glancing between Mom and Dad, and took another sip of the dour wine. "I'm going to Florida."

Veronica touched Mom's unmoving hand. "That sounds fun."

"I'm going alone." Dad sat back in his chair, his bitter gaze locked on me. Mom nibbled on her lower lip, and tried to avoid everyone's inquiring look. "My best friend invited me." I said that as if it explained everything.

A few seconds elapsed, but they might as well have been minutes, or hours. Or days, if the pit of my stomach was any gauge. The silence soon grew deafening. Veronica tried to put a good face on it. "I'm sure you'll have a wonderful time." Honey, when you're at ground zero, there's only one direction you can go.

"Maybe we should talk about this at home, baby." For some reason, Mom looked genuinely hurt. I couldn't imagine why.

"What, and interrupt your divorce?"

That wasn't meant to be thought out loud.

Uncle Alex looked to his beloved Rika and Simon for something in the way of an elucidation. Mom began to cry as she got up and hurried out of the crowded dining room. Dad's eyes continued to burn into me as he hurled his chair backwards and stormed away. A few of the displaced-person cousins, undoubtedly starved from their long voyage on the canned ham boat, tucked back into their meals. Nobody seemed ready to chime in and play referee, and, one by one, they fell back into the morass of their own private skirmishes.

My uncle looked at me in complete dismay and confusion. I looked back in outrage. Sure, my family had a near Olympian skill for papering over and lying about their troubles, but I still could not believe Dad hadn't mentioned a single word to Uncle Alex about their split. Talk about ground zero.

Mom practically screamed out my name from the front door. I finished my wine as Uncle Alex took me by the arm, pulling me down to his lips. "I don't know what the hell is going on, but we'll come over tomorrow morning, to try and sort this out. Stay cool until then, huh?"

"Yeah, right. The funeral parlor opens at nine."

Aunt Hilly let a long sigh out through her nose as I walked away to Santa's Detroit sleigh.

*

Dad swung me into the back seat by my collar. The wheels of the station wagon squealed as we spun out of the icy driveway onto the empty suburban avenue. I heard Mom sniffling and gasping, trying to keep the flood gates at bay, staring into some unknown space outside of her window. The further we got from Aunt Hilly's house, the faster Dad accelerated. His hands were wrapped like coil around the steering wheel. I closed my eyes, trying to picture a silver and blue Eastern jet rumbling down the runway and screaming off into the December morning sky. It was almost nine p.m. Only thirty six hours to go.

Suddenly, I jolted forward as the wagon skidded to a noisy, barely controlled halt. Before I could get my bearings, Dad's hard palms began to rain on me, bouncing my face from his hands to the car window. Mom cried out and lunged sideways at him, but he knocked her out cold with a swing of his arm across her chin.

I flung my door open and scrambled on my hands and knees onto the wet road and up a small, weed-covered incline that led to the train tracks. I heard him coming and panicked, stumbling in some mud as I tried to get up and run. Dad pulled me to my feet with his shaking hands, clawing at my ears and mouth to hold me still only to slap me back down into the muddy snow when he did, before finally dragging me by my hair back to the car.

"Get in, you little bastard!" He slapped me to the pavement again. I landed near the belching exhaust pipe. I could taste blood inside of my mouth. I forced myself to stand up and face him directly, even as my legs seemed weak under my weight as I shivered from the cold and the adrenaline shooting through me.

I didn't see my father anymore. He was just some strange abstraction, some idle memory as outdated as the White Sox's red pin-stripe uniforms. My facial expression and tone of voice were dull and remote. I would sooner die than let go of my feelings in front of this suit impersonating a father. "Go to hell," I whispered.

He drew back his hand to strike me again, and I flinched, bracing myself for the blow. He stood there for a few seconds, savoring his little victory, before he stormed back to the car. "You can come back in the house when I'm gone in the morning." I heard Mom start to scream at Dad before he closed his door and drove off, just like that.

A beautiful sight, we're happy tonight, walking ... where?

I sank to my knees with my arms wrapped around myself, trying badly to keep my breathing level. I wasn't going back to Aunt Hilly's. I spat out some blood and wiped my lips across my sleeve. I didn't know where Uncle Alex was staying. Felix was already in Florida. An Amtrak passenger train roared past on the tracks above me. Hanging my head, I noticed a bent red envelope a few inches away from me in the tall, brittle weeds.

I had completely forgotten about Nicolasha's Christmas card.

It was a terrific color lithograph of classic nutcrackers, with an inscription in German. There were also two tickets inside - box seats, for Friday, January 10th, at seven o'clock. The Chicago Symphony Orchestra was playing Symphony Number Fifteen by our old comrade Shostakovich.

I looked up into the clear night sky, and, through my swollen cheek and bleeding lip, smiled. The stars glistened down at me as I took a deep breath of frosty air and headed up to the tracks, hoping I didn't freeze to death before I got to Hyde Park.

X

Receive what cheer you may.
The night is long that never finds the day.
Macbeth

It was almost midnight by the time I reached Roseland, passing the dark and empty 111th Street platform and climbing down the corner of the train line's cement overpass. I fell down the last few feet, landing on the sidewalk behind the tiny twenty four-hour diner built into the side of the overpass. I used to love their hot dogs when we lived a few blocks away, and I'd been tempted to stop for one coming back from school, but it looked shabby and a little dangerous, the neighborhood's 'change' and intervening years having had unpleasant visual effects on the place.

(Yes, the neighborhood *changed*. We were too sophisticated to say blacks had moved in, or we had moved out. We weren't sociological enough to speak convincingly about natural urban migratory patterns, or clever enough to see the fast-spreading rot strangling all the nearby heavy industry. The neighborhood just...changed. Attendance at all the Catholic churches dropped off. No one wanted to go back. The surrounding frame houses and bungalows suddenly seemed more run-down and ill-kept. The local Catholic boys' high school quietly grew a fence. Palmer Park started looking like an unmade bed, because Roseland *changed*, everyone would hiss. Not because the city stopped maintaining it, of course, like the very white Streets and Sanitation stopped bothering with the alleys and side streets, which began sporting potholes we could have used for our toy boats on rainy days. Not even the cops would go into the Chicken Unlimited on 111th Street. My favorite toy store on "the Avenue" (Michigan) went out of business. My favorite candy store on 115th Street, where I used to gorge myself on grape-flavored Twizzlers, turned into a Baptist meeting hall, and the State Theater, where Scott and Roberta took me to see "Dr. Who and the Daleks" on a bizarre midnight showing with "Night of the Living Dead", became a Baptist church. The Normal Theater, on 119th Street, where me and anyone else I could drag in sat through the grandest double-feature of my childhood - "Thunderball" and "You Only Live Twice" - four out of the seven days it played, went on its merry neighborhood theater way, still dispensing ice cream bars from a cooler tucked in a corner away from the concession stand, still selling pineapple-orange and cherry soda (with the choice of carbonated or non-carbonated a matter of pressing a button), its wide and open lobby still lined with 8x10 glossies of upcoming features, but no longer thronged with chattering neighborhood kids on weekends, since the Saturday and Sunday matinees were the first thing to go. I guess the only films black kids wanted to see were "The Klansmen", "Super Fly T.N.T.", and "Mandingo", right? I wanted to go back and see "Sounder" one week, but no one would take me. I'll bet they didn't stock Black Crows licorice chews by the time one of the new neighborhood patrons left a smoldering cigar in the bathroom and set fire to the place one night last year. Dad had taken me for a quick recon through the old neighborhood on the way back to Holy Rosary, for a nearly-deserted Easter Mass given in Polish. I asked if we could go past the Normal before heading off to our little Rhodesia in the suburbs, and it broke my heart. The burnt-out wreckage was still there, and the marquee's final feature hung there in some bitter, festal defiance against the increasingly desolate poverty of West Pullman: "Fort Apache - The Bronx". But what did I expect, Dad had asked? The neighborhood had *changed*, for Christ's sake.)

I was tired and cold and sore. If the diner was in the middle of the heart of darkness, I couldn't have cared less.

A fireplug of a woman with her hair in a bun, the various layers of her in a tight-fitting blue dress, stained white apron, and a name tag reading **Irma** looked at me like I was the Ghost of Christmas Past. The white teenaged Ghost of Christmas Past. Two over-the-hill truck drivers huddled over coffee at one end of the C-shaped counter eyed me peculiarly. I felt like a cue ball. I sat across from the truckers in the corner, leaning my head against the wall as Irma placed a coffee cup and saucer in front of me, holding a steaming coffee pot in her left hand. "You want some?" I nodded. She filled the cup and returned the pot to the large stainless steel warmer. "What about food?"

I smiled tiredly. "Is it too late for a hot dog?"

She laughed. "Not in here, it ain't." A small kitchen radio played below the counter. Irma turned it up and started singing *Every Day Will Be Like a Holiday* with The Sweet Inspirations as she began cooking my breakfast. I felt the numbness across my face and the cold stuck in the tips of my fingers and toes. My mind drifted off to Nicolasha's apartment. I wanted him to sing this song to me while we took a Comrade Bubblevitch bubble bath together. It was pretty obvious my visit was a novelty for Irma and the truckers, but they were too polite to just come right out and ask what the hell I was doing in a place like theirs on Christmas morning. And I was too exhausted to think about it myself. I was content to keep smelling the meal she was preparing. Irma grilled a large hot dog in a mound of onions and peppers, and scraped them into a wide poppy-seed bun, which was spread out in a red plastic basket, before showering the entree with freshly-cut fries. Heart attack heaven!

I finished the delicious meal and a fourth cup of heavily sugared and creamed coffee as a pair of slightly out-of-shape white Chicago Police officers came into the diner. Everyone waved at one another. Regulars, I thought. Irma threw a pair of hamburger patties on the grill and made two coffees to go as I tried to ignore the funny looks from the policemen. It seemed like they were talking about me. Uneasily, I dropped my last five dollars on the counter and went to leave. The older cop sitting closest to the door smiled as he took my arm in a gentle but authoritative grip. "It's a little late for a walk, isn't it, son?" I was afraid, and it showed. "I know it's too fucking cold for a walk!" The group laughed in agreement. "You want to tell me why you got dried blood on your face?" The cop guided me to the stool next to him, but I looked down at my feet and the slush-stained floors, resigned that my nighttime adventure was drawing to a close. The other cop paid Irma and took the food outside to their grimy squad car.

With an impatient sigh, the officer with the red face and silver hair picked up an aluminum napkin dispenser and held it in front of my face as if it were a mirror. I looked like I had been thrown from a moving train, head-first. Even though I was full from Irma's delicious cooking, my stomach began to knot up, and my cut and swollen bottom lip began to move on its own. He lifted my face up with his gloved finger. "Well?"

My mind raced with lies to tell. "I live with my brother in Hyde Park, near the University." I let my eyes fill. "We got into a fight." I looked away from him and Irma. One of the truckers hid a smile. He knew I was lying like a cheap rug. "I was running away."

"A hundred and ten city blocks is a helluva hoof." The cop wheezed to his feet and patted me on the back. "Well, I can't leave you out on the street. You want to come down to the station and file a report?" I hadn't thought of that. Now there was a gift idea! Blame Dad and his ass thrown into stir on Christmas, some therapy to soothe his restless nature. Maybe it would make up for that last slap that never arrived. Why did that one hurt more than the others? But no, I reflected, he'll be gone soon enough. I shook my head. "Then we're gonna bring you home, son."

I played the reluctant passenger and nodded sadly, opening the door for the officer. Irma put her hand on her hip with righteous indignation. "Hell, I don't see no meter in that broken down squad of yours, Captain!"

"Come on, Irma. You see the decal - 'We Serve and Protect'. The punk gets a ride home, we threaten his brother, and we all get some rest before we open our presents in the morning. See how simple law enforcement can be?"

"Well, God damn, I ain't ever got no taxi rides from your ass." She picked up the money I had left on the counter. "No tips, either, you shanty Irish pig. Least the kid leaves a tip!" She winked at me. "Must not be Irish."

"Irma, you can ride my ass anytime."

"Get the fuck out of my restaurant, both of you!" I gave her a little Felix wave as I left, and Irma waved me off with a little Felix smile. I decided to take Felix here for lunch when we got back from Florida.

*

The police Captain knocked on Nicolasha's door with controlled anger. The officers stood on each side of the doorway - did they think my fictional brother was going to fire a shotgun at us? I stood behind the Captain. Our ride into Hyde Park was uneventful and quick. Traffic wasn't very heavy at two a.m. on Christmas morning.

They asked me to elaborate on the fight I supposedly had with my supposed brother, so I spun another yarn, one that made it seem like I, as the bratty little sibling, deserved a few of the slaps they could see I got.

There was no answer. The Captain glared at me. "Are you sure he didn't go out?"

"His car is still outside," thank God.

"Maybe he went looking for you." I could only dream of such an event. I shrugged. "Don't you have a key to your own apartment?"

"We were screaming and hitting each other." What do you mean I only got an **A-** ?! "I wasn't thinking about my keys."

The Captain shook his head and pounded on the door. "This is the police," he yelled, "open up!" He pounded again, so hard the middle wooden frame of the door gave a little with a sharp squeak. We heard movement inside the apartment. The Captain nodded and pulled me in back of him, in case my brother wouldn't come quietly. I hoped Nicolasha was good at lying on the fly. The door opened a crack. Nicolasha peered out. The other officer, a young, weak-kneed Pillsbury Dough Boy stuffed into an ill-fitting police uniform, stepped forward in case Nicolasha didn't have a good view of his badge, or his revolver. I peeked around the Captain, and our eyes met. The door opened at once.

Nicolasha looked pretty funny, wearing a bed sheet wrapped around his waist like a giant towel.

The Captain spoke up. "Are you Nick Strauss?" Nicolasha glanced at me. I tipped my head discreetly. My teacher nodded. "Is this your brother, Mike?" Nicolasha nodded again quickly. "Good. Now, I'm going to make this short and sweet. Number one, it's too late for him to be running around the city alone." The Captain almost stepped on Nicolasha's bare feet as he moved closer to him, jabbing my disoriented teacher in the shoulder with a thick forefinger. "You guys want to fight and yell? Go right ahead, but don't hit him in the face like that again, period. No punches, that's number two." He pulled his baton from his equipment belt and shook the end of it under Nicolasha's sincerely terrified face. "You do, and you'll look pretty funny walking around with this night stick shoved up your ass sideways." Not as funny as you'll look <u>putting</u> it there, Captain, I privately mocked. "Merry Christmas." He put the baton away and cocked his thumb for his partner to follow. And, with that, the policemen went off, to serve and protect somebody else.

*

Nicolasha closed and locked his apartment door and brought me into his bedroom, the only room with a light on. He sat me down at the edge of his disheveled bed and knelt in front of me, turning my bruised face from side to side to have a better look. I tried pretending nothing hurt, until Nicolasha touched my lower lip and made me flinch. "Stay here. Let me get some medicine."

"I'll be fine, Nicolasha." I stood up, but his hands ushered me back to the bed.

"Just sit still, little friend." He headed for the bathroom with a sad smile on his face and the bottom half of his bed sheet trailing along behind him.

The bedroom was plain - pale blue walls, white ceiling, unpolished hardwood floor, no pictures or anything, and a fresh Persian throw rug between the bed and a long, bare dresser. A reading lamp and an alarm radio were placed on a short bed stand, and an antique-looking leather easy chair sat in the far corner of the room, next to the closet door, which was closed. Nicolasha's cello sat in its case beside the chair, where his clothes were tossed.

Nicolasha returned, with a wet rag, towel, iodine, and rubbing alcohol. He handed me an ice pack, which I bounced in my hand while he tut-tutted over me. "You should be fine." I grunted. He lowered his hand over mine and held the ice pack to the bottom of my jaw, watching my reaction closely. I didn't show any, even though I felt a flash inside of me upon meeting the warmth of his palm. His fingers slid inside of mine. "We have two, how do you say, sure fire cures for such wounds back in old Siebenbürgen."

Nicolasha's eyes drew me into his. I felt the flash again, and felt a little fear, too. I gently pulled my hand away from his and dropped the ice pack on the floor noisily. "I think they're only bruises, *Freiherr*."

Nicolasha shook his head mournfully. With great tenderness, he began running his hand through my hair. "No, my young friend, they are wounds, as grievous as a bullet or a blade. I think I know who gave these to you," he whispered as I closed my eyes, blotting my Christmas Eve festivities out with the picture of Nicolasha's unlined, unshaven face staring with morbid oblivion at an invisible camera, "and that is why they cannot be mere bruises that will go away in a few hours."

I tried to put the photo album out of my mind. His fingers playfully circumnavigated my scalp. "So tell me about these two famous cures from the old country." I couldn't. I felt myself get hard with another flash.

"One is to get blind drunk on the strongest homemade wine you can find." I laughed as he wagged a finger at me. "But you are too young for that." Right, tell that to my baseball buddies when they raid their parents' wet bar supplies. "The other is...a different sort of medicine." Nicolasha's free hand timorously brushed across my crotch.

Flash.

I didn't react. I didn't know how to. But I didn't back away, either, or make a sound. I was scared, that's for sure, but there was a thrill in that fear that made me shake in my seat. "The other is a tender kiss from a loved one." I looked closely at Nicolasha's soft, white body, afraid to touch him anywhere else except his face. I could hear the wind blowing outside of his small bedroom window. It was the first time since Nicolasha ran his hand through my hair that I was aware some other world existed outside of the room. My eyes stayed closed. My stomach was full to bursting, yet I felt hungrier than I'd ever been. I cried out continuously, almost happily, as it hurt. I could barely breathe, panting and moaning myself silly, when the throbbing turned into a warm ocean. The music I felt, the vibrations across my body, they all seeped into the dark and bounced into a swirling delirium that swallowed me whole.

*

Nicolasha returned from the bathroom and switched off his reading lamp, curling me into his arms and legs beneath the chaos of the bed's multiple blankets. He carefully kissed every corner of my bruised face while his hands massaged my spent and naked body. I bungled along, trying to follow his lead, stopping only when my teacher lay down beside me and tucked me into the thickest of the quilts, content to run his fingers through my hair again. "I love you, little friend."

106

My breath choked in my throat. "I love you, too, Nicolasha." My chest heaved once. I spit out a tired, hurt, disoriented sob, but did not cry. My fucking God, I was so sick of crying.

Nicolasha rubbed his lips over my hair and hugged me underneath the covers. We lay in the dark of our thoughts for many minutes. "When you are ready to tell me what happened this evening, little friend, don't be afraid." His warm feet slid under mine.

"Tomorrow?" I asked, hanging on to him until he pulled away.

"It is already tomorrow," he reminded me with a chuckle. I squinted at my Omega before Nicolasha took my hand in his, playing with my fingers. It was almost dawn. Nicolasha made me squirm as he ran his wet tongue along my ear and the side of my neck before he fell back onto his limp feather pillows. I moved into the only available arms that would have me and fell asleep while the snow continued to fall on the cold and nearly motionless city I called home.

XI

Sorrow breaks seasons and reposing hours
Makes the night morning and the noontide night.
Richard III

I slept forever.

The soft warmth between our tangled bodies was something I had thought about and something I had dreamt about for a long time. When it came to me like a gift on that blinding, sun-drenched Christmas morning, I let it sweep over me like the crashing, childhood waves off of Nags Head, North Carolina, the ones that would pick me up and hurl me onto the beach like I was a rag doll, the ones I used to visit with my mother and father, when they still loved each other.

I felt Nicolasha's breath near my face before he kissed me once on the chin. I woke up and smiled up at him. "Merry Christmas, little friend!" He was kneeling beside me on the floor, wearing a ridiculously old-fashioned thermal underwear jump suit that drooped from his shoulders, goofy long-johns right out of a B-western. He took one of my hands and kissed it, before I glanced down at my lap, where a tray of hot food had been placed. There were four slices of that salty black rye bread, a block of soft white cheese that was as big as a pack of cigarettes, a small carafe of steaming tea, two of Nicolasha's demitasse teacups, and a plate covered with a mound of scrambled eggs, filled with slices of onions, peppers, potatoes, and a sweet pork sausage, not to mention about a pound of garlic. No sign of any homemade wine, however.

He peeled off his faded red underwear and crawled into the covers next to me. We ate in silence while Handel's *Messiah* played quietly in the background. The little speaker of the clock radio didn't do much justice to the oratorio's joyous expanse, but complemented the warm sunlight pouring into the bedroom over us. And I felt another wave crash over me, a wave of contentment and reflection that aroused and odd, fast-motion meditation of my life as a confidential agent those last few weeks that lead up to my fateful Christmas holiday, making secretive visits, clandestine phone calls, stealth research, and a few private conversations in search of a father-type I could talk to without being slapped or getting mortified into further, acrid silence.

A few days after I met Felix, I made my first, tentative inquiry at the Pilot Institute's normally well-stocked library, but found nothing, except dry and discouraging medical definitions that told me nothing.

Later that week, I moved on to our school nurse, a shy, frail Mexican-American who had served as an Army medic in Vietnam. He listened to my questions and tactfully ignored the anxieties that had to have dripped like rainwater from my timid overuse of genderless pronouns, doing his best not to be judgmental or give me any advice that would indicate his own attitudes on the subject, except that I should continue my inquiries "until I was satisfied with whatever answers materialized".

The following week, I found texts at the University bookstore that were more forthright and spoke to many of the questions I had been troubled with for what seemed like a long time. A few nights later, I got up the nerve to phone the professor who had assigned those books at his office. We talked for hours, and he even invited me to visit one of his classes, but I couldn't think of an easy way to ask Felix to come with me, and was too intimidated to go alone.

With only a week to go before the Pilot Institute let out for the holidays, I showed up to take confession at our local church, a typically suburban, under-architected spiritual banality that wouldn't pass muster as a city church cry-room. Quite unexpectedly, I ran into Christian, one of the guys I used to play pick-up ball with, sitting in a corner pew. I didn't expect him to be waiting for me after I stormed out of the box, angry and humiliated after a thoroughly negative exchange with the local priest about guilt and fidelity and sin and some more guilt thrown in, just in case.

Christian and I walked through our old playing field, a large, grassy corner of one of our local parks. We were chilled to the bone, but kept each other company until the sun went down. I surprised myself by actually talking to someone my own age, live and in person, face to face, about...well, everything. And Christian listened, and didn't laugh, or hit me, or make me feel bad, or run off. He told me to find some other priest to talk to, and made me promise to call him over the Christmas break.

With a smile, I remembered holding out my frozen hand, and Christian pushing it away to give me a tongue-tied hug that helped me muddle through the rest of that night.

I went back to Holy Rosary the next day. A little old lady in the office sent me to see a visiting priest from Poland, of all places. He was a young guy with wavy blond hair and a wiry build who had just finished giving morning Mass when I arrived. He sat us down on the marble steps leading down to the front door of the church, and, in surprisingly good English, urged me to speak freely to him. So I did. He was either the best actor in the Warsaw Pact or genuinely cared about me and my stupid little problem, because we talked for an hour, stopping only because he had to perform another Mass for the other ten Poles still living in Roseland. He invited me to attend, but I chickened out. Instead, I insisted he give me absolution. Just in case. The young priest was convinced I had nothing to be forgiven for, but grudgingly obliged. He sent me off to school with parting words, rich, sublime words that kept ringing in my ears: "You are God's child. He made you what you are. He loves you as you are, no matter what people may say. Be what you are, or you will indeed be a sinner against Him."

So this was it, I mused. Being what I am.

What is it about superb food or being naked with someone that makes it so easy to ruminate over the vital emotions and key moments in your life, like you were watching them over and over again, ala instant replay on television? I cut a slice of the cheese and swallowed it with a mouthful of eggs, and let another wave of tranquility flow over me as the meal and the morning and our time together continued. I decided to call the professor, the priest, and Christian to wish them a Happy Christmas before my flight to sunny Florida departed, to thank them all.

Maybe Uncle Alex would come down to Florida with me, I speculated. God knows what sort of tangled plots and conspiracies would emerge from Jason and my uncle getting together.

Nicolasha lifted the tray from my legs and leaned across me to set it down on the floor beside the bed. "What would you like to do now, little friend?"

I considered the question with mock gravity. "Do you have any more Mr. Bubble?"

I sunk back into the covers and let my teacher take me in his arms, content to stay there with Handel's chorus in the background, singing to me and my young teacher:

Let us break their bonds asunder, and cast away their yokes from us.

*

The air was clear and icily fresh. There was no wind coming off of Lake Michigan, only a few blocks away. It was still below freezing, but not by much, a veritable heat wave compared to the Ice Station Zero temperatures and wind chill that had besieged Chicago much of that December. Nicolasha lived on a quiet street by Hyde Park standards, but the neighborhood itself was a busy and vibrant one. You could always hear traffic going past on South Shore Drive, buses coming to a halt or crawling away from a stop, commuter trains clattering along the overpass tracks that bisected the neighborhood, the occasional police siren, or some combination thereof. But the street was unusually soundless. You could almost hear the drops falling from the cluster of icicles that had formed on the corners of the porch roof. The sunlight bounced off of the fresh, fallen snow, making both of us squint as we stood next to each other outside the building's glass front door. I didn't immediately notice the colorless sedan parked behind Nicolasha's Volvo, even though it was the only car on the block that had no snow over it.

"Thank you, *Freiherr*." It had been some time since I had taken a bath, rather than a shower. I had certainly never taken a bath like that one. I felt like I was still sopping wet under all my clothes.

Nicolasha shifted uneasily on his feet, his eyes fixed on the deep, cloudless blue sky flying above us. I touched his arm, and he smiled, but not at me. "No, little friend, thank <u>you</u>. Thank you for coming...for being here."

I laughed quietly and reached up to pull an icicle off of the gutter. "I didn't have any other place to go!" I examined the icicle closely before tasting the tip of it with my lips, making sure there wasn't too much air pollution frozen into the thing.

"You could have gone home."

I snapped the icicle in half with two fingers and glared at my teacher, who seemed small and timid, all of a sudden. "But I didn't. I came here because I wanted to." Or needed to, I wasn't sure.

Nicolasha put a hand on my arm and smiled. It was a careful smile, perhaps a tired one, but definitely sad. "And I am glad you did." But...? My music teacher took a deep breath and crossed his arms over his chest with his head down. Slowly, he began to pace over the chipped paint of the wooden porch. "There is so much in my mind and in my heart, little friend, so much I would like to say."

I shrugged my shoulders and leaned against the railing. "I'm not going anywhere," I said in a matter-of-fact way, the same emotionless voice I'd used so much with Mom and Dad of late.

"I don't want to hurt you, or...confuse you."

Nicolasha still wouldn't look me in the eye. I hated that. It made me feel colder inside, a little blue flame of anger deep in my heart that came out through the computerized tone in my voice. "I'm not a little kid."

"No. I know that." Nicolasha's arms dropped to his side as he glared at some invisible dot floating around in back of my left shoulder. "There is little 'kid' about you."

"I'm going to be seventeen in August."

"And I'm going to be twenty five next week." Next week? An edge had crept into his soft voice. Our eyes finally met and stayed locked together, while our bodies didn't move an inch. "I do not know if that should matter. Or what does, anymore." Well, nothing, if you want to be existentialist about it, I responded to myself, thinking about Camus' *The Stranger*, which we were reading in Mister Granger's ball-busting Literature class. "All I can be sure about is what I am feeling." Which is...? "I believe I love you." Flash. "I do not know how, or why. But it is what I feel, and I am afraid of that."

My voice sunk to a murmur. "How come?"

"You are so young. You are my student, as well." His eyes begged for me to look away, or make a joke, or push him aside and walk off, but I didn't. I stood my ground and stared back at him, making him say what I couldn't even bring myself to think. "Because I feel so alone so often, and it is less so when you are with me." I could see his eyes begin to fill. "I would like us to be together, even though I know we cannot, or should not. Or..." His eyes closed tightly. "But I love you, and do not know how to stop from feeling that in my heart."

And the last warm wave I would feel inside of me for many, many days came teeming down like a burst dam onto a defenseless little *Mitteleuropan* village below. I heard a car door close behind me, but didn't turn around to look. I took a step closer to Nicolasha, and touched his breast under his leather jacket with the tips of my gloves. My voice was still a whisper, but was no longer unvarnished with emotion. "I love you, too." I couldn't help but smile. Perhaps it was my groping use of one of the great romantic cliches of all time. More likely, it was the sense of power I felt, watching Nicolasha's trembling, bare hand reach up and wait for my gloved fingers. "Nicolaus Matthias Székelyvon Straußenburg."

"So that's your real name." We spun around to see the old police Captain from much earlier that Christmas morning. He wore a plain white t-shirt under a loose, overstuffed yellow parka, fading blue jeans, a yellow stocking cap, and a battered pair of work boots, whose laces hung loose. His face had a strange mixture of relief and seriousness about it. Nicolasha visibly recoiled upon recognizing him. I stood my ground, again. "I was pretty sure this was the house we dropped you off at, son." He winked at me like a proud father might. I was confused. "Merry Christmas."

"Yeah. You, too, Captain."

"Thanks." His eyes glanced over to Nicolasha, who had backed up against the front door of the three-flat. I looked at my teacher with a smile.

"He's from Romania, Captain. They're scared of the police over there." The Captain nodded, as if he already knew that. I heard the hydraulic doors of a bus open down the street. It broke the awkward silence that had crept between the three of us. "Mister Straußenburg was about to drive me home."

The Captain's rosy red face crinkled with what looked to me like a painful indecision. "That's what I came here for."

Nicolasha hurriedly spoke up. "Please, officer. There is no need." He tried to smile at the old Captain, whose narrow eyes scrutinized Nicolasha's face with the beguiled cunning of a veteran Irish cop.

"Son, I think it'll be better if I take you home."

"Why?"

Ignoring my question, the Captain's eyes continued to size up my teacher. "Got a call into the station this morning, some older guy asking about a teenager that looked a lot like you do." He pointed his thumb at me. "Says he was your Uncle Alex."

"Strasse?"

The Captain nodded once. Instinctively, Nicolasha drew closer to my side, while the policeman continued. "My partner dialed me at home and told me about your uncle's call. So I came out to look for you." In Chicago, old neighborhood cops did lots of things in funny, personal ways, but, for the life of me, I couldn't imagine what had brought him here. Another car, this one a proper squad car, pulled up in front of the three-flat. The Captain waved him off with a smile that disappeared when he turned back to face me. "It's up to you if you wanna bring your...teacher...back with you." What if I didn't want to go back, I thought? The old Irish bastard must have sensed me wondering that. "You need to go home, though."

Nicolasha's hand squeezed my shoulder. "What has happened, officer?"

"Tell me." My voice became cold all over again.

The Captain stuffed his hands into his jacket pockets and looked at the sky, Nicolasha, the steps in front of him, and the sky once more before meeting my eyes. "Your parents, son. They...they're dead." Nicolasha's arm slid across my back, holding me up as my legs weakened. "Some drunk at a stoplight, last night. I don't know." The Captain's voice was trapped in the back of his throat. "I'm sorry, son."

My eyes drifted to the icicle I had snapped in half. It laid there at my feet, slowly melting in the sunlight that still hung over the porch, the bright sun's unsullied veneration to the birthday of the son of God. God...some divinity I suddenly felt I couldn't hear, or touch, one that had left me in the mists of that daylight, deadened by the frost of a winter afternoon in hell itself.

My God.

*

I sat in the back of the Captain's unmarked Chevy and let Nicolasha hold my gloved hand as we drove to the southern suburbs. The sun was beginning to set. The passing noise of the expressway and the occasional crackle from the police radio were the only sounds that broke the silence I had imposed on everyone.

My mind had wandered to a night last summer, when I had invited all of my baseball buddies to stay over at my place. None of the other parents wanted a platoon of young teenaged boys in their house, but I was "lucky": Dad was downstate on business, while Mom was working that night. The next morning, everyone complained about how I was the last one to go to sleep, and the first one to wake up. Mom teased me in front of the guys, reminding me about how I would never go to sleep when I was a baby unless my little fingers were wrapped around someone's hand.

Nicolasha leaned forward and whispered directions into the Captain's ear. He sat back gently and turned his head sideways to look at me. I paused for a moment before deciding not to return his stare. I couldn't make out his features in the dark of the car, anyway.

Whenever we used to drive someplace, Dad would always insist on traveling at night. Traffic was lighter, moved faster, and there weren't nearly as many State

Policemen out when it was late, he reasoned. I thought it had to do with his favorite kind of music, jazz, which always sounded better at night. I used to fall asleep with my body curled sideways against the front seat and my head resting on his thigh, that is, until he bought his Stingray, which had its gear shift mounted on a large center console. He purchased it around the same time we stopped doing road trips.

I took my gloves off and put a bare hand back into my teacher's.

*

The wide circular driveway in front of our pristine home was filled with cars, few of which I immediately recognized. The Captain had difficulty finding a place to park. He and Nicolasha flanked me like bodyguards, and walked me slowly toward the front door. Some idiot had turned on all of the Christmas lights that lined the house and hung from the naked branches of the young trees Mom had planted last spring. My cousin, excuse me, Mayor Lawrence Poiregaz, peered out from one of our living room windows and pointed at us. He opened both sides of the front door and met us about ten feet from the house. There were a cluster of relatives staring out from within the doorway. "Thank God, you're here. We were all worried sick."

The Captain cleared his throat, about to speak, but I cut him off with a slightly raised hand and my very best, ice-cold tone of voice: "Who is this...'we'?"

Lawrence the Laughing Lawyer, Dad's contemptuous behind-the-back nickname for his Aunt Hilly's pride and joy, was stunned. I think my bodyguards were, too, but the little blue flame inside of me, smoldering through the ride from Hyde Park, had become rather fierier. He diplomatically ignored the visible bruises on my face. "It's...we're your family."

Damn my family. I jabbed my finger toward the house. "Is that mine now?" I ignored Nicolasha's gentle hand on my shoulder.

"Uh...what?" Lawrence sputtered.

"The house. You were my Dad's lawyer, weren't you? Is this house mine or not?"

Lawrence fumbled trying to light a cigarette. He nodded repeatedly until he took his first drag.

"Good. Then I want everyone to leave, right now."

The Captain spoke up. "Now, son, you can't..."

"Yes, I can. It's my house, isn't it?" The Captain nodded his chin once. "Then get them out of here."

Nicolasha stepped between me and Lawrence, putting his hands on my face. "Little friend. Listen to me," he implored. I took a step backward, out of his reach.

"Where's my uncle?"

Lawrence cleared his throat with a deep series of smoker's coughs. I could see the Huns at the door getting restless. "He's taking it very hard." Nicolasha and the Captain withdrew to the unmarked squad car. "We all are." I don't know if Lawrence heard my snort of a reply. He coughed again. "He said he'll be here tomorrow morning."

I watched the Captain drive away, but forgot to wave. Nicolasha stood where the car had been parked, holding my gloves and waiting in the darkness for the blue flame to subside. In vain.

"Who's making the arrangements?"

Lawrence started to regain his composure. "Your uncle asked me to, help make it easier on both of you." One of the immigrant cousins began to walk outside the house. Lawrence waved him back. "If that's OK with you," he added, with a degree of sincerity I couldn't place.

"It isn't." Everything inside of me was being gobbled up by the blue flames. I felt like I was about start spitting fire from my mouth like a nuclear dragon on a bad day. And my maybe well-meaning lawyer cousin became ground zero for the blast. "I'll to do it myself." I wheeled past him and headed for the side of the house, the secret passageway to my empty backyard. "And get those people out of here. I want to be alone."

"No problem at all." Lawrence's voice was equally cold and insensitive, and had hurt woven throughout the syllables, as well. I spun around on my heels and glared at him with a pointless hatred. He lowered his head and mumbled an apology before retreating back to the house.

I gestured rudely for Nicolasha to follow me.

*

After waiting for the last door to slam and the final car to drive off, I sunk back into the large wooden lawn chair that faced out from the patio toward the end of the snow-blanketed yard, almost two hundred feet away. I felt like Michael Corleone at the end of "The Godfather Part II", cold and alone, incapable of doing anything about my pain except to stare off into some distant space. Nicolasha pulled up a wooden stool and sat next to me. A good deal of the white moon radiated brilliantly in the star-studded night sky above us. The yard and the suburban neighborhood surrounding us were utterly silent, except for the supernatural rustle of the icy breeze as it passed through the leafless tree branches that towered like barbed wire over our barren property. I could smell traces of pine being burnt from a local chimney. We sat just beyond the shadow of my empty house made by the moon. My only thoughts stayed with my eyes, which scanned the heavens, looking for that one shimmering star the wise men were said to have followed those many, many years ago.

"You were very harsh back there, little friend," Nicolasha said gently. I nodded, still playing at Copernicus. "I am trying to understand, however." Waiting for my reply, he held out a hand for me to take, which I declined to, choosing to enjoy a few final moments of lifeless wonderment at the twilight instead. "Would you like me to come inside with you?"

"I don't want to go in," even if I was freezing to death.

"You cannot sleep in the snow."

Our shadowy features gazed at one another. "Alone, or with you?"

"Even together, little friend."

I looked away. "I should be more upset than I seem." My voice remained impassive. Nicolasha couldn't see the tears about to fall from my eyes. He stood up in front of me and offered me my gloves. I closed my eyes as I put them on, trying to keep any tears from falling. Strained with an odd sort of fear, I felt myself being pulled up from the chair and into his arms. I slowly relaxed after Nicolasha did not reach downward with his hands, or touch me with his lips. He just held me close to him, leaning his face over my head.

"I am so sorry, little friend." Nicolasha's voice broke with a terrible snap. "Sweet baby Jesus be with you tonight." Only a messianic Siebenbürger would say such a thing. We cried together. Or, rather, Nicolasha sobbed quietly, for me, for us, for sweet baby Jesus knows what, while I let forth with a heaving, choking, hyperventilating, practically screaming hailstorm of tears that would have been embarrassing in an opera.

*

I had just seen Nicolasha off to the train station, his having balked at spending the night in my house, before retreating to the timeless sanctuary of warm, sprinkling shower water, with Shostakovich's fun if slightly surreal *Hamlet* Suite, voluminously playing in the background. I spent many minutes standing naked from the door of my bathroom, staring down into the dark hallway where Mom and Dad's bedrooms were. I knew a little about Shakespeare's *Hamlet* (and a few of his other works) thanks to the cool, nearly sadistic baritone reading voice of Mister Granger; whatever tenuous relationship this Suite may have had with the neurotic Danish prince, et al, Soviet artistic sensibilities aside, was beyond me. The damned piece sounded like vast music for a silent movie comedy. But I was thankful for the distraction provided to me by the crashing, cacophonous potpourri of musical vignettes in this Shostakovich oddity. I particularly enjoyed the allegro Tournament, a vast, classic waltz for those precious twinklings of Stalinist intimacy one might be possessed with. I listened to it twice. Mom loved waltzes.

*

I sat in a hunter green tartan flannel robe one of my aunts had bought me for Christmas, with a fresh pair of white gym socks on my feet. I tried on the matching shirt and pants that came with the robe when I got out of the shower, but they were unbearably stiff and itchy. I had already called the Polish priest at Holy Rosary to ask him to preside over the funeral service, and to reserve the church for that purpose, my parting shot to the Huns, who would no doubt be shivered to their timbers about making such a fateful trip back to the old neighborhood. The Pole was a little terse on the phone, carrying on like maybe to hide his dismay at the grim tale I'd just told. I was, too, I guess.

I then called Lawrence's house. I was relieved he picked up the phone instead of Aunt Hilly. I apologized briefly and he accepted with gushing grace, insisting I let him take care of the wake the following night. He wanted to hold it at a client's funeral home, a friend he had gone to the University of Illinois with. I agreed, and apologized again, mostly because Nicolasha had prevailed upon me earlier to do so.

The professor wasn't home. Neither was Christian, damn it.

That left my phone call to Florida.

I ran my hand through my wet hair, waiting for the other line to be picked up. I was nestled in the corner of our sofa, where the raging fireplace warmed my legs, which were propped up on a bulky hassock placed in front of me. I had brought my Shostakovich record downstairs to listen to again, but hadn't switched it on yet, unlike every single light in every room I could turn on in the house.

"Happy Holidays."

"Mrs. Cromwell." I could hear a festive gathering in the background. My mind spun in turmoil, trying to decide whether I bitterly resented the cheer, or desperately wanted to be there. "Is Felix there?"

"The Hitman! Sure, let me get him." She called for her other son. "I'd spank you for that 'Mrs. Cromwell' but I think you might enjoy it!" Could she hear my involuntary smile? "We can't wait for you to land tomorrow!"

My jaw and eyes closed tightly. I couldn't bring myself to say anything else until Felix took the phone and said 'hello' twice. "Felix?" I was determined to keep myself composed, like I had with the priest and the lawyer, but my voice betrayed everything that was fermenting deep inside of me. Felix yelled for everyone to be quiet. The rest of his family ignored him.

"What's the matter, buddy?" I had trouble talking, again. Deep distress flooded into his gentle voice. "You're not coming, are you?"

"No." That I could say out loud. "I can't." I fought with my heaving chest and short breaths, but lost to the few tears that rolled down my face and rested between my cheek and the receiver.

"Is it your parents?" The festivities quieted down considerably. Felix sounded furious. I didn't know he even had a temper. "Tell me what they said. Please."

I refused to speak until I was sure I wouldn't break down in the middle of a sentence. My best friend probably thought I was blowing him off, or trying to think of a really good lie. "My Mom and Dad...they're dead...got killed by some...by a drunk driver." I covered the mouthpiece with my hand to keep my halting sniffles a private affair. "Last night."

"Oh my God..." I heard Felix start fumbling with the phone. He took a few seconds before coming back on. I couldn't tell if he was crying, too. His voice sounded completely different, though. "Are you OK? Were you

124

hurt?" I listened as Arlene whispered urgently to Felix, wanting to know what was going on.

"I wasn't in the car." I ran out of things to say. Felix told his mom in a vicious whisper what little I said. "I have to go."

"I'm flying up in the morning. So will my family, if they can."

"You don't have to, Felix." I didn't expect him to say that. I don't know what I expected, aside from bursting out in tears for the three hundredth time that year. I wondered if all these crying sessions meant I was a manic depressive. My voice winnowed down to a squeak. "I'd rather be there with you guys, anyway."

"I'll be there by lunch." His voice was collected and serious. I knew there and then he'd come, and almost began to feel a flash deep inside of me. "Try and get some sleep now, OK, buddy?" It was almost midnight in Florida.

"I will," I said, even though we both knew I wouldn't. The fire needed some more logs. "Thanks, Felix." I was too disoriented to wonder why I was thanking my friend for being a part of the most difficult phone call of my life.

His voice was filled with emotion and pain. "You're my best friend."

He hung up before I could reply.

*

I turned off all of the lights I had just turned on before I began my phone calling. I was convinced I would stay up all night to watch the flames in the fireplace run their course, only to turn my attention to the vast, intricate patterns of blackness I would find on the ceiling above me. But I didn't. Still wearing my new robe, I huddled myself in one of our hand-woven blankets from Mexico and plunged into a leaden, dreamless sleep well before the logs had extinguished themselves or *Hamlet* had finished playing.

XII

I turn my back.
There is a world elsewhere.
Coriolanus

It was the longest day of my life.

While I took my morning shower, I presupposed that the wake would go smoothly, as smooth as such events can go, while the funeral itself would be the "hard" part. After all, when Papu Kasza passed on to the great ward organization in the sky, I was devastated by the wake, and assumed the burial would be that much worse. Sure, I was younger and slightly more foolish when that happened, but why would that impact on my assumption? Thus did I begin my interminable voyage across the tumbling and uncharted seas of the ritual of death, Roman Catholic-style.

*

Uncle Alex and Veronica came over around ten that morning. My Uncle had quite obviously drank himself to sleep only a few hours before, but I was relieved that he hadn't found any other form of pharmaceutical morphine to help him... cope, inhaling a few bottles of gin fell under that category. Veronica suggested we needed to pick out what Mom and Dad were going to wear. I stared at her without comprehending. Was this a party or something? They're dead, missy. I wasn't sure appearances were the most important thing on their minds now. What the hell was she on about? "For the wake, baby." Baby? Don't you call me that. My Mom called me that. "We have to decide what clothes to bury them in."

I thought they were being buried in coffins?

Uncle Alex stood uselessly in between us, staring at the family pictures lining the hallway leading to my parent's old bedrooms. Veronica glanced sideways and unhappily at him. "I'll pick out something." Fine. Dad was probably in the middle of negotiating with Saint Peter as we spoke. She emerged a few minutes later with one of my Mom's best dresses, a blue silk with silver piping, tailor-made to show off her breasts and her antique pearls, an outfit that screamed 'I have more money and more taste than the rest of you whores'. Was there a dress code in the afterlife? "Isn't that a little bit much to be buried in?"

Veronica shrugged her shoulders, and held out her other selection, Dad's Navy dress whites. I nodded at that choice. Uncle Alex began shaking his head like there was something rolling around inside of his skull. "We can't have the caskets open. They told me." Veronica turned away. I went into my bathroom and washed my face and hands until I heard them go downstairs.

*

A young guy with a black crew cut, maybe a few years older than I was, greeted us in the lobby of the funeral home. Why do funeral homes smell so distasteful, like the doctor's office, or a confession booth? He introduced himself as Roger and shook my hand like an ape. Must be the son of Lawrence's school mate, I thought. He had the hands and shoulders of someone who worked in construction during the summer, and wore an ugly beige suit so badly cut, it had to be a hand-me-down.

Roger escorted us into a large room in the back of the parlor that was filled, wall-to-wall, aisle-to-aisle, with coffins. Fucking coffins! He cleared his throat and asked us to choose a pair, before running down the portico to answer a ringing phone. I gazed out at the showroom of coffins. Choose a pair, huh? Hey, everybody, look! We're shopping for coffins! "What about that one?" I pointed to a sleek, jet black model directly in front of us.

Veronica shook her head. "It's too masculine for your mom."

"Fine." I pointed at a creamy white oblong job next to it. "That one for her."

Veronica shook her head again, taking a closer look at the white casket. I noticed she was wearing one of Mom's French scarves. "It's still...well, old-fashioned."

Old-fashioned? "Fine." I walked over to a pair of caskets in the corner that were molded from aluminum alloy. One was silver, and the other was a light gold. "These are modern."

"Don't you think they seem...cheap?"

I grabbed at the silver's price tag, hanging from one of the side grips. Fifteen hundred dollars? "They aren't."

Veronica shook her head yet again, her eyes locked on a casket I could see was made out of ebony. "What about this one?" How many clarinets could you make out of that?

Uncle Alex beamed back down to Earth and spoke up. "That looks too expensive."

I exhaled angrily through my teeth. Roger came back into the room and smiled stupidly at me. Jabbing a thumb over my shoulder to indicate the burial box boutique, I snarled, "Which one of these things are popular?"

Roger hurried over to a rose-colored casket with a metallic finish. "This one is, sir. It's very nice." He said that as if he were pointing out a sunroof on a Jaguar sedan. I stormed over to him and pushed my hand down inside the box, testing the mattress, as it were.

"It feels like raw springs with a bed sheet over them."

Roger blushed and looked away from me. "They're all like that, sir." Well, what if they're not dead yet? Hm? Laying there on that lot, they'll come back and haunt us, I was convinced. "But look at these!" Look at these whitewalls! He pointed wildly at the casket's handles, miniature sculptures of Biblical scenes, not unlike the Stations of the Cross.

*

The florist was a friend of Mom's. Her hands shook as she leafed through a large binder which contained hundreds of pictures featuring different floral arrangements, wreaths, bouquets, and so on. All the ones I really liked were meant for weddings. Uncle Alex dropped a hand-blown crystal swan. Veronica insisted on examining each of the funeral setting pictures like they were plans for the latest Soviet nuclear submarine. I played with the florist's shaggy Chow, who took a liking to me after I kept feeding him Christmas cookies, which I took from the pocket of my pea coat.

Veronica was torn between a pair of full settings, raised flower pots, church pew decoratives, and wreath. One was mostly purple. The other had a lot of yellow and blue. Uncle Alex liked them both. The florist was delighted. They were both expensive. I reached across the three of them and flipped the page to an even more elaborate full setting, which had been initially rejected because it consisted solely of costly red roses.

"That's the one. I want these."

No one argued with me. The Chow tried to follow me out the door. It was beginning to snow again.

*

"Are you hungry, baby?"

I swore, if she called me that again, I would strangle her with Mom's scarf. The back seat of Uncle Alex's rented Ford Granada was uncomfortable. "Yeah, I guess."

"Alex?" My uncle stared out of his window, evidently counting snowflakes or something. She called his name again before he looked back at her with glazed eyes. "Would you like to stop for lunch?" He nodded. Veronica kept to her driving, rather than fish for any more bad conversation.

I saw a Greek-owned family restaurant coming up on the right. You know the sort. Open twenty four hours with a huge menu (even though the burgers and breakfast were the only things worth having), complete with a giant, flashing tower that proudly featured the words **STEAKS CHOPS COCKTAILS FOUNTAIN**, and, of course, **FINE FOOD**. The only thing missing was **EXP WAITRES WANTD** on the marquee, but that was because it was **HAPY XMAS SEASN**.

I was in the middle of my salty French onion soup when Veronica looked at me with the kind of cheery, perky, **HAPY** smile that would irritate me when I watched one of the local newscasts on TV. She crushed an unopened bag of crackers before pouring the remains into her thick bowl of mushroom soup while Uncle Alex busied himself with over-buttering a pair of Ry-Krisps. The waitress refilled our coffee, unable to keep from looking over her arm at my face.

"I was thinking." This is good, I thought. She thinks. "After all of this is over," you know, like a long, boring movie is eventually over, "maybe we should all go down to Miami, or San Diego, someplace warm." Why, in God's name? "The three of us. They would have wanted us to." 'They'? *They* aren't even in the ground yet, you scavenger. "What do you think, baby?"

Where was Mom's scarf?

*

It was the day after Christmas. We should have been returning all the gifts we really didn't like, and snapping up the half-price discounts on the good leftovers.

Three-thirty, and the low, grey sky outside the funeral home was already turning dark. Flurries of snow had been blowing since lunch. Someone mentioned there was a blizzard on the way for the entire Midwest. Every time somebody came in the front entrance, cold, fat gusts of wind followed them through. I was hit by one of these drafts as I exited the men's bathroom, where I had just washed my hands and face again. The florist's delivery man, an older black gentleman with kind eyes and a grey moustache, struggled with his goods as Roger nervously escorted him into "The Resting Room" without lifting a finger to help the man carry anything. I caught the young-and-old pair of ladies in the funeral home office looking at me like I was a Bengal tiger or something, locked in a small cage they didn't want to get too close to. I slammed the glass door against its supporting glass wall to give the hags something to talk about as I withdrew to watch the gloomy December sunset.

I stood restlessly in between Uncle Alex's rent-a-car and the funeral home's early model Cadillac station wagon. The florist's van was parked in the middle of the parking lot with its side door open. The delivery man glanced sadly at me as I ignored the dropping temperature and let the falling snow build up on my hair and grey tweed suit jacket. "You should go back inside, child." He reached into the van and handed me a short-stemmed rose before he continued bringing in the various floral arrangements. I looked at the incongruous flower for a long time, watching the edge of the petals roll backward as snowflakes landed upon them. I broke off the bottom of the stem and inserted the remainder into the button hole of my lapel. I wasn't sure if wearing the thing would be considered untoward. I could still make out a hint of the rose's fragrance as I stalked back into the chilly and silent Resting Room, now festooned with flowers, empty chairs, and Mom and Dad's matching coffins, which were decorated with an odd assortment of framed pictures showing them in rather a better state than they were today.

*

"Oh, I'm so sorry."
"God bless you."
"What a terrible, terrible thing."
"If there's anything you need..."
"We were such good friends."
"You look charming in that suit."
"He was my favorite cousin."
"They've gone to a better place."
"We're here for you."
"You look tired."
"The flowers are beautiful, just beautiful."
"Our prayers are for you."
"How could this happen?"
"Why? Oh, why?"
"She was a wonderful woman."
"God be with you, little friend."
"What happened to your face?"
"I can't find the words."

"You've grown so much."
"Be strong."
"Can we do anything for you?"
"Horrible."
"I know they'll always be with you."
"Everything looks so nice."
"Call if you need anything."
"At least there was no suffering."
"We'll all miss them."
"Aren't any of your friends here?"
"Try not to take it very hard."
"If there's something I can do..."
"How are you holding up?"
"I didn't know you could buy so many roses in December."
"My God, on Christmas Eve!"
"You poor dear."
"We have to keep in touch."
"I miss them already."
"God will keep them for you."
"If there's anything I can do..."

*

I sat alone in the Reflection Room. It was decorated with dark paneling, uncomforting religious prints, and burgundy leather furniture that hadn't been broken in. One wall featured rows of leather-bound volumes, much like an attorney would own. I wasn't surprised to note the almost complete absence of any worthwhile literary works, aside from Balzac's *Pere Goriot* and Graham Greene's *The End of the Affair*. Tiny snowmen and Santa Claus lights were hung around the borders of the stained glass windows. There were two black wrought-iron lamps in the suffocating box. I kept the one furthest from my seat on. The only piece of furniture in the room I really liked was a large cherry wood radio console.

Nobody came into the room after I had retreated into it. Nicolasha and Roger talked quietly amongst themselves outside the door, discouraging anyone from doing so.

I spent the first part of the evening playing greeter while Uncle Alex tried to sober up, and then took to walking back and forth between the snowy parking lot, the wash basin in the men's bathroom, and the Resting Room, where the family had grabbed half of the seats to hold court, a chatty swarm of locusts whose company served only to reassure me that my cage really was too small that night.

I almost prayed for Felix to walk in the door.

After sitting in silence for I don't know how long, I plugged in the radio and switched it on to the Mom and Pop classical station, just in time to hear one of their three announcers intone his best wishes for everyone's happy holidays, and introduce a live recording of the Orchestra del Teatro ala Scala di Milano playing a few overtures of Rossini. I'm glad I was alone in the room. No one saw me smile. My wandering mind alternated between images of Elmer Fudd having his hair done by Bugs Bunny, and lines of robed guests wandering about the Roman health spa in glorious Felliniesque monochrome. *Il barbiere di Siviglia*...bravissimo, indeed!

I decided I wanted to visit Milano with Felix to catch an opera.

"Little friend, your uncle would like you to come out." Why? "It is time for the closing prayer." Nicolasha and Roger beckoned me with a pair of melancholy smiles. I stood up and made them wait until the last few bars of *Semiramide* finished.

That's it, I thought. I'm going to Italy over Easter Vacation. To hell with reality.

Nicolasha brushed his hand over my hair as Roger shifted back and forth on his heels. The funeral home heir said, "If there's anything we can do..." I walked past him, laughing under my breath.

I always knew God had a sense of humor.

*

The snow continued to fall through the endless night of the wake. Urged on by a bitter east wind, the snowstorm was still going strong by the time we met at Holy Rosary the next day. The ride to and from our old church was slow and treacherous.

Earlier that morning, the Polish priest had called me at home, to ask if I would say a few words during the church service. "About what?"

"Your parents, of course. Whatever you might be feeling about them, or their passing. Maybe something you remember from your childhood. It is up to you."

Fine.

"No longer mourn for me when I am dead
Than you shall hear the surly sullen bell
Give warning to the world that I am fled
From this vile world with vilest worms to dwell
Nay, if you read this line, remember not
The hand that writ it; for I love you so
That I in your sweet thoughts would be forgot
If thinking on me then should make you woe.
O, if, I say, you look upon this verse
When I perhaps compounded am with clay,
Do not so much as my poor name rehearse,

*But let your love even with my life decay,
Lest the wise world should look into your moan
And mock you with me after I am gone."*

I read Shakespeare's seventy first sonnet in a cold, even voice that unsettled the drafty, echoing church into a tense silence that continued through the mercifully brief service at the suburban cemetery's ultra-modern glass chapel.

*

The mourners filed out to their cars while I sat down on the carpeted cement floor, staring at my Mom and Dad with the book of sonnets pressed between my chest and my crossed arms. The Huns would be off to the local country club for the post-burial lunch arranged for by Dad's partners, I noted idly. "Are you coming, baby?" I glared at Veronica and Uncle Alex until they turned around and left.

The cemetery people came in to take the coffins away. I stood up and let Nicolasha wrap his arm around my shoulders and walk me out to his snow-covered Volvo. I heard the chapel door close behind me.

Many Christmases ago, me and Mom and Dad spent the holiday at Uncle Alex's new Minnesota redoubt, which he called Der Schloss. It was the last really happy Christmas we had together. I don't think it got above zero the entire time we were there. The front of Unc's Schloss was built on top of a big hill that rolled down to a good-sized lake that the town was built around. The lake was frozen solid, of course, and so was Unc's hill, after Dad snuck out and hosed it down one night. We spent the next day with Unc's hick neighbors, trying to kill ourselves sledding, rolling, sliding, and falling down the hill of glass. It was some of the best fun I've ever had.

Nicolasha cleared the snow off his car with a tiny broom. As I sat and looked out of windows, the whole world seemed white. The sky. The grass and the trees. The air. Everything.

XIII

'Tis bitter cold
And I am sick at heart.
Hamlet

My teacher dropped me off at home. He kissed me once on the cheek and waved at me as he drove away, leaving me to face my empty house alone. As I unlocked the front door, I saw a yellow envelope sticking out of the mailbox. I left it there to answer the phone. It was Felix. The snowstorm had stopped almost every flight in and out of the Midwest. He didn't know when he would be able to come, but promised he would, even if he had to sleep another night at the airport to get a seat. I believed him, and was happy to hear his voice, even though I'm sure he couldn't tell that, because I didn't say much. He said he loved me before he rang off. I trudged upstairs to take another long, hot shower. Offenbach's *Orpheus in the Underworld* kept me company.

*

I threw my suit into the corner of my closet and put on a brand new pair of long underwear and jeans, a fresh t-shirt, wool hiking socks, and a thick, itchy, and black V-neck sweater given to me by Veronica. It crinkled with static over my uncombed hair as I slipped it down my arms. I walked into the family room to lace up my hiking boots. I had planned to take a walk in the park before ordering a pizza and going to bed early. Instead, I stared out into the backyard and watched the sky get darker and darker. It still hadn't stopped snowing. The phone rang. I switched on a light before answering it on the third ring. "What?"

"Hey! This is Christian. Merry two days after Christmas!"

"Hi." I plopped onto the couch with relief. It wasn't a family member, thank God.

"How are you?" My voice was a mixture of happiness and exhaustion.

"Who cares about me? How are you?" My tongue-tied silence replied for me. "I'd be happy to get back home." Speak for yourself, bud. "We're stuck at my Grandpa's place in Terre Haute." Talk about being in mourning. "The local Interstate is all screwed up."

I remembered the limousine almost being broadsided by a Chicago Transit Authority bus as we slid across a red light at Halsted Street on the way to the cemetery. Wow, I thought, almost got the entire family in two days. "I tried calling you on Christmas."

"Really? I tried calling you, too, but all I got was a busy signal. The same thing last night." I had taken the phone off the hook before going to sleep. We bantered on about our presents and the weather and going back to school and playing baseball again, until I finally told him about Mom and Dad. I also wanted to tell Christian about the wake and the funeral, about all the bizarre things I had to do and listen to and watch, but chose not to after I almost started crying again, just thinking about it. I looked forward to the day when I could go more than twelve hours without wanting to break down and cry. "I don't know if I'll see you before school starts again." Christian's voice sounded regretful and unhappy. He had been so cheery when the conversation began. "My parents are talking about staying here until after the first."

"That's okay. I'll see you when you get back." I tried to sound as hopeful as I suddenly realized I wanted to be.

"No, it isn't. I should be there now, with you."

I felt a small flash inside of me.

There were about ten of us who played ball together. We didn't have teams. We just took turns coming to bat and switched positions when we weren't up. Most of the guys went to the local public high school, and they were the closest friends. They saw each other every day, no matter what. Christian and Ozzie went to the nearest Catholic boys school, but didn't seem to hang out much, except with us. I was the only one who left the immediate suburbs every day and always seemed to be the last one called out to play, even though everyone was cool to me. I suppose if you counted all the games and all the cookouts and all the times we'd drink and light up together since I moved in from Roseland, we were actually a pretty good group of buddies. But I never pictured any of them as friends, or ones that would last, and never felt like anyone was picturing me that way either. Christian all of a sudden did. Another close friend? I was still getting used to the one, and now out of the clear blue I had two. Flash.

"Are you still there?"

"I'm sorry. My mind's a wreck." I wasn't day-dreaming. I couldn't focus long enough to do that. I was tired, but not terribly sleepy. My stomach felt like it was a pretzel. I wasn't sure if I was hungry or I had some queer ache that wouldn't go away. Since the Captain had brought me home, I had washed my hands and face more than Lady Macbeth. My teeth ground together, picturing Christian playing in the untouched Indiana snow. I had two close friends my own age in the entire world, and they were both in different states, I protested to any god that might have been listening. I sighed heavily. "I'm glad you called, though."

"I feel real close to you right now." Sure. Terre Haute might as well be in France, for all intents and purposes.

And Fort Myers? How about the Seychelles? "Hey!" He barked at me like I was standing across an outfield from him. "Did you get my Christmas card?"

The envelope I left outside? I felt a little life creep back into me. "That yellow thing? What are you trying to say to me, hm?"

"It's all they had left down here," Christian replied defensively. "They ran out of fluorescent pink envelopes."

"That's because you kept them all for yourself."

"Fuck you!" I heard a single, loud "hey!" from an older man in the background, probably his dad. "Fuck you!" Christian whispered.

"No. Not unless I can fuck you back." We burst out laughing, nervously you could hear it, but laughing all the same. Terre Haute didn't seem so far away right then.

The doorbell rang. I flinched. "Someone is at the door." Oh, please, I pleaded to the ceiling, don't let it be a relative. We listened to each other not say anything for almost a minute. The chimes rang again.

"Okay. I'll call you in the morning." Christian's voice got cheery again. "Don't stay up all night drinking."

Where could I score some homemade wine? "Good idea!"

*

Wait. Oh my God! I knew it! It was those damned coffins! Mom! Dad! I <u>told</u> them they were too uncomfortable!

"The eaglet has landed." Felix's usually dapper trench coat looked old and wrinkled. Snowflakes dotted his shoulders and were strewn all over his wind-blown hair. He held out his hand with an apologetic look on his sunburnt face, which looked funny in the cold. "I'm sorry I couldn't get here any sooner."

I shook my head in disbelief, but seized Felix's offered hand in both of mine. I had resigned myself to a long night alone. Now I had Felix standing in front of me, smiling me into submission. "I thought you were still in Florida," I said dumbly.

"My pale face is."

We practically knocked ourselves over trying to hug each other, the snow, wind, and cold be damned.

*

The entire house looked like the Red Army had just gone through it. Dishes and glasses, clothes and boxes, wrapping paper and books, everything was everywhere it didn't belong. Felix peered into our arid refrigerator. "What were you planning on doing for dinner?" He took out a bottle of Coke for the two of us. I shrugged. That was thinking too far ahead. "Well, there's nothing in here. You go order a pizza and I'll start cleaning up."

"Felix, I can do it myself later on."

"Later on when? Next year?"

"Next year starts in three days."

Felix brought the mini-debate to a halt by turning on the kitchen radio, which was set to Dad's usual jazz station. He nodded his head with satisfaction. "This is pretty cool music." My friend pushed me toward the wall phone. "You won't do any work if there's some symphony on."

*

We gutted every room in the house. The kitchen was now spotless. Every dish and glass was washed and put away. I started a fire while Felix tended to the couches, the book shelves, and the wet bar. He did two loads of laundry while I dusted and vacuumed both the living and dining rooms. He even scrubbed my bathroom down while I changed the sheets and made my bed, which I hoped we would share later that night. I put away the clothes Felix had washed while he went through my record collection.

"Have you listened to all of these?"

"Not yet. That's my Christmas project." We smiled at each other. "Want to help out with that, too?"

"We didn't shovel the driveway yet."

"That's what American technology is for. We have a snow-blower."

He put a hand on my arm. "I know. Let's get up early tomorrow and take it out and do a bunch of driveways. We'll take turns so we don't get tired, and make a ton of money." His eyes sparkled at me, but I turned away from him and idly fiddled with my record player.

"I think I've got a lot of money, now." The doorbell started ringing, another fine friendship moment broken by the bell. I looked at my Omega. Two hours for a pizza? I handed Felix a ten dollar bill from my jeans pocket, and said in an empty voice, "We didn't do my Mom and Dad's room yet."

Felix put himself in my arms. I closed my eyes, fighting off another attack of tears, when my best friend whispered, "Tomorrow." He held my face for a few seconds before going to get our sumptuous dinner. I knelt down and began picking out albums I wanted to listen to with Felix, still trembling from the feel of his warm hands.

*

Felix asked, "What are you thinking about?"

"Nothing, really."

I wore my tartan robe and a pair of white socks. Felix wore its matching pajama top, which hung down below his underwear. He sat on the carpet, propped up on an oversized pillow against the couch. I lay next to him in front of the warm and colorful fireplace. His arm was draped over my chest while my head rested in his lap.

"Who're you trying to fool, bro? You're always thinking about something."

I placed my hand over his, pressing his palm over my breast. Felix slid his other hand beside my face. "I'm trying not to think in the first place."

He lowered his voice, as if someone might hear him. "What are you feeling, then?"

"I feel loved." The words came without hesitation or thought. So did his.

"You are." I sat up slowly and moved beside Felix, pulling a blanket up over our legs. "Am I?"

I nudged closer to him and touched his face with the side of my fingers. "More than I can probably say out loud."

"Do you mean that?"

I shifted around to face him, taking both of his hands in mine. "Sure I do. Doesn't it sound like I mean it?" Felix looked embarrassed as he nodded his head. "Why would you even ask that?"

Felix pulled his hands out from mine, only to take them inside of his. "My Grandfather always says that people already have an answer in mind when they ask a question."

"He's probably right. So?"

"I know you meant what you said. You always do." Felix let go of my hands and looked away from me to the fire. "I just wanted you to say it again."

I sensed something was wrong. Felix sounded afraid and defensive, nothing at all like his usual optimistic, playful self. His happiness made him such a source of strength for me. "Well, just for the record, I'll say it again." He tried to laugh me off, but it didn't work. "And again and again, until you finally believe me."

"I believe you."

"No, Felix. I mean, believe me, deep down, in your heart of hearts." I put my arm around his shoulders and drew my face close to his, making him finally look me in the eyes. I all but smiled at the unease I saw. We were back on the carpet in front of his apartment. "You're my best friend, Felix." I watched his bottom lip begin to shake. "I love you." His eyes shut fast. I started to speak softly. "Do you hear me? I love you." I moved my lips closer to his. Excitement coursed through my body, as tension gripped Felix's. "I love you, OK?"

"Sure," he whispered. "But if you love me, will you tell me the truth, no matter what I ask you?" I could almost smell the alarm inside of Felix's voice. I leaned my forehead against his before sitting back beside him, regret seeping into the warm waters that only moments before were flooding throughout me.

"You're my best friend." I crossed my arms over my chest and took a few deep breaths. "You left your family back in Florida just to be with me. Do you know what that means to me? Everything that's happened, the last few days, they seem...less horrible, now." I sensed the night was coming to an end. My voice shifted into neutral. "I love you, Felix. You can ask me anything you want."

"You said you weren't in the car when..." I could hear him swallow, "your parents..."

"No."

"How come?" I told him every detail of my family's Christmas Eve. He listened closely and unhappily, noting the leftover bruises still visible on my face. "Where did you go after they drove off?" I paused before telling him every detail of my trek to Irma's diner, and, afterwards, to Nicolasha's apartment. There was a lengthy pause before he spoke up again. We were sitting together under the same blanket, alone and half-naked, but, in the pit of my stomach, it felt like the Berlin Wall had been dropped down in between us. "You spent the night there?" I nodded. He looked at me in a strange way. I couldn't tell what he was feeling. "Did he give you that photo album upstairs?"

My heart sank. I closed my eyes and my fists, trying to escape the chill that began to smother my heart. Felix must have run across Nicolasha's album while I showered. I shook my head slowly. "No. I brought it home the first time I went to his apartment." Stole the damn thing, actually. "I just never gave it back." I guess I never really tried, either.

"Did you, you know, sleep together?" I took a long time before I nodded my head. Felix let out a pained breath through his mouth. Now I finally understood Uncle Alex's taste for unusual and exotic forms of liquid and narcotic restraint. I suddenly and completely regretted what I had said, and wanted to run clear out of the room, out into the snow, away, away from everything. "Why?" Felix sounded like he was fighting back tears. "Do you love him, too?"

"No," I replied angrily, "it's not like that." My voice wound down to a peep. "It's not the same thing."

"Did you say you loved him, too?"

I stared at Felix as he fought for his breath while tears rolled down his cheeks. "No," I lied.

"Did you...?" I shook my head. I reached for Felix, but my friend bolted up and stood by the bar with his back to me, trying to catch his breath while he talked and cried at the same time. "You're the best friend I've ever had. We're so different, though. I knew that on the first night you stayed over at my house." What was it, four, five weeks ago? It seemed to me like an eternity ago, right then. "But I didn't care. You were my friend, and that's all that mattered. I didn't care if you were different." Oh, different. Separate development for me. Apartheid for the androphiliac. "You say you love me, but I don't know what that means." Who the hell does? "I keep on wondering about what I really feel about you. I came here to be with you, but now..."

I chortled through my closed teeth. "But what? I'm the same friend tonight that I was the first night we spent together, except we're both still wearing clothes, and

I'm down a few family members." The statement was fired like a missile, and landed like one, to judge by how Felix spun around with anger, guilt, and sorrow all burning in his eyes. "Nothing's changed, Felix." Just the temperature of my soul, that's all. I tried to put some effort back into my voice. "We're still best friends, right?"

He came back to the fireplace and knelt down beside me. I hesitated before reaching up to wipe a stray tear away from his lips, making him smile. "Will we still be friends after I leave?"

Now I understood a little more. "You haven't left yet."

"I will, when school ends for the summer."

Six months, and my best friend would leave. "Do you know where you're going?"

"Out west, someplace," Go west, young man. "I think New Mexico." I'd never been there. Uncle Alex told me it was gorgeous. Felix's voice took on another unusual edge. "Now Dad wants to be a horse rancher."

I tried to lighten the mood somewhat. "That sounds a lot more fun than commercial real estate, Felix. Look at it from his point of view."

Felix agreed. "I'd rather rustle doggies than schmooze a bunch of filthy rich investors and lawyers any day."

Lawyers. I liked Dad so much more when he was an officer and a gentleman. *Let's kill all the lawyers.*

We giggled together. Felix sat back down next to me. "What is that from? *Richard II*?"

"*Henry VI*, dear boy." I mimicked our Mister James the Literature Fiend Granger's rich voice.

"I can't believe you read Shakespeare in your spare time." Felix looked at me with respect, and then, affection, mixed with lonely fear. I knew that lonely fear look. I saw it every morning in the bathroom mirror. "Will you still love me after I leave? As a friend?"

"As a best friend, you mean." A reflexive urge to reach up and kiss Felix mushroomed through me. The gesture came out in words, instead. "I love you now, Felix. I'll still love you after you leave. I just won't be able to say it to you in person. Not as often, anyway."

Felix braced himself visibly before speaking again. "Would you keep loving me, as a best friend, if we did it? Like what you and Mister Nicolaus did?" He spoke the simple little word 'did' with the same awkward inflection all teenagers use as a tenderizer for a more explicit sexual description. So, hey, Paco, did you do it with Betty? You bet your ass we did it, Jack. We did it until my rocks hurt. I did it all over her face. I did it.

The fire crackled in the background. I ran my finger along Felix's lower lip, but he didn't move away. Slowly and without interference, I began to unbutton his pajama top, while neither of us looked at the other. "Do you want to?"

"I don't know," he whispered, "I don't know." He bit his lip. "I feel so afraid, and I shouldn't, because you're my best friend." He laughed uneasily. "Maybe that's why I'm acting like such an idiot tonight."

I painted Felix's soft cheeks with the teardrops that dribbled out of him in the pause. "You're not an idiot at all. Believe it or not, I know exactly what you're feeling."

"I thought we'd stay best friends if I...if we..."

"We might not stay friends at all. Who knows?" I let out a tired laugh. "We might be dead before school ends." Dead. I decided I didn't want a wake. I wanted the defector priest to perform the service in Polish at the gravesite, *His cares are now all ended* inscribed on my tombstone.

"Did you ever think about it?" Felix kissed my fingers. He made my waist squirm beneath the blanket. Our eyes locked up, the same way they did the first day we met, sitting on Felix's bed making promises to each other neither of us really thought we'd have to keep. I was going to pretend he was talking about dying when he pressed my closed hand against his lips. "You know, with me?"

I considered how honestly I would answer Felix's question. "At first. Yeah. The first night, definitely." I was the first friend to look away from the other.

"What about after that?"

"A little bit." Ha, try nearly every day. "The more we became buddies, the less I thought about it." The more I tried not to think about it, which hurt. A lot, as I recalled.

"And now?" There was pressure and dismay in the soft tone of his voice, the same feelings I was aware of, deep inside again.

"I don't know." I sounded as unconvinced as I felt. We sat in my family room's echoing stillness without touching or looking at each other, until the fire finally burned itself out.

*

My bedroom was freezing. I had forgotten that I closed the heat register when we were playing "Hazel". I left it that way. My heart needed company, and the cold would have to do. I switched on the radio in time to catch the beginning of Schumann's piano suite, *Carnival*. Felix climbed into my bed first. I followed, still wearing my robe. We laid side-by-side in the dark for the duration of the deeply sentimental piano composition, before he rolled to his side and faced the wall, away from me.

The bedroom's chill began prodding my heart in the wrong direction. "I don't think I'm what you're really mad about. It's not us, either."

"I'm not angry," Felix mumbled.

"Oh, yeah? Maybe we're not so different, after all." I pulled my robe off and threw it across the room. Let him deal with me being naked, I thought. I couldn't even hear Felix breathe. I thought about kissing the back of Felix's neck in apology, or cradling him in my arms like Nicolasha had done with me a few nights ago, but I didn't. Instead, I pretended to fall asleep, and listened hard while my best friend used his pillow to keep his sniffling to himself. I was actually happy someone else was doing the crying, for a change. I should have felt bad about that, but didn't.

Mom and Pop Radio moved on to their next selection.

XIV

You have such a February face.
Much Ado About Nothing

Lawrence the Laughing Lawyer was very businesslike
and cordial. The office staff looked at me with over-
solicitous pity. Dad's ex-partners each came out of their
suites to say hello, shake my hand, ask how I was doing,
and, of course, inquire if there was anything each of
them could do. Such was the glory of being reduced to
the role of poor, lonely orphan. The whole office, from
the walls to the jewelry, seemed painted in a rainbow
of conservative grays and blues to me. It always had.
Felix and his trench coat fit right in. My blue jeans and
hiking boots didn't. None of legal eagles made open
notice of the fact I was wearing Dad's favorite greatcoat
like a vampire hunter in a Hammer Film.

Uncle Alex waited for me in Lawrence's dull "Better
Homes and Garden"-approved office. He was alone. He
did, however, look refreshed and alert. Maybe it was
the bracing cold he loved so much. Felix stayed in the
anteroom.

Lawrence slid his large leather chair close to his tidy
and empty desk, empty except for a single, open file,
which he rested his hands over. "I'll try to be as brief as
possible." He lit a short, unfiltered cigarette. "I'm sure
none of us want to linger over this stuff." He cleared his
throat with a smoker's cough and looked at me directly,
without emotion. "You understand your parents
arranged for me to look after their affairs, take care of
things." I nodded and returned his vanilla stare. "We can
have one of the other partners handle this, or any other
matter, if either of you would prefer."

Uncle Alex winced with impatience, and turned to me
for my decision. I could picture Aunt Hilly grinding

Lawrence's knees over the phone, making him agree to ask such an inane question. I smiled thinly. "They don't give family discounts, do they?"

Lawrence smiled back. "No." The ice was broken. "Now, everything's yours." He indicated me with his cigarette. "There aren't any wills, but nothing ends up in Probate Court or creates a tax issue, because you're the only survivor. Your name is on the house, as you know, and it's going to be paid off out of the firm's bereavement annuity." My eyes widened. "It's one thing you won't have to worry about." He coughed again. Stop smoking, for God's sake! "You're listed on the bank accounts, so there's no problem there, unless you decide to run away in style."

Uncle Alex gave me a humorous look that said, "That's what I'd do!" I laughed to myself, even as a numbing sensation grew inside of me. "It's kind of funny." Lawrence's voice was sadly ironic. "Your dad put all those utility stocks in your name, alone, right after he said 'yes' to that New York firm." In a rare moment of emotional lucidity two anniversaries ago, Aunt Dutch had given Mom and Dad all her electric and gas company shares. I didn't know what they were worth, but I knew there were a lot of them. The whole family had come a long way from our decidedly working class, immigrant background in Roseland. I used to think it was funny we weren't happier as a result. "They're very conservative stocks. Our money man, Mister Sheehan, could definitely do better with their cash value."

"What do you think?"

My lawyer cousin shrugged the shoulders of his light grey suit. "Utilities are slow and steady, but they get you there in the end. You can probably live on the checks until you're done with college." He gave me a quick, hard stare. "You are planning on college, aren't you?"

"My lit teacher sent a few of my poetry samples to some of his Ivy League friends back east. I guess they like them. They're interested in having me come visit them." Lawrence nodded approvingly. Uncle Alex rolled his eyes.

"Good. Good." He flipped a number of pages in the file. "Now, your uncle and I spoke last night..."

Uncle Alex was my Godfather, and agreed to be legal guardian. He would sell his Minnesota property, and move in with me. No mention was made of Veronica. Once I made plans for college, Lawrence and Uncle Alex would help me decide what to do with the house. The water level of the conversation kept getting closer to my face. I was underwater by the time Lawrence told me about Mom and Dad's substantial life insurance policies. The payoffs would be put into a sheltered trust that I could access for college, and anything else, once I was twenty one.

"So I've got a lot of money now, huh?"

Lawrence waved his cigarette in the air. "It's not all liquid cash, per se, but you'll have to go on a terrific drunk to end up as poor as our great-grandparents were."

We both looked at Uncle Alex, a man well familiar with spectacular lost weekends. "You want my advice? Fuck the Ivy League. Go to the University of Hawaii."

"Why?"

"You won't have far to go to the beach when you skip classes."

*

Dad's office was decorated like a Captain's cabin on an important ship. It was one of his very few childish indulgences, besides the Stingray. I realized I loved them both, for what they were, and what they represented, and Dad, for breaking down and having them in the first place. His secretary, a large, grey-haired woman named Paula, was still shaken by what had happened. She had trouble talking to me as I showed Felix the office. She was on the verge of tears. Dad used to treat her like a dog. No, he treated dogs better. "I'll have one of the clerks pack up your father's belongings. I'm sure you'll want the photographs."

Dad had that irritating habit of lining his office of all the pictures he had snapped of me as the number one son, and us as the number one family, a desperate effort to shout down his own doubts about it all to the rest of the world. Felix was impressed. Paula got sadder. I got irritated. Look at them all, I carped to myself. My birthday parties. Christ, even the Bus-O-Fun! My Halloween costumes. It figures he wouldn't have proof lying around the office that I once chose to be "Blacula" one year. Ah, yes, opening presents every Christmas morning. There's my favorite: the motorized cable car and ski lift from the extraordinary F.A.O. Schwartz catalog. That was the year Mom became a nurse. All the Easter Sunday Masses, in our sharp three-piece best. Stolen moments from all of our trips. I looked pretty funny falling, not diving, from the Fontainebleau's diving board in my zebra-stripe bathing suit. And how could I forget? Every single one of my school portraits, from Kindergarten (spot the dimwit smiling away in his checkerboard suit jacket and red bow tie) to this year, as a "tough" and detached Junior (white button-down, black sweatshirt, bleak "take the Goddamn picture" sneer).

I handed Paula a 5 by 8 picture of me and Mom and Dad, equipped with hats and pennants, sitting along the upper deck railing of White Sox Park, bundled up for the ever damp and cold Opening Day, smiling like we might actually win the game. She began to cry and left the office. I sat down in Dad's chair, swinging myself back and forth with my feet. "Can I have one, too?" Felix asked.

"Take whatever one you'd like."

He didn't hesitate. He reached for the shot of me as a little kid, floating in the middle of a Playboy Club life preserver. A scuba mask was propped up on my forehead, and I was wearing flippers. Two cute teenaged life guards, a guy and a girl, were each holding a side of the inner tube and one of my feet out of the sparkling indoor pool waters. I was grinning from ear to ear.

"I like this one." I don't know why I thought he'd take my most recent school portrait. "You look so happy in this." I remembered I was.

*

Earlier that morning, me and my best friend entered the atrophied, suburban universe of talking without saying anything, listening without hearing anything, and carrying on without living. We were there together, clearing the driveway of snow, making breakfast, and crossing the invisible line that is drawn on a person's belongings when they die, sorting through Mom and Dad's remaining effects like busy little beavers, packing away Mom's stuff for anyone who wanted it, and trying on Dad's clothes, to see what I wanted to keep and Felix thought his dad might like.

The night before didn't happen. Nobody cried. No conversation of import occurred. No hand or heart or any untoward body part was touched. We left the lawyers, laughing and otherwise, and returned to my home. We sat together inside Dad's Stingray. As always, the gleaming white fiberglass body was polished and waxed like new. The red leather seats were cold and stiff from the weather. Felix picked up on the glimmer of excitement I felt, pretending to pilot the car. I already had my learner's permit. I would get the license before my birthday, this summer. Felix admitted he could hardly wait to take the car out for a test drive with me, but didn't say where. He didn't mention any place special, or far away, like New Mexico, for instance. My only reply was a phony smile. It was a pair of performances for the ages.

XV

The orphan pines while the oppressor feeds.
The Rape of Lucrece

I sat with my bare legs folded over each other, staring at my record collection. I had just gotten out of the shower. I was now taking a shower before I went to bed and another after I had finished jogging in the morning. It seemed like I was running further and further with each passing morning, and stayed in the shower longer and longer. I was cold, sitting in my tartan robe, but wouldn't put on any more clothes.

The Firebird. Cinderella. Der Zarewisch. The Magic Flute. Die Meistersinger von Nuremburg. Katerina Ismailova. A Soldier's Story. Symphonic Metamorphosis. The Water Music. Samson et Delilah. Romeo and Juliet. The Alpine Symphony. The London Symphony. The Leningrad Symphony. The Unfinished Symphony. Heligoland. Billy Budd. Babi Yar. Carnival of the Animals. Brandenburg Concerti. Les Nuits d'ete. Finlandia. Spartacus. The Age of Gold. Enigma Variations. Faust. Jewish Folk Poetry. Jeux d'enfants. Death and Transfiguration.

Requiem. A couple of those. *Requiae? Requiea?*

*

I wandered into Dad's bedroom. The large dimensions seemed even bigger with the shadows of emptiness hanging over the old-fashioned colonial furniture and the half-full, half-empty moving crates still cluttering up the floor. I wasn't sure Uncle Alex would want the room, even as a painting studio, or whatever he called the room he did his work in. I wouldn't. My hand slid across the bottom of Dad's sock drawer until it reached the hard leather holster concealed in the mass of unsorted hose. I pulled it out of the drawer and took the vintage .25-calibre Beretta automatic into my right hand, balanced it in my palm, and slowly held it up, extending my arm fully, moving the pistol around the dark room until the reflection of the moon on the edge of the backyard window was in my sights. I unchambered the hollow-point round and pushed it back into the small clip, which I slipped into a side pouch of the holster. The bullets were hand-loaded by Salvatore, a maddeningly fastidious tailor who had a small storefront in town. The elderly Neapolitan immigrant had evidently once worked for Beretta itself, and maintained, modified, and crafted ammo for Dad's little automatic as if it were his own. I liked the gun. It fit my hand perfectly, even though I knew it wasn't all that powerful a gun.

Seven shots. Aunt Dutch. No jury on earth would convict me. Aunt Melody. A bullet before the gin got to her. Cousin Julia. Think of the price I'd get from her twenty or thirty ex's. Cousin Matt. Forget a head shot with his thick skull. Uncle Albert. Who could tell the difference if he had been shot? That lunatic twelve-year-old cousin just off the boat that wouldn't leave me alone at the wake. Veronica. Save Uncle Alex a lot of trouble, down the line.

Back in my bedroom, I began to level the pistol at Felix, who was sound asleep, curled up facing my side of the bed, but felt another wave coast over me, a cooler, more penetrating one that made me stop in mid-gesture. I quietly put the gun in its holster and stuffed it into my own sock drawer, before slipping into the covers next to Felix, who stirred as I moved closer to him.

I could see his eyes open slightly from the moonlight that touched the top half of my bed from outside the frosty bedroom window. He asked in a whisper, "Are you okay?" I nodded my head, but started to cry without much in the way of sound effects, something I considered an achievement at that point in my life. I let him pull me into his arms and hold me like I was his little brother who had just gotten roughed up by the bullies down the block. I didn't realize until I had finished that Felix's hands were both settled along the waistband of my underwear, and that he had cried, too, just not as long as I had, and much more discreetly.

*

I woke up the next morning after hearing the front door close behind Felix, as he left to go back to his apartment "for some clothes", according to the note. I watched him walk slowly across my backyard and through the neighboring small park, both still covered in snow. The cloud cover was low and grim. It would probably snow some more, I thought, crossing my arms over my chest as I trudged to the bathroom. I tried not to think about Felix when we showered separately, pretending I didn't really believe he wasn't coming back that night. Well, he didn't. I let Lawrence take me to his house for dinner with his family, his macabre, intact, happy family, hoping someone would try to call me that night and not get an answer.

*

The light snowfall pasted itself over my face and in my hair as I walked to the cemetery, in lieu of having a good jog the following day. I had deliberately overslept. I didn't much feel like jogging or getting out of bed. I lay there, leafing through Nicolasha's photo album, until almost noon, when I decided to walk off a few of my blues.

Hah.

If the temperature had been seventy-degrees, under a bright, clear sky, with a soft spring breeze blowing in the air, the cemetery, hell, any cemetery, would be depressing. A giant field decorated with granite slabs and statues, stuffed with boxes that held the leftovers of people you used to share life with. Christ, I thought, what a concept. The ocean sounded more appealing to me. "Where is so-and-so buried?" someone might ask. You would then point outward, to the warm blue Pacific or the cold green Atlantic, and reply, "out there". I began to consider other appropriate burial grounds, vast and forbidding, edge-of-the-world kind of places, like the Alps. I'd take a chopper through the middle of Switzerland and scatter the ashes. "Where did you bury them?" I'd smile, sweep my arm toward the line of perpetually snowcapped peaks, and respond, "In there". Or Baja California. Land or sea would work down there. The Australian Outback. Never been there, I said to myself, but it looked pretty edge-of-the-worldish to me. Or New Mexico.

Winter was much nicer up at the Schloss Unc in Minnesota, I decided. Lake Geneva, too.

I knelt over the pair of red stone burial markers and brushed the falling snow from the lettering. I didn't bring flowers. They would be covered in snow in an hour. It was cold again, and gloomy. The streets were swimming in dark grey slush and pulverized road salt. All the cars that passed me were filthy. The cold wasn't a fresh cold, but, rather, an unformulated, damp, smoggy, clammy sort of cold. And why not? It was New Year's Eve. After tomorrow, the holidays were over. No more ornaments. Take the lights down. Put away the presents. Burn the tree. I was certainly going to burn that awful, white-flocked artificial tree of ours.

From Thanksgiving to New Year's Day, the cold and the snow and the wind chill are all a perversely romantic addendum to the Chicagoan's holiday season. On January second, they're just cold and snow and wind chill, officially a pain in the ass and something to despise until winter finally went away, which, in Chicago, could be as early as Easter Sunday, or as late as Mother's Day.

As I walked through the snow-covered graveyard back towards our empty and unlit house, I felt alone, absolutely, terribly, completely alone. It didn't matter if Uncle Alex loved me, or Aunt Hilly and Cousin Lawrence were there, or that they all cared. It made no difference that my teacher Nicolaus was a friend, or lover, or whatever I was supposed to call him, and that he would be there if I ever called. It was irrelevant that Felix and his entire family shared my grief as unselfishly as they shared their love for me, and trivial to mention the depth and sincerity of what had grown between Felix and me. None of it mattered. There were people in my life, and love came from those people, it was true, a gleaming treasure trove of love, freely given, received, and sometimes reciprocated. But it didn't matter, because I <u>felt</u> alone. I may not have been, but that's how it <u>felt</u>, deep inside my heart, and my soul. Alone.

My God, I kept whispering out loud to myself, like a broken record skipping over a piece of ice from the empty winter around me. Alone.

XVI

By his face straight shall you know his heart.
Richard III

When I first spotted someone waiting for me at our front door, I thought it might be Felix. Or hoped it would be, I don't know. As I got closer, I could see they were too tall to be my best friend buddy ol' pal from school, whoever it was.

Christian DeVere stood two inches taller than my six feet. His shoulders weren't as broad as mine, and his chest and waist were slightly thinner, which made him seem lankier than he was when he wore his school baseball outfit. His fingers and feet were long and, well, elegant, as was his long blond hair, which was thrown back from his ears and hung well below his shoulders. His coaches left Christian alone over his hair; he was too good to pick on. He'd stuff it into his baseball cap when he played. Everyone gave him hell when he put it into a pony tail. He had bright green eyes that sparkled when he grinned or laughed, both of which he did a lot, because he was always telling jokes and playing around with people, at least when I was around. His lips, eyebrows, nose, and ears were also thin, complementing the sharp lines of his cheek bones and chin, a warm handsome face that only closed on the pitcher's mound.

On a good day, I was lucky to get a scratch single off him.

His mom and dad were unrepentant hippies, cheerful dropouts who kept the better part of the sixties alive and well and living in their Volkswagen minibus, mature stoners that owned a small nursery on the edge of town, the edge that bordered the unfashionably working-class (and integrated) suburb to our east, flower children whose only little boy did his pre-high school growing up in communes and collective farms somewhere in the Pacific Northwest. All their money went to political groups that they called progressive, we called liberal, and the rest of my family called communist, so Christian didn't expect to have a car of his own until after college, and bought all his clothes at the dingy Army / Navy surplus store he worked at all every evening to pay his own tuition at the Catholic high school he chose to attend.

The DeVeres lived in a grey brick Cape Cod house on a side road near the nursery. Their backyard blended into a small corner of Cook County Forest Preserve land, so it seemed like there was a miniature forest just outside their back door. The living room, family room, all three bedrooms, and the basement each had a separate stereo system equipped with an 8-track tape player, as did their minibus. I had only visited Christian at home once, and that was with the rest of the guys, but I loved his basement, which was lined with psychedelic posters, many of which were lined with black felt and glowed in the black-light mounted on the ceiling. Christian had one of those sound boxes, a molded plastic box the size of a stereo speaker that flashed different colored lights in a wild pattern, lights activated by talk or the music from their late-'50's style juke box. The room was filled up by a full-sized pool table with real leather side pouches and genuine ivory balls that Christian was banned from using. The fabulous antique looked out of place, surrounded as it was by cheap head shop posters. They even had a strobe light, too.

And all I could do was hang a stupid grin on my face, I was so happy to see him, to see anyone, waiting for me to come home.

"Is there a good reason why you haven't opened my Christmas card?" Christian waved the yellow envelope ny nose. The mailbox was stuffed with unopened .. I felt like an ass. He slapped the side of my cheek with the card and smiled into my eyes. "At least you didn't throw it out." I paused awkwardly. I didn't know whether I should have held out my hand or moved closer to hug him. I wasn't sure if our only other hug was just to cheer me up. There was a lot about our walk home from the church that I wasn't sure about. Why had I felt so comfortable in telling him about what was hurting me so much, instead of holding it in and crying, like I had so often with Felix? Christian grinned at my indecision before putting the card in my gloved hands. "Read my card, first." It was the cheapest, tackiest drug store Christmas card I had ever seen, with a bad Japanese cartoon-like drawing of Santa Claus falling down a chimney into a lit fireplace. Wow. It cost a whole thirty-five cents! Kind of a step down from the gilt nutcrackers and village people at play. I opened the small card, read the inscription quickly, and looked up at a Christian DeVere I had never seen before. "Aren't you going to read it out loud?"

I blushed. "Why would I do that?"

"That's the least you can do, considering you didn't send me one, and left mine out in the cold for a week."

"A day or two," I corrected him.

Christian leaned sideways against one of the house's front picture-windows, looking wistfully at our Christmas tree inside the house. "Dad says, when you write something down, it becomes real, but when you read something written down, it becomes forever."

That sounded like something his dad might say. Shyness overcame Christian as I made him wait for a few more seconds. "Okay, okay." I cleared my throat as if I were about to recite from Shakespeare.

To my friend,

Have a merry Christmas - get lots of cool presents - and a happy New Year - hit lots of home runs, just not off me! We've played ball together for years, but never played friends like we did after meeting in church. You opened up to me with honesty I didn't think I earned, or deserved. Thanks for that, and letting me be your friend that night, now, and for a long time to come, I hope.

I need you too.

Love, Christian...oooo.

The impact of what Christian had written, intended or otherwise, began to sink in after I had read it aloud. The words were alive, deep inside of me. We looked at each other carefully, beguiled by our shared hesitation, but neither of us moved to close the three-foot gap between us. Our little stalemate was broken by the sudden flash of blinking and twinkling Christmas lights hanging in the front windows and the trees lining the driveway. I had forgotten about the timer I'd hooked up the night before.

Lights.

"What do the zeroes mean after your name?"

"Come on!" Christian shook his head with a pursed grin. "You really don't know what they mean?"

"Nope." I shrugged my shoulders. I honestly didn't.

My baseball buddy and friend glanced down at his cheap and wet Converse All-Star gym shoes, silly looking red things, if you asked me. "X's and O's?! I <u>know</u> you know!" He looked back up at me and smiled. "They're hugs."

With another blush, I asked, "Then what does an **X** stand for?"

Christian blushed back. "A kiss." Hugs and kisses? I looked at the card again and felt myself shiver as a rare and welcome tide of warmth poured across me inside of Dad's greatcoat. "Haven't you ever written anyone a card or letter?" Actually, I hadn't. Silly poetry and worse stories, yeah, but none of that. Until the last couple of months, who would I have written to, anyway? "You're just making me say it all out loud."

"What?" I tapped the top of Christian's head with the card, yellow envelope and all.

"I want to give you a hug."

Camera.

I began to laugh, but stopped when Christian seemed hurt. He didn't look away, however. I ignored the distant sound of a ringing phone inside of the house. I wanted to hold him, too. "Me, too."

The time and the place didn't seem important. I don't remember if it was still snowing, or how cold it was, or felt. I'm not even sure what kind of look I had on my face, but I can remember every detail on Christian's: his long, blond hair, slicked back over his head and over his ears, dark from the moisture of the falling snow, the reddish tint on his ears and nose from the wind, the slight quivering of his bottom lip, the small wagon train of freckles at the top of his cheeks, and the wide open pair of bright green books that left themselves open for me to see, books that watched me read them with indulgence and a touch of desperation.

He was beautiful.

"Remember what you talked about? You know, after Confession?" I nodded, at once admiring and resenting how calm Christian appeared as he looked into my eyes when he spoke. I felt like the little boy with the violin I had written about, the one in the courtyard, turning to stone as an angel carried me in their arms and music swirled up in the background, except that the music now was the invisible bridge connecting my eyes, and heart, with Christian's. He started pointing his thumb at both of us. "So am I." His voice suddenly disappeared into a whisper. "Me, too."

I closed my eyes for a moment and lifted my head toward the heavens I was pretty sure were hiding behind all those winter clouds. Christian stepped forward, put his arms around me, and pressed us softly together.

Action.

It wasn't like our first, hurried, awkward hug. It was weird the way one of his arms went across the top of my shoulders and neck, and the other went under my arm and around my back, weird like that was the correct way to hug and we'd been doing it for years, not seconds. The sides of our faces rubbed together like chilled fleshy pieces of jigsaw. He slid one of his legs in between mine under the open greatcoat. Our bodies, despite our winter layers of coats and shirts and t-shirts and long underwear, fitted around each other perfectly. We stood in each other's arms, closer than even Nicolasha and I had, longer than I ever hugged anyone before.

It had to be the best hug anyone ever got, and it came from someone I had only known as a nice smile and a fearsome split-finger pitch, someone, I then realized in a second warm flash deep in my heart, I was going to be friends with for, yes, "a long time to come."

"I'm sorry I couldn't get here sooner," Christian softly told me in my ear.

"That's okay," I murmured from his neck. "You're here now. I couldn't ask for anything else." Well...maybe just one or two other things.

We reluctantly pulled away from each other. Christian reached up and straightened my scarf under the collar of the greatcoat he looked over with envy. "It's, uh, really been a rough end of the year for you." Yes, I nodded with a blank, almost stoic look on my face, it kind of had. "Well, tomorrow's a new year." He wrapped an arm over my shoulders and shook me gently, smiling his way through my mock stoicism. "And we're new friends, right?"

I nodded again, holding open the front door for my new friend to enter. Warmth from the house poured over us as we shut out the cold and snow behind the closed door and headed into the family room to start a fire, which would soon include that damned flocked tree.

Flash.

XVII

Lovers and madmen have such seething brains,
Such shaping fantasies, that apprehend
More than cool reason ever comprehends.
The lunatic, the lover, and the poet
Are of imagination all compact.
One sees more devils than vast hell can hold,
That is the madman.
A Midsummer Night's Dream

"Hello?"

"Young man, I've been calling all afternoon."

"Hi, Unc. Where are you?"

"The Schloss. Where've you been?"

Pause. "I took a walk."

His pause. "To Hyde Park?"

Giggle. "No, not that far."

"I'm having some trouble putting my affairs in order. I don't think I'll be back down until some time next week."

"That's okay. I'll be fine."

"Are you sure? You can come up here and miss some more school, if you'd like."

"It sounds fun, Uncle, but I'm actually looking forward to going back to class. It'll keep my mind busy."

His second pause. "I understand. You really like that university place, don't you?"

"Yeah, I do. A lot. I don't know why, though. They work us like we were serfs there!"

"Have you thought about just staying on there at the university itself?"

"Well, yeah, I did, for a while, until my Literature teacher breathed on me about it. He said I should go someplace totally foreign to me. A whole new world, he keeps saying. Sticking around wouldn't be much of a change for me. Besides, I think I'm ready for some new geography, now."

Mutual silence.

"You're right. Pretty smart guy for being seventeen."

"Sixteen, Unc."

"What's a year or two between family?" We both giggle. "I should set fire to this place for the insurance money."

"Well? Why don't you?"

"That little rag would probably sue me for that, too."

"Who?"

"Veronica. Or Sybll. I should call her Sybll to her face and see if any more hidden personalities fall out of her hair. Psychotic wench."

I giggled again. "Should I ask what she's suing you for, Uncle Alex?"

"Hah! The usual! 'Mental anguish' or some other twaddle!" I heard a wine bottle pop. "I personally think she smelled some of that money you've come into, and flipped when I said no."

"To my money?"

"No, nephew, to marrying her. What you do with the money is your affair."

"A responsible adult would keep it their affair until I finished college, or started a career, or got married. Something like that."

"Oh, yes! Now you sound like some of those mummies we're related to." I laughed. Uncle Alex didn't. "Have you even picked out a college, yet?"

"No."

"What are you going to take up, besides space, once you break down and pick one?"

"Writing, or poetry. Something like that."

"Something like that. Fine. Something like that, someplace presumably in North America. Right?"

"Well, yeah, I guess."

"You guess. You guess you'll take up writing or poetry or something like that at some college or university someplace in the Western Hemisphere."

"Fine! I'm going to the University of Geneva! I'm going to major in French language, and minor in 16th Century English Literature! Is that okay, Unc?"

"I'd go to the Sorbonne myself. Paris nightlife rather puts anything in Switzerland to shame." He took a short drink. "The point, dear heart, is that you can't possibly be expected to have any idea about what you want the rest of your life to be, or where you want it to take place, or _why_ you do, which is the only really important question you can ever ask yourself. Not at your age, despite that brain of yours. Even if the rest of your life begins next year, or whatever."

Uncle Alex wasn't drunk, but it didn't sound like it was his first bottle of wine or champagne, either. The only time he became overly contemplative or philosophical was after a full bottle of wine. I loved him when he got like that. Unc talked about things no one else wanted to think about, much less talk about, and he did so in such a brutally common-sensical way that it drove anyone who tried to argue with him nuts.

"I think the rest of my life began a few days ago, Unc."

I looked at the bits of flock that had fallen from the grate inside the bright and crackling fireplace, and suddenly thought of Christian, who sat across from me, pretending he wasn't listening.

His third pause. "You're a clever little bugger, aren't you?"

"I hope so, Unc. I can't do a whole lot else, except hit a baseball and write poetry nobody understands!"

"Send some of it up to me. I'll read it. If I don't get it, I'll hit a bottle of port. After that rot, I can figure out anything. Even a prenuptial agreement."

"Really?"

"No, not at all. Can't stand the stuff. Just wanted to lead you along. Yes, of course, I mean it! Send them first thing the post office opens. And don't send anything you haven't copied."

I realized Uncle Alex was the first relative to ask for some of my poetry to read, and it made me feel like I was Czar of the Russias. "Okay. Thanks, Unc."

"No problem. By the way, happy New Year. I'm getting drunk to bring in the new decade. You should, too. It'll make the old one look better."

Christian and I exchanged smiles. "A friend of mine is spending the night here."

"Then get drunk together. Incoherence is much more fun when you share it with someone." His fourth and final pause. "Is it that teacher friend of yours?"

My second but very large, fearful, and defensive pause. Uncle Alex was pretty clever, too. "No. It's one of the guys I play baseball with."

"Well, don't play tonight if you're going to get drunk. Bats and baseballs and beer don't mix, unless you've got upper deck seats and there's a Yankee fan close by." We laughed together. "And don't you dare touch that Corvette. Do you hear me?"

"Oh, yeah? What if I got all the cash I could earlier today, and I'm planning the ultimate road trip, a crime spree across the country? What then?"

"Set the house on fire for the insurance. There's better money in it, and it's a whole hell of a lot easier to pull off than armed robberies, of which the only worthwhile ones are Federal offenses, and who needs that?"

"There's a much better grade of cell-mate in a Federal prison, Uncle Alex."

"Ah, yes, Club Fed. Think of all the interesting senators and bankers you'll meet."

I heard the front door open and close. "My friend is here." Christian waved at me from the kitchen with a large Army backpack slung over his shoulder.

"Go start your drunk. Call me sometime tomorrow. Late."

"I will. Take care."

Uncle Alex grunted his reply. We hung up without saying "I love you" or anything else awkward.

*

"Are you ready to go?" I put my hands on Christian's arms. They were shaking. "What's up? What's the matter?"

He shook his head with a smile. "Nothing. I'm just cold."

"Do you want a different coat to wear?"

"I'm fine. Thank you, though."

"Okay, how about another hug to warm you up?"

He blushed and smiled anew. "I'd like that."

"Me, too." I held Christian until he stopped shaking. Our arms reluctantly withdrew from the other's body, but we kept standing very close and face-to-face. "How come you only put hugs on your Christmas card?"

The blush on Christian's face began to look permanent. His arms began to shake again. "I was too scared to ask for a kiss." He lowered his head to my shoulder, with his lips close to my neck. "I still am."

Christian took a step backwards. "That's okay," I sighed. "I guess I'm scared, too." I wanted to wrap my arms around his entire body like Nicolasha did to me on the last day of school, but Christian beat me to it.

It was just as good as a kiss.

*

The movie theater was surprisingly crowded. I didn't think very many people would be interested in a Woody Allen double feature on New Year's Eve, besides me and my reluctant companion, who had never seen any of Mr. Allen's films before. The local screen had only just converted itself into a revival house, of sorts, instead of what it had been, a last port of call for films that everyone had already seen, or had no intention to in the first place. It was actually a homey sort of place, not too big, not too small, clean, featuring good sound, seats that weren't completely useless, a nice downtown location in the business center of the neighboring suburb to our north, and the trademark of excellence of all real movie theaters - a single screen.

We sat in the back row, taking up the four-seat aisle on the far right for ourselves. An older couple sat in the row in front of us. Movie-going couples of all ages filled the big aisle in the middle. Everyone enjoyed the management's quaint slices of free angel cake and cheap cold duck and the overheated warmth of the dark auditorium. Christian and I were the only pair of young guys watching the movie as a couple, which derailed my train of thought, even thinking the word 'couple'.

"Manhattan" was fabulous. Christian laughed throughout the whole movie, and seemed to enjoy the Gershwin music as I much as I did. The black-and-white photography that filled up those loving Panavision frames blew me away, but not as much as the fact the film hadn't won a single Oscar. During intermission, I waited for Christian to come back from the men's room before I went myself. I don't know why. It embarrassed us both. I was excited about seeing "Love and Death." Nicolasha had once mentioned in class that the soundtrack was entirely made up of music by Prokofiev, something I wasn't sure would work in a Woody Allen film, but wanted to check out, nonetheless. Well, what did I know? It was great! *Lieutenant Kije* was always a favorite of mine, and I doubted I would ever hear it again without thinking of Woody and the Grim Reaper dancing together through the woods as the film ended.

Christian remarked on the music more than once. I was excited about digging out my Prokofiev records and listening to them together. Near the end of the film, he quietly thanked me for bringing him to see the double feature. I took a deep breath and reached behind his shoulders, leaning over to whisper a reply in his ear. I didn't say anything, however. I kissed the side of his ear and ran my closed lips across his neck for a stolen moment before straightening myself in my seat and returning to the business on the screen. Christian didn't move a muscle for a couple of minutes. "That was awesome," he finally whispered, smiling at me in the near dark as he ran the palm of his warm hand over mine for too brief an instant.

Dad's old Omega said the New Year would start in less than an hour, but it had already begun, for me anyway. For Christian, too, I hoped.

*

We sat on a large strip of cardboard we found in a dumpster near the town's commuter station and perched ourselves near the top of the incline where the train tracks were laid. There were people everywhere in the park below, our suburb's largest: families, couples young and old, partiers, cops to keep the partiers in line, and a few singles, who looked as lonely as I vaguely remembered feeling earlier that day. No one seemed to mind the thin layer of snow they were standing or sitting in (if they had brought lawn chairs), or went the economy route, like we did. Everyone was in too good of a mood to give any notice to the vile wind chill, which helped us to run to the park in good time before the fireworks began.

Mom and Dad and me had never done this, I groused. We should have. Damn those asinine parties we had instead, cells of attorneys and nurses refusing to coagulate. Shabby substitutes for this here.

We counted out loud with everyone else to midnight, and contented ourselves to shaking hands and patting shoulders with rue we could see on each other's faces. We weren't alone, or in the dark.

"Happy New Year, dude."

"Happy New Year, Christian."

We did sit very close to each other, for warmth and for the fun of doing it. I had given Christian my beret to wear. Dad's greatcoat kept me a lot warmer than Christian's Army surplus field jacket was keeping him. Christian continued to scan the crowd of spectators below us, anxiously looking for any of our baseball buddies. I ran Handel's *Royal Fireworks* through my mind as the multicolored explosions launched themselves into the starry black sky above us.

"To Catch a Thief"-a-rama.

Christian suddenly turned and looked at me with serious, almost frightened eyes. A gigantic green hailstorm erupted in the icy heavens with a loud pop. "Kiss me. I don't care if anybody sees." Two bright red umbrellas of streaming light cascaded into the air, with the trumpet of sharp, staccato crackling, the sound of the world's largest firing squad opening fire. We didn't stop until some of the saliva that was running down our mouths began to freeze.

"I don't know if what I'm feeling is love," Christian panted, "but I know I want it to be."

Flash. A stupendous flash of exploding silver balls fired upward towards the watching stars, accompanied by the shrill whistle of incoming artillery. But it wasn't as big or as loud as the flash I felt inside of me, inside of my hand as I squeezed Christian's and more or less smiled.

"Let's go home."

*

We started the second blaze of the night in the fireplace, which was filled almost to the grating with ashes from our earlier effort. It was the only light in the family room. I had taken our large Inuit mural, a patchwork of different Arctic animal furs Unc probably scored from some poor Eskimo over a bad bet, off of the wall and laid it at our feet. We moved into the other's arms at the same time, our second, perfect hug, before I took a step back and slowly undressed Christian with hands I could barely keep from shaking. I left his socks on. I wasn't sure how to take them off with him still standing. He kept his face close to my body as he returned the gesture. He left my socks on, too. We threw ourselves onto the mural almost as one and wrapped the fur around us. The logs continued to crackle and burn in the fireplace.

It tickled. It hurt. It was the highest high, warmer than the fire, wet and tight and smooth all at once. We didn't say a word. Our hands, our lips, our legs, and our bodies said everything we each wanted to say, and each wanted to hear.

*

It was I don't know how many hours later. I was at last beginning to fade into sleep when Christian shook me awake. "Let's get dressed."

"I don't want to," I moaned.

"Come on. It's a surprise." He smiled me into submission. I complied wearily.

The next thing I knew, I was sitting in the passenger seat of the DeVere's freezing Volkswagen minibus, teeth chattering, staring out into the deep blue eastern horizon at the edge of Lake Michigan as the sun crept out through the scattered clouds and over the murky, churning body of that Great Lake. Christian had driven to Rainbow Beach, the fairly dreadful strand of the rag-tag neighborhoods of the Southeast Side that always seemed to be in the toxic grey pall of the nearby and rapidly-diminishing steel mills. That New Year's Day morning, however, Rainbow Beach looked as good as the south of France to me. The sun actually sparkled off of the lake and the large, flat chunks of ice that floated on the surface. The further the sun rose, the fewer clouds there were in the bright blue sky. The windows on the bus were beginning to ice up. We could see our breath in front of us. I could feel Christian's on the side of my neck. He held me from behind the seat he was kneeling against, resting his chin on my shoulder.

"I always wanted to come see the sun rise on New Year's Day." I leaned my head against his as I caught a squad car turn into the beach parking lot in the corner of my eye.

I yawned long and loudly. "Don't worry. It's not the company, it's the hour." Christian pressed me tighter in his arms. He was about to kiss the side of my face when we heard a gravel-voiced cop on the squad's rooftop bullhorn order the lot of us out of the parking lot. A few other cars fired up and left. Christian slid back into the driver's seat with disappointment. We were the last to go.

Well, almost as good as the south of France.

*

Despite how bleary-eyed we were, we got home somehow, got undressed without incident, and fell into the cocoon of my bed. Without inhibition or embarrassment, Christian moaned softly as he crawled into my arms and closed his eyes. If I wasn't tired to the point of collapse, I might have reflected about what I was thinking and feeling about myself and us, there in bed together. But I didn't. I exhaled with greedy satisfaction and went to sleep with Christian's face in my eyes, not feeling alone at all, not caring what would happen after that, exulting, dead bodies and frightened so-called best friends notwithstanding, that Jesus loved me, this I knew.

XVIII

Love sought is good, but given unsought is better.
Twelfth Night

I woke up after the phone rang for the twentieth time.

Nicolasha was crying. Was he drunk? He kept saying he loved me, and begged me to let him come over to our house, locking me in some twisted stage fright. I kept trying to talk to him, to somehow calm him down, but he wasn't listening. He wouldn't let me interrupt either his tears or his nearly incoherent wailings, which drowned out my urgent whispers. Christian didn't hear me or the racket on the other end of the phone, even though he was curled up alongside of me under the covers, with his face resting next to mine on the pillow. And then the doorbell started ringing, over and over again. I accidentally hung up the phone as I tried to move out of Christian's arms and the warm bed without waking him. Our clothes were nowhere to be found. Someone began pounding on the front door as the doorbell's irritating chime melodies blended into themselves without pause. Christ!

I threw Dad's greatcoat on over my naked body and opened the front door. Felix burst into the entryway and slammed the door behind him. Before I could say a word, he tore the overcoat from my shoulders and wrestled me to the cold ceramic tiles, which were wet from the snow on his shoes. Felix knelt onto my chest and pinned me to the floor, his eyes burning with jungle frenzy. The phone began ringing again. Felix shoved me back to the floor and ran up the stairs, toward my bedroom. Without putting the greatcoat back on, I stumbled up in chase. I thought he would attack Christian, but, instead, he was kneeling once again, this time at the foot of the bed, sobbing like a child, mumbling my name, and demanding to know why he wasn't in the bed instead of Christian.

My eyes burst open as I gasped for air. I was sweating, even though I was cold, lying outside the pile of covers that Christian remained tucked into. He woke up with a start. I looked away from him and sat up at the edge of the bed with my head hanging low. I ignored the cold air on my body as I sat in silence, catching my breath and feeling the depth of my own exhaustion. I regretted not getting us drunk last night, and suddenly felt alone again, momentarily, until Christian reached up and pulled me back into the warmth of his arms and the bed. My eyes floated absently toward the ceiling, bright with morning sunlight. Christian draped half of his body over mine and snuggled his face close to me on the pillow. Neither of us spoke for a long time.

"Happy New Year." I smiled involuntarily as I looked into Christian's eyes with sad relief. He began running the tips of his fingers over my bare chest, ice skating along my rib cage and over my erect nipples. "It'll be a while before all the hurt goes away." I nodded. A couple of years? "It will, eventually. You just need time. And love." 'Love'. "My Dad has an expression for it."

I tried to hide my amusement. "Your father has an expression for just about everything."

"Didn't yours?"

"No," I sighed. "Not for the last couple of years."

"I'm sorry."

"Forget it."

"When you're hurt or confused," Christian continued, "you know, like an animal that's lost its way? You want answers and you want to stop hurting, but you have to keep going."

"Why?"

"If you stop, the hurt will get worse. You'll die, somehow."

"Everyone dies, Christian."

"I don't mean die as in dead, but die, here, inside." He put a warm fist over my heart. "So you put up walls around you, around your spirit, in your soul." He leaned down and kissed my chest, near my heart. "Rifles go up. Cannons. Missiles. You shoot anything that comes near you as you keep running away."

"Running away sounds good to me, Christian."

"But it won't change anything."

"Yes, it will. I won't be here." My voice was level and cold. "I won't sleep down the hall from where my Mom and Dad used to. I won't have to take the train through what's left of my old neighborhood. And I won't have to pretend to be happy, or loved, or some person hardly anyone knows doesn't really exist."

"I know. Your teacher knows."

My teacher. I shook my head. My God, I thought. "I want to go away." Suddenly, I felt tears welling up inside of me, and the rest of my body straining against them. Christian pressed himself closer until I relaxed again.

"You'll still hurt. Whatever you hurt about here, you'll hurt about there." He shook his head and ran a hand through his hair, brushing it back off of his face. "Time and love will make the falling of walls and the lowering of rifles happen. That's what Dad says." All you need is love...DA da da da da DA... It sounded hackneyed, at first, but the earnest intimacy in Christian's voice carried the words past my reaction into my heart. I began fighting tears again. The damned things followed me into the New Year, I thought! I was comforted back into a semblance of restfulness by Christian's continued proximity, and the relief I felt when neither the phone nor the doorbell rang as we laid there together.

"The falling of walls and the lowering of rifles, huh?" I hated the sound of my voice, pock-marked with the tears I refused to let go.

Christian kept staring at me with his compassionate green eyes. "You should just cry."

"No." I then realized Christian had been writing something on my body with his finger. "What are you writing?"

He grinned shyly. "Do you want me to read it out loud?"

I grinned, too. "Yeah. Make it forever."

"Make it become forever, you mean." Warmth and silence. No bells and no chimes. "I wished you a Happy New Year."

"That isn't what you wrote."

"Yes, it is."

"Is it?"

"No." Christian closed his eyes and took a short breath. "I wrote I loved you."

I was so shaken by hearing those words and believing them, somewhere deep inside, I tried to make it into a joke. "So, you've decided, then. Love, that's what you were feeling last night."

"No, I was feeling the two of us all over each other," he chuckled. "But I feel it now." Christian began writing again. "I love you."

"You don't know me so much." My wall wasn't ready to fall, yet.

"I think I know more than most people do. I know I'd like to know more, over time. You know, time?"

"I don't know you very well, either."

"You will." Christian smiled. "How do you like me, so far?"

I smiled back as a few stones fell off the top of that wall. "I think I love you, too." I should have felt afraid to say that, but I didn't. "I know I want to."

Christian didn't comment on the appropriation of his very tender, very special expression of our previous night together. We stayed in each other's arms for another sweet, long time. I considered staying there for the rest of the day, the Rose Bowl be damned. "If you're gonna take your pain and go somewhere, don't you dare go without me," Christian whispered.

I didn't think I would, either.

*

It was six o'clock am. The deli had just opened. The old brothers from Brasov were amused to see me almost an hour earlier than usual. I ordered a bowl of their over-spiced oatmeal and some raisin toast, and sat alone, reading the paper without paying much attention to the stories my eyes glanced over. I kept wondering if Felix would be there to meet me by seven, like we always used to, last year.

"How are you?"

I looked up from the dull editorials with faint surprise. Nicolasha smiled poignantly at me, and took a seat at my table.

"I'm okay." He raised his eyebrows a bit. "Really."

"Good. You know you can call me, for anything."

"I know." I surprised my teacher by taking his hand for a moment. "Thanks, *Freiherr*."

Nicolasha pulled his hand back awkwardly as the older brother placed a carafe of fresh-squeezed grapefruit juice and two glasses on the table. We both glanced at the steady stream of commuters and students passing the deli in their morning rush until we were alone again. "Who are you taking to the symphony, this Friday night?"

"I thought we were going together," I said, taken aback.

He laughed quietly. "That would not be *kulturny*, giving you a gift, and using half of it myself."

"Oh." The juice was insufferably tart. It needed some vodka, and a pound of ice.

"Another close friend has invited me already. He doesn't have box seats, unfortunately." Close friend, huh? I wondered if it was the person who took the pictures in the photo album. My teacher gave me another one of his melancholic smiles that hung so naturally on his soft face. "Thank you for considering me, however." It was almost seven-thirty, and there was still no sign of Felix. "Wouldn't your uncle enjoy going?"

"He's still in Minnesota." My tone revealed my personal misgivings that Uncle Alex intended to come back at all. Nicolasha looked uncomfortable. I decided to brighten things up a little. "A friend of mine from home wants to go. He's never been to see an orchestra."

"Considering your love of Shostakovich, I'm sure you'll be the perfect companion for him."

We walked to school together without speaking further.

*

Felix walked up to me at my locker as I stuffed my satchel full of morning textbooks. There was an immediate and enormous tension in the air between us, one you could almost reach out and touch with your hand. I tried to keep my face blank, but could feel my eyes narrow with a touch of anger that made the impassivity of my voice that much more cold. "I thought you were coming back the other night."

Felix looked like a young deer caught in an auto's oncoming headlights. "I was going to." A senior made Felix move to get into his locker. "...I wanted to." His voice trailed off.

"You could have called."

"I'm sorry." I closed my locker and began walking to class, with Felix following a step behind. He suddenly took a breezy tone. "My parents were hoping you could spend the weekend with us." I stopped and turned around to face him. He offered me his hand, but I didn't take it.

"I'm going to the symphony Friday night."

"Oh."

I walked off first, and felt bad about doing so almost immediately, but not bad enough to go back and shake Felix's hand, or smile at him, or even turn around, for that matter.

*

The small but elegant white marble and gleaming brass lobby of Orchestra Hall was packed with its well-dressed and well-heeled subscribers, fat-cat patrons, and a few interlopers, like Christian and I, who just came to hear the music.

That was the problem with orchestras and operas, Uncle Alex would often remark. They were patronized and supported by landed gentry-types who gave their money and presence easily, but little of their real appreciation. They went to these performances to go, to be seen, rather than because they really liked Bruckner's symphonies or a Verdi operas. I supposed Unc would know, because the same orchestra crowd of "culture vultures", as he derisively called them behind their crusty backs, were the ones who dominated the art gallery scene that kept the Uncle unit in funds. I saw what he was talking about. We worked our way through the crowd and damn nearly choked on the grotesque mélange of cologne, perfume, hair spray, cigarette smoke, and garish and highly visible jewelry worn by women that all the makeup in the world couldn't salvage. Not once did I overhear anyone remarking on that night's upcoming performance, or discussing either Soviet classical music in general or Shostakovich in particular. I would even have been happy to hear somebody complaining about the modernity of the night's program, something else that irritated Unc about the average orchestral customer's sensibilities, the conceit that any classical music written in the 20th Century was necessarily modern. I mean, is a Marilyn Monroe film or a Benny Goodman record modern?

I felt bad for Christian the minute I saw the crowd was largely made up of the sort of tight-lipped, grey-suited rich (and almost rich) folk that so often made him and his parents out to be little more than low-end white trash. He wore my black tweed suit, one of Dad's expensive silk ties, and his own pair of black cowboy boots, which he polished just for the occasion. I thought he looked great, if a little unnatural in the suit and tie. He was the only guy in the lobby with long hair. I made do with my favorite of Dad's suits, a maroon double-breast with silver pin stripes, which made me look like a young Capone protégé. "Do you see your teacher anywhere?"

"No. He said he'd be here, though."

I glared at anyone I caught staring at Christian and his long hair with a disapproving look on their face. There was some goof who kept staring at both of us, however, with a little smile on his face. He had bright blond spiked hair and a black moustache and pointed goatee, and wore little granny glasses on his thin and shifty face. As he approached us through the happily oblivious and chattering crowd, I noticed his silky jacket, which looked like an old Beatles outfit.

"My name is Basilio." He handed both of us a stylish business card. "Forgive the way I was staring, but I do a lot of work for magazines in Europe, and I'd like to do some business with you. Both of you have a great look."

"What kind of work," Christian asked? He seemed bemused by the whole thing. I sensed something about the Eurogeek that I couldn't quite place, something I didn't like.

"Photography." No - it couldn't be. "I have a studio up near Wrigley Field." Christ, I knew there was something about him I didn't like! "Give me a call and we set something up. I might plug you into some good money, maybe." I could see Christian was interested, and looked that much more so when the magic word 'money' was used. This Basilio person was certainly interested in him.

"Little friend!" Nicolasha stepped beside me to warmly squeeze my shoulders. He touched Basilio's thin leather tie with his free hand, and smiled at Christian, who nodded his head respectfully to the music teacher he had heard a lot about as the minibus wound its way into the city earlier that evening. "Have you all met?"

"Well, Nicky, I was just introducing myself to the young men." 'Nicky'? "You must be the star writing student." His eyes appraised me uncomfortably, despite Nicolasha's reassuring hand, which remained on my shoulder. "I hear you have shot at an Ivy League school."

I shrugged. Christian, however, looked like someone who had just been slapped in the face, but was determined not to show any reaction to the rest of the world. I knew that look!

"He has to go someplace with plenty of rain and snow," Nicolasha said, "a place where *bella musica* is at home. Besides, no real writer can bear the sun until they have become famous and alcoholic!"

Christian and Nicolasha and Mister Photographer laughed, but I didn't.

"And what about you...?"

"Christian. Christian DeVere."

"Ah. Christian. I like that name." Christian was embarrassed, but enjoyed the attention, all the same. "What are your plans for college?"

My friend's fluster became acute and apparent. Over pizza the other night, I discovered Christian was self-conscious about the subject of college, afraid that he wouldn't be able to attend a good college unless it was on an athletic scholarship of some sort, something he felt cheapened by. While he tried to coming up with a decent answer, Nicolasha cleared his throat diplomatically and gestured to the crowd, which had begun moving to their seats. "We can talk after the performance." Christian and I both nodded toward Nicolasha.

"Maybe dinner," the strange photographer added.

I shot a final glare at Basilio before leading Christian up the winding staircase toward the box seats.

*

Dmitri Shostakovich wrote fifteen symphonies, an unusual but powerful and important body of work that made him the premiere symphonic artist of the twentieth century. While a few of these works were written as Soviet political vehicles, rather than purely aesthetic compositions, the overall quality of this canon is hard to overstate. Any listener with a shred of interest in the symphonic form can discern in these an enormity of style, line, and sensibility that far surpasses the idle carping of critics, who can't see Shostakovich as anything more than a noteworthy composer of the Soviet Union. But what do critics know, anyhow?

We sat alone in our small corner box, overlooking the bright and clean stage where the Chicago Symphony players got comfortable and adjusted their instruments. The applause for the first violin was polite. The applause for the conductor, Sir Georg Solti, was vigorous. He was well on the way to making our CSO competitive with the very best orchestras in the world.

The old Magyar alone was worth the price of admission. Christian pretended to whisper something in my ear when he in fact kissed me as the auditorium silenced itself and Sir Georg raised the baton to beckon the triangle to sound, the flute to blow, and the bass to play, beginning this oddly enigmatic symphony.

I did a Charlie Chaplin and mimicked a silly person moving bits of their body in a strange rhythm to the trumpet solo of the second subject, almost making Christian burst out in laughter.The quotations of *William Tell* brought both of us to act like we were riding horses. We could <u>feel</u> the icy vibrations from our neighbors, all but willing us to sit still and stop enjoying ourselves. I personally think Shostakovich would have enjoyed the bizarre facial expressions and devilish physical gestures Christian and I exchanged, trying to make the other one laugh out loud first, even though, if either one of us actually had guffawed like we wanted to, Sir Georg himself would have stormed up there to beat us into submission.

The pause between movements at a live concert has always been a point of hilarity for me, what with a couple of hundred people suddenly being switched "on" to cough, hack, wheeze, groan, sniffle, and sneeze, only to be switched "off" by the fearsome conductor, a few scant seconds later. We ran through quite a repertoire of coughing wheezes and hacking sneezes before we stopped and were plunged into the driving elegiacs and inner sadness of the second movement Adagio. Christian listened intently, but kept turning to his side, watching my face harden and then withdraw from the crowd as the violin solo filled the white shell of the concert hall. I was assaulted with faces, Mom and Dad's faces, the different faces I had seen on both of them throughout our last Christmas Eve. The funeral march made me look away from the orchestra and close my eyes. I wouldn't let Christian slip his hand inside of mine until I began to cry silently, despite my every effort not to, and took his hand in both of mine, crying the faces out of my sight.

I wondered what Nicolasha was thinking of, hearing the same notes.

The third movement Scherzo came and went through my shaken mind. It was as seemingly random and dissonant as *The Age of Gold* introductory and dance allegra, but had such superior depth I decided I needed to listen to it many more times before I even began to understand what Shostakovich was getting at.

I became convinced that Basilio character was the person who took the naked photographs of Nicolasha. It made me dislike him even more than I already did.

It was funny to watch and feel Christian take his turn at drifting off into the murky depths of his own thoughts as the richly individual fourth movement Adagio-Allegretto played on. Unlike me, he spared himself the indignity of public tears, but seemed to welcome and appreciate it when I wrapped the palm of my hand over the back of his warm neck and squeezed gently a couple of times.

The final applause was thunderous. I was gratified to see Christian yell out a few "Bravos!" for the band. Before we left the box for good, Christian took a good, hard look at the interior of the hall, memorizing it for future reference. "No telling when I'll be back here, especially in seats like these."

"I'm glad you liked it." I fiddled with Christian's tie.

He nodded with satisfaction. "I feel pretty wild, hearing music like that. Thank you."

Christian Albert 'Thank You' DeVere. Thank you for coming over. Thank you for breakfast. Thank you for having me over. Thank you for calling. Thank you for a wonderful time. Thank you for inviting me. Thank you for being my friend. Thank you for letting me be your friend. Thank you for staying up all night to have jungle sex with me.

(He never said that.)

We left Orchestra Hall without seeing Nicky the Music Teacher or Basilio, his faithful Euro companion. If Christian was disappointed, I couldn't tell. I wasn't. We sang loudly along with The Moody Blues on the chilly ride back to the gulag of suburbia.

*

I switched my bedroom stereo to Dad's jazz station, turning the volume low enough for us to hear, but quiet enough for us to sleep, when we eventually got around to doing so. I was getting used to the sensation of sliding between the cool sheets and under the heavy quilt on my bed, and then to be met by another warm and naked body, which would surround it with mine. You've no idea how much pain seemed to slip away with each second spent like that.

"How come you changed the channel?"

"Don't you like jazz?" A rich Duke Ellington indigo played softly in the background.

"I haven't heard a whole lot of it, but sure I like this. Very cool, like a black-and-white picture of a rainy city at night, you know?"

"Dad loved this station." Christian reflexively kissed me on the forehead, like I might forget he was there in bed with me. "I guess I'm classical music'ed out."

"It doesn't matter. Anything they'd play would sound shitty compared to what we heard tonight. By the way - "

"No. Don't say it."

"Say what?"

"Thank you. You don't have to thank me for everything. I don't want you to."

Christian laughed quietly. "Why not? It's polite."

"It's insecure. I don't want you to be thanking me every five minutes. If I'm giving you something or doing something with you, it's because I want to. If you want or need something, well..." I felt an enormously soothing, warm flash across my body that made me tingle. "I want or need to give it to you, not because I want to hear you say thank you, but..." Christian felt the flash, too, and pulled us closer together. "You don't have to keep saying thank you."

We were silent for a few minutes, both struggling to ignore the urge to reach below our waists for the other. That's why we were upstairs in my frigid bedroom, instead of on the floor, in front of the fireplace. "Can I ask you a question?"

"No."

Christian ignored me. "You want or need to give something to me, not so I'll say thank you for the umpteenth time today, but...?"

"But?" I could picture Christian's face getting all lemony with being needled. It turned me on, too. All of a sudden, I wanted to go downstairs and start up the fireplace. Damn it!

"Well? You said it. But...?"

I exhaled noisily. I was genuinely tired. I hadn't slept in twenty hours, but I then recalled how it used to feel when I slept alone. Sleep could wait. I sat up and slipped my arm around Christian's shoulders and draped the other across his chest and held his face with my hand, like we were posing for the movie poster of "Gone with the Wind". I slid a leg in between his and lowered my face closer to Christian's. I could see him smiling in the dark. "The point of being friends is filling in some want or need in each other, whatever those happen to be. And I want to, for you. With you. And from you. Not because I want you to say thank you, or because I want to have sex with you -"

"Or because you want to make love to me?" His voice was almost as quiet as the Thelonious Monk solo tinkling in the dark beside us.

"No. Not that, either."

"Did we have sex, or make love?"

"Does it matter?" His fingers tightened on my arms. "OK, it feels like making love, to me. As if I'd know."

"Me, too."

"Shut up, Christian." He pulled his head up and kissed me on the lips. "I do it because I love you, and I want and need you to love me back."

"I do." He kissed me again. "I love you."

A chill crossed through my consciousness, recalling Felix saying he loved me, before he ran off; thinking about Nicolasha, how afraid he was to say the same thing; remembering Mom and Dad, how they used to say it all the time, and how little it was said between any of us for...too long. How it would never be said again. Nonetheless, the chill was momentary. The moist warmth of Christian's thin lips rolling along mine broke my thoughts, and I eagerly let them, until his lips drew close to my ear. I could feel him giggling in his closed mouth.

"Why do you love me?" Christian's playful words came to me in ticklish puffs of air, but dropped like mortar fire. It took a long time for him to realize I wasn't responding to his kisses.

My lost words fertilized the garden-variety fear inside me. "I'm alone, without you."

Christian's hands took my face and felt the wetness along the edge of my eyes and my shaking lips. "You're not alone."

"I am..."

"No."

"My God..." My voice went to pieces. "Alone!" Some kind of scream began to retch outward before it was stopped dead by Christian's mouth, sealing itself over mine. His fingers closed my wet eyes, keeping me from another selfish cry and keeping us locked together. Somebody, presumably in a heaven someplace, sent us to a merciful sleep on the same tear-dampened pillow.

*

Bits of the sun managed their way through the corners of the storm clouds, which could not decide if they would come together and have at it, or just drift off toward another city in need of wintering. I finished my REM-interrupting pee and stared out of the bathroom's icy rectangle window as the toilet flushed. I didn't hear Christian open the bathroom door behind me, but, without a start, I smiled when his hands reached around my waist. We stood wordlessly in the dark and held and touched and rubbed and licked and sucked and pushed and pulled and pumped and drained each other senseless.

*

"I have another question."

"Christian, shut up until the sun comes up."

He ignored me again. "Does love last forever?"

"How would I know?"

"You're the smart one."

"Christ, Christian, I'm no smarter than you or anyone else. I just remember everything I read." And feel. And think. My voice tensed up and rose. "Do you have any idea how that separates me from others, like you and the guys, or the other inmates in my classes?"

"I'm sorry," he whispered. "You are smarter, though, or more talented, maybe both, to judge by your poetry. I've read some, you know."

I rolled over from my back to my side, facing my friend in the fading darkness of the bedroom. I could distinguish a Stan Getz ballad somewhere in the background. "That's funny, but I don't remember ever showing you any."

200

"Before the symphony, when you took your shower without me." I figured we'd miss the symphony, if I hadn't gone in by myself. "I hope you're not mad."

"No," I mumbled. "Did you like any of 'em?"

"I sure did a whole lot." Another flash overcame me, the bastard. "Especially the one about going to the ballpark with your mom," he added. The frosty currents of silence took me away from the exploding scoreboards and flaming Cubs pennants and into Christian's soft arms. "I think you're super-special, and you'd be a happier person if you accepted that."

"Stop it, Christian."

"I love you."

"Stop it." My voice was crushed by the tears that began falling from my eyes. More damn tears. I felt like a weakling, such a helpless, useless fairy. I wanted a dollar for every time had I cried in the last calendar year. I'd buy the White Sox, by God!

Christian ignored my tears, too. "So, do you think love lasts forever, or what?"

"I don't know," I choked through the end of the light rain. I managed a laugh. "I love the White Sox, even when they're no good."

"Which is most of the time," Christian added. We laughed together and kissed. "Hey, the sun's up. What would you like to eat for breakfast?"

"How about you?"

"You."

"Huh?"

Christian pointed at me and said quietly, "You. I want you for breakfast."

Aren't you stuffed from dinner? I knew I was. Ouch. I brushed a curtain of his long blond hair away from his face. "You can have me for the rest of the year, Christian," I replied in a hush.

"What happens after that?"

"Ask me again next year."

We laughed again and kept kissing, until a further three more songs finished after Getz'. I had a mind to call the station and ask if they'd play "Cheek to Cheek" for me, no, for us, but my breakfast kiss kept me busy. Kept us busy, actually.

*

Much later, the phone kept ringing, and it wasn't a bad dream. It was Felix. "Good morning, sir. This is your wake up call."

"Felix..." What time was it?

"How was the symphony? What was on the program?"

I rolled over and moved closer to the edge of the bed. Christian kept his eyes closed, but followed my body with his.

"Shostakovich's Fifteenth Symphony," subtitled: The Evil Photographer.

"How was it?"

"Superb." I only cried once, and didn't laugh out loud at all.

"I'll bet it was. Have you ever been snowmobiling?"

"It's been a few years, but, yeah, I have. I love it."

Christian mumbled he loved me from the nape of my neck. "What did you say," Felix asked?

"Nothing." I covered the mouthpiece and whispered for Christian to be quiet. He stuck his tongue out at me. "Why?" Had Jason bought a stable of snowmobiles?

"Dad saw something about snowmobiling on TV last night, and wants to drive to Michigan, like, right now." Jason Cromwell was mad, and would live a very long and happy life, I reflected. "We'd all love for you to come with us."

I smiled. "Right now?" It sounded fun. Christian pressed his erection between his stomach and my lower back, moaning very loudly in the process. I clamped my hand over the receiver and told him to shut up. He pulled a strand of pubic hair from my balls in reply. I screamed out, pushing Christian and his playful tool away from me. Felix hung up. I tried calling back, but the line was busy, and stayed that way. I dropped the phone into its cradle and fell back into bed. I felt bad. Christian said he was sorry. I shrugged it off and went back to sleep in his arms, thinking about how I might try and make it up to Felix next week.

*

We drove back to Christian's and strolled through his backyard into the connecting forest. The morning sun gleamed through the tall grey trees around us. We had trouble keeping our footing on the uneven ground and the loose layer of snow over it. Christian took my hand as soon as we couldn't see his house. "You have to have the biggest backyard I've ever seen. It's so cool."

"The guys always come over after school to light up out here."

It was good to hear the team hadn't changed much. "How are they?"

"I don't remember so many of them being such jerks when we were younger. Still, they'll always be the team."

"I guess."

Christian stopped walking and held us still. He bit his lip while he looked around us, as if we were in a Belgian forest, surrounded by enemy soldiers. Confirming no mustard gas attack was imminent, he took an uneasy step closer to me. "Now what's up?"

"You never answered my question."

"Jesus, Christian! Maybe you can use these sleep deprivation interrogation techniques with the CIA!"

"I'm serious."

I sighed. "Which question?"

"The one about love. You didn't say if you thought love lasted."

"I don't know. People don't last. Why should love?"

"Love is better than we are."

I tried not to smile. "If love comes from people like us, how can it be much better?"

"The same way a symphony can be better than the guy who wrote it."

"You sound like Nicolasha." I squeezed Christian's hand in mine, but got no visible reaction.

Christian began looking around the empty and frozen preserve once again. "Well?"

"I don't know, Christian. Real love should last forever, I suppose. I'm not sure." I usually have trouble with real like." No return smile. "Does that answer your question?" He nodded. "Good. Can we go inside now? I'm still tired, damn it, and now I'm hungry, too." Well, for food.

"One more thing. Please." I looked down at the snow and shook my head, keeping my grin to myself. "Can I kiss you again? Out here?"

I finally laughed out loud, making my friend blush. "Like I'm gonna say no. But you'd better make it quick, Christian. Some raccoon might see us."

We had come a long way in a short amount of time. It seemed our mutual walls were falling, the rifles lowering, every time we were together. Did we really respect and trust and care about each other enough to call it love, or were we just greedy and horny and saying whatever shit sounded good enough to get what we wanted from each other? We weren't even seventeen; I was at least smart enough to have doubts about, well, everything on that basis. Or maybe we just weren't brave enough to admit we actually had found love in the other, certainly not smart enough to admit it to ourselves and make our lives a whole lot easier - or unimaginably worse, as the case might be. Not even me, the reputedly smart one.

*

I ran through the transcripts of our most recent bedtime conversation as we drove back to my house, away from the enemy lines, not to mention any ex-hippies who might see or hear their son and his close friend re-interpreting a few Commandments. "I think you're super-special, too."

"What?"

"Last night. You said I was super-special. Well, so are you."

Christian eyes glazed over. "You're not alone. Not anymore." The grip between our hands became so tight our arms shook.

XIX

For many men who stumble at the threshold
Are well foretold that danger lurks within.
Henry VI

I was surprised to make it to school alive.

It began snowing the instant I walked out of our house. The old reliable commuter line struggled to stay on schedule, even though its new aluminum double-deckers had this irritating habit of flying off the tracks in snowy weather. And it kept snowing, very hard. If it weren't for the maniacal zealotry of the old man, our beloved Principal, classes would have been canceled, and we all could have spent the rest of the day horsing around in the snow by the lake, or prowling around the University, or playing chase in the nearby museum, or even risking life and limb in the dilapidated remains of the Loop's movie theaters. But, no, unless you could measure the snow in terms of feet, we were going to get educated, by God, and the weather would just have to wait.

Well, I thought, let it snow. If the trains break down, I could stay over at Nicolasha's.

On my way to Literature class, I saw the old man talking, or, rather, issuing directives, to Mister Granger, who then gestured for Zane to come with the Principal. Over a flavorless cafeteria lunch, Zane once told me his father had named him after the famous cowboy novelist, which I thought was funny, since there was very, very little of anything cowboy about Zane and his asymmetrical blond crew cut, glasses, nasal voice, and dimpled smile. He was a shy, wooden preppie who couldn't walk down the hall without careening into something, he was such a klutz. Zane was one of those poor chumps brought up not so much as a son, but as a colony, of a domineering architect father who always picked him up from Pilot School every afternoon, "to make sure he got home safely."

We exchanged puzzled glances as we passed each other, and I went in to be regaled by a few unimportant sonnets by Marlowe. Felix made a very active effort to ignore me, even though we sat next to each other in every class, right near the door for quick getaways. Zane didn't return to the group until we had moved on to Asian History. Felix was then summoned by the old man. The lecture on the pre-Nationalist warlords of China was stultifying. I tried making eye contact with Zane, but he sat on the other side of the room, and didn't look up from his notebook until the bell rang. Felix wasn't back yet.

I followed Zane heading up the dark staircase to Italian class, and stopped him near the base of the steps with a hand on his briefcase. Other students filed past us with irritation. "Hey, Zane, wait up."

"We have to get to class." He didn't look at me.

"There's still time. What did the old man want?"

"I'm not supposed to talk about it." Zane began to walk away, but I held on to his arm. He glanced at me for a very defensive moment before shaking his head and almost running away from me into our classroom.

Felix gave me a blank look as I approached him and the old man, who sent my friend into Signore Abbado's care. I was taken into the old man's Interrogation Room downstairs.

*

"I'm very sorry to hear about your parents." I nodded, looking for something beyond the affected pleasantries on the cool but witty ex-History professor's face. "Do you think you'd like to take some time off?"

"No, sir. I'm just glad Christmas is over."

"You're sure? All of your teachers would understand." He looked at his lap. "They're all very proud of you. You're an excellent student, one of our best." I was mortified, and it showed.

Principal Connelly, in his appalling orange-and-navy blue tartan blazer, waved his hand dismissively. "I personally think you could show more collegiality and leadership. Join one of the clubs, for Heaven's sake." Join? <u>Join</u>? "You'd take over in a month. The newspaper, for instance." Please. If there were a bigger bunch of geeks in the Western Hemisphere than the paper people, someone would have to show me. "You're too introspective for your own good. Be young while you still are." I nodded in polite agreement, not feeling like debating him or anyone else about who I was, or what I was supposed to be. "At any rate, you're a fine poet for somebody so young. The works you handed in for the mid-term were very, very good, even though I'm not much for poetry." No, I thought, anything less than a thousand-page ordeal on some drab historical figure wouldn't appeal to you, sir.

"I've asked you down here to discuss a very delicate matter." He looked away from me again. I wondered, what was on his legal pad that was so damned interesting? "I'm no good at this sort of thing. I don't like questioning people as if I were a policeman." A secret policeman, you mean. I imagined what Principal Connelly would look like in the grey-green uniform of the East German Stasi. "Subtlety isn't one of my strong suits."

"Can I ask what's up, sir?"

He smiled without showing any teeth, looking me over for a few moments, before turning in his chair and watching the snow continue to fall in the manicured hedgerows outside of his window. "We should all go home," he said under his breath, "forget the day ever happened."

"I beg your pardon, sir?" My voice was aggressively firm and pronounced. I'll bet his chagrin at thinking aloud was in hyper-drive right then, hee hee.

"Tell me about Mister Straußenburg."

Click. So much for my voice being firm and pronounced. "What would you like to know, sir?" The radiator was louder than I was.

"Your impressions." Did _you_ ever wish you were in a train wreck? "Anything at all."

I cleared my throat nervously and shifted in the old man's uncomfortable wooden "guest" chair. "He's a great teacher. One of the best I've ever had."

"Why?"

"Because he knows his subject. To death, I mean."

"He's paid to. All of them are." Connelly's voice was clipped and emotionless. I hated staring at the high back of his leather executive chair.

"He cares about us."

"He's paid to."

"I mean, really cares. Like we were friends."

Principal Connelly turned his chair around and met my furtive eyes directly. "Are the two of you friends?"

I blushed, but didn't mean to. I looked away first, but didn't want to. "Yeah."

"Yes," my Principal suggested.

"Yes, sir." I couldn't look up from the edge of his desk.

"What kind of friends?"

"Good ones." Hah! I knew I could look up at him again! "He's been like the older brother I've never had. Through... through...all kinds of bullshit."

The old man folded his hands on his desk, returning his eyes to the legal pad. I felt his disappointment in the air. Our parents paid a lot of money to purge such vulgarity from our souls, I could hear him thinking.

"Has Mister Straußenburg ever invited you to his apartment?"

"Yes, sir." My voice began to regain its composure. "He loaned me some of his records, one evening."

"Records," the old man mused. "Which ones?"

"Symphonies by Prokofiev and Shostakovich," I lied. "Number Five of Prokofiev. Numbers Eleven, and Twelve of Shosta - "

"Did you visit him during the Christmas break?"

"Yes sir, on Christmas morning, to give Nicolasha his gift." I felt good about finally using the term of endearment that probably grated on the old man.

"You didn't bring one for him on the last day of classes, like everyone else?" He peered curiously over the rims of his large black glasses at me.

"I did. But I only found this record after school was out, and I thought I'd surprise him."

"Nicolaus means a lot to you, then."

"Yes, sir, he does," I replied in my newly firmed up and pronounced voice. "He's a great teacher, and a great friend. I wish I had met him before I did."

"Why?"

"I could have used some of his hugs a long time ago," I admitted, then furiously regretted. But at least I wasn't stupid enough to make a joke about bubble baths.

"Does Mister Straußenburg hug all of his students?"

"Yes, sir, as far as I can tell, Nicolasha hugs all of his students, and everyone else's students, too. That's the way he is. That's why everyone loves him." I blushed again, knowing I had used the wrong word. "He's beloved."

I girded myself for being asked if I loved Nicolasha, and, intending to say yes while looking the old man right in the eyes, thought about what I would say when the big "Why?" was launched in my direction. But the question didn't come. We had gone as far as we would. Principal Connelly brought back his jets back from my airspace.

"Do you think teachers should hug their students?"

I was sure of it. The old man had an unknown twin who was a high-ranking officer in the Stasi. "Yes, I do. We used to get hugs from the nuns and the priests when I was in grammar school, more so when we were younger. We used to get slapped, too, if we got out of line, but most of us didn't. Where does it say older kids don't want or need hugs anymore?" The old man held open his hands in agreement. "Aren't you allowed to get hugs once you're in high school?" I hoped the radiator would explode, like I suddenly felt like doing, in that small, peeling room. "Especially when you don't get them at home, anymore."

"I hug my children every day," Principal Connelly said.

"I will every hour, if I ever have any."

The hallway bell rang sharply. It was lunch time. "You will." He smiled at me and stood up, offering his heavily veined and strong, dry hand. I took it, managing not to show the looming sadness I felt, doubting the old man was right about that last bit. He escorted me to the door and opened it. Students hurried up and down the corridor outside his office, careful not to run in front of the Principal. "Tell me. What special record did you buy for Nicolaus?"

"An opera by Satie."

In dismissal, he touched the side of my arm like a jeweler would touch a fragile diamond, and I headed for the my locker. Snowstorm or not, I wasn't going to stay in the building. I needed some air. I turned into a rest room before exiting the building. I was in the middle of washing the "conference" off of my hands and face, when I looked up at my reflection in the mirror with water dripping down my cheeks and dread in my bloodshot eyes.

I couldn't remember if Satie ever wrote an opera.

*

I walked to the middle of the huge, empty plain that lies to the immediate south of the Pilot School and the rest of Hyde Park. The locals called it the midway. The dense falling snow peppered my face and clothing and the rest of the city, creating an eerie silence in us both. The sky, the air, and the ground blended together into one tremendous, snow-white painting. If I smoked, I would have been smoking. I wished I had some vice like that. Chewing gum, cigarettes, booze, hell, even pills, something to occupy me, rather than always having my thoughts to bounce off the sides of my mind until I was half-nuts from it. I supposed I could call all my crying a sort of vice. I did it enough for it to be a bad habit. It wasn't very cold, perhaps a few degrees below freezing, which would make the night's travel across the slushy city that much more difficult. My pants were soaked halfway to the knees from the snow.

My lunch period was almost over, but it felt like I had just gotten outside. I didn't want to go back. How much trouble would I get into if I skipped the rest of the afternoon? What would I miss? What would it matter? Who would school report me to, anyhow? I filled my mind with this idle nonsense, desperate to ignore the trembling worry I was gripped with.

*

I could see Felix looking at the snow that was still caked on my hiking shoes and the bottom of my pants. The classroom was silent as Doctor Clive bantered on about the finer points of adjustment disorders. I suppose I should have been listening, since a lot of what our Psychology teacher was talking about sounded more than a little relevant to what I felt was going on inside of me, but I couldn't.

Nicolasha and me, the two of us. That's all I could see or hear. I re-animated every moment of our making...having sex...in the Christmas twilight, while thousands of pounds of metal and rubber were smashing into each other, somewhere in the far southern suburbs of Chicago, with my Mom and Dad being reduced to dead massacres of broken bone and torn flesh. Yep, I was being strangled by barbed wire made out of Christmas lights.

Most of the class had already left when Doctor Clive and Mister Granger, who shared the classroom, both called my name. They looked at me with a mixture of kindness and sympathy that only made me angry. Granger said, "You can go home now, partner."

"Home?"

"If we don't leave now," Clive added, "we might get stuck here."

"Oh." I gathered my belongings and tried to smile back at my Literature teacher as he left the room.

Doctor Clive approached me with his customarily gentle face warming up the room. At least the pity wasn't in his eyes, anymore. "I just learned about your parents this afternoon." I hope it didn't put you off your soup, doc. "We're all sorry, quite sorry."

"Yeah. So am I."

"Any death is difficult. This? Beyond tragic, I'd say. No consolation in anything one can say, but we all feel deeply for you."

"Thanks."

Clive sat down on the edge of a desk. I was content to lean against the side chalk board, facing him and Granger. Clive was by far the most stylish out of our teachers, a salt-and-pepper rake who wore expensive Scottish tweeds and wry good looks with the aplomb of an expatriate Brit. Granger looked like a CPD detective who got into a lot of trouble for conduct unbecoming. Like the rest of our teachers, both could easily be teaching at the university next door, but chose not to, for some private reason.

"Carried yourself pretty well last week, considering what's happened, you know. If the old man hadn't let on, wouldn't have suspected a thing, the lot of us."

"You mean Nico - Mister Straußenburg, he didn't tell you?"

Granger shook his head. "Haven't seen him all day. Don't think he made it in, tell you the truth."

My face fell as those Christmas lights drew tighter around my throat. "I should go," I murmured.

"Yes, well, so do I." Clive took out a small cigarette from his jacket and lit it. "You live in the bush, don't you? Out south?" I nodded impatiently. "Let me give you a lift. I've got one of those Jeep contraptions, so we won't get stalled in that muck outside."

"But you live near Lincoln Park, don't you?" On the North Side. Yuk.

"Certainly do, but I've got a dinner appointment with a lady that's worth a drive in a snowstorm for. Radio woman. Lives near you, I'm pretty certain."

The German in me sensed a trap. "You don't have to, sir. I'll be fine on the train."

"Until it takes flight? Come on, kid!" Granger almost slapped me into the wall as he patted my shoulder before plodding away.

"Bad company or not, I insist."

"I have to pick up a book from Margo, first." I was getting too good at this lying-on-the-fly bit. "She lives just around the block."

Doctor Clive eyed me carefully before sending me off with his cigarette. "I'll meet you in the parking lot. Fifteen minutes, then?"

I ran out the door and out of the building, straight to Nicolasha's apartment. There was no sign of his Volvo. Nobody answered his doorbell. There were no lights on in his apartment. His mail hadn't been removed from the box. I punched the side of the building as I left.

*

Clive was an excellent driver. We were in my driveway in less than an hour. We had listened to an obscure alternative rock station on the far left of the FM dial. I could tell he wanted to sing along with the screaming, peroxided punkers. The DJ, who sounded as young as I was, took a moment to intone that a traveler's advisory had been issued, and for drivers to use caution, due to the snow. He paused, and then screamed "Duh!" We both laughed, but that was it for any conversation, until I climbed out of the Jeep.

"I suppose you've heard a brigade's worth of people saying things like 'If there's anything I can do'."

"Yep."

"Won't add m'self to the list, then. Call if you need to. Student rates apply."

"Thanks, I will." I glanced toward my empty house. I didn't want to go inside. "Can I ask you a question, Doctor 'C'?"

The Brit switched off his Jeep and put on his game face. "Of course, you can."

"Is there something the matter if you..." I had to sift through a number of subjects before crying rose to the top of the list "...if you keep breaking down?" You know, all the time? In the shower? Making love? In your sleep? In the dark, at the movies? When nobody's looking? In the same bed with someone?

"You mean cry?" My look lowered Clive's arching eyebrows. "No. Not unless you're British." I nodded curtly. He winked at me and left.

*

I called Nicolasha every fifteen minutes until I went to bed, but there was no answer. I even dug out that Basilio's business card and called him at his studio. I couldn't tell if he was surprised to hear from me, with his strange, squeaky voice. He hadn't heard from "Nicky", either, but promised to tell my music teacher I needed to talk to him, "if they ran into each other." How the hell do you run into someone in a snowstorm?

The phone didn't ring all night, and I slept badly, on the couch and alone.

*

I took another early and deserted train to Hyde Park the following morning. The deep and fresh snow made everything, from our backyard all the way to Hyde Park, look beautiful. Untouched. Peaceful. I was reduced to being thankful I could still identify something to do with peace. No Volvo. No answer. No lights. The same mail in the same place. I skipped breakfast and sat on a bench in the middle of the University, starting and restarting a poem I didn't like in the leather notebook Christian had given me over the weekend. I ignored the curious glances from the passing university students as my wheels spun almost out of control, retracing the past few weeks in my mind with nearly possessed detail, sitting alone and out of place in a Gothic courtyard that would seem haunted, if I had taken the time to notice. I broke off a large, round piece of ice from the side of the bench, and held it in my bare hand, squeezing it until my hand and arm shook from the effort. It was too thick to break. The cold water dripped out of my frozen fingers and down my wrist and shirt sleeve, until the ice finally melted into a shape that collapsed under the pressure of my grip. My hand still hurt after I put it back into my gloves, but not as badly as my heart did, turned inside-out by the conclusion I found inescapable.

God damn you, Felix.

*

The entire class looked at me strangely as I walked into Mister Granger's room after the bell had rung, a few seconds before. I was never late. None of us were ever late. I didn't even show up in the two classes before that, which was unheard of. Felix didn't look at me, Granger barely so, a brisk nod that understood, forgave, and forgot, in one fell swoop. 'Forgiveness' - I wondered what that was.

Our Literature teacher had published a gripping and horrific fictional memoir of his service in Korea a few years ago, but kept teaching while he toiled over his follow-up novel. He had wound imagery and gestures into his storytelling without a shred of effort, and demanded the most out of our readings and writings. Every class was an emotional roller-coaster, but it was so real, so visceral, whenever his wide, rounded eyes scanned the room while Granger's rich baritone voice began discussing or reading something.

We had come to **Richard III**.

"It's time to read. Anyone?" He avoided my side of the room, even though I was the only guy to raise his hand. Of course Kim raised hers. Felix looked like he was about to raise his hand.

"I'd like to read." I met Felix's eyes very hard. The room was uncomfortably silent. Granger finally acknowledged me with another clipped nod. He sat in his seat like he always did, with his elbows dug into his knees, his face resting on his folded hands, his eyes half-closed, in order to take in the reading fully. "Read to the cheap seats," he would always say.

But I was reading for only one seat. Each syllable and phrase hissed through my clenched teeth and jaw. The words became forever, and mine.

"Now is the winter of our discontent...cheated of feature by dissembling nature, deform'd, unfinish'd, sent before my time into this breathing world, scarce half made up...since I cannot prove a lover...I am determined to play a villain and hate the idle pleasures of these days..."

The emotionless, icily enunciated reading I gave rumbled in the classroom long after Mister Granger raised his palm and brought me to a halt. A strange, exciting power had flooded through my senses as I read, making those centuries-old words fly off of the typeset pages in front of me and into the collective consciousness of my classmates and teacher. I took my time before I sat back down.

Granger coughed twice to clear his throat. "What did you hear in this **Richard**," he asked? The responses given by my fellow classmates gratified me.

"A lot of pain."

"Someone crushed by their separateness."

"Defiant hatred."

"Consuming emotions."

"Loneliness. He's so lonely from the rest of the world, he wants to destroy it."

"Sadness turning into something else."

"An unjust life being rebelled against."

"The pain everyone feels about their place in the world."

"The edge of madness."

Personally, I heard myself. And I dared Felix to look back at me.

*

When I went to Nicolasha's apartment after school, the mail had been removed, and, from the front porch, I could see his entire living room had been, too. He was long gone.

XX

Rude am I in my speech,
And little blessed with the soft phrase of peace.
Othello

It was Friday night. I had spent all week trying to reach Nicolasha. His landlady had no idea where he had gone, and seemed concerned about how he was acting before he disappeared into the evening sunset. Basilio kept denying he knew anything at all, and hung up on me after I called the fifth time. Nobody at school would even talk about it, except to say that Mister Straußenburg had resigned. I even tried to contact his parents in Washington D.C., but they were on tour with the National Symphony somewhere in Europe. I left a message, along with all the others I had spread out across the city of Chicago.

It was Mister Granger who told me what had happened, hidden in the privacy of the Pilot School's ancient library stacks during lunch period. A student claimed he had been molested by Nicolasha during a visit to his apartment, and another anonymous note professed that an attempt was made on him, as well. A faculty Board of Inquiry refused to take a position, citing inconsistencies in the stories told by the students interviewed. Evidentally, the entire Junior-level faculty backed Nicolasha. In a million years, I could not picture Messieurs Abbado, Clive, Granger, Tanaka, and Wheatley, our highly eccentric calculus professor, agreeing on anything, above and beyond what day it was (and, even then, Wheatley would probably cite some astronomical anomaly to suggest it was in fact Wednesday...). Nicolasha had burst into tears during his "questioning" by Gruppenfuhrer Connelly, and withdrew on the spot, unwilling to confront the charges in another forum.

I asked Mister Granger why he was telling me things I was clearly not meant to know. "Because I don't think Nicolaus did anything, either."

*

The phone rang twice. I leapt at it each time. Uncle Alex would finally arrive Sunday morning, flying down with his easels, oils, and steamer trunks. It sounded like he had a send-off party going on in the background, so the conversation was short. Christian was on his way over to pick me up for a night at the movies and, later, a fireside chat. He complained about getting busy signals all week, but I didn't explain.

As I was cleaning up the family room, the doorbell rang. I ran to answer it, looking forward to a good, long, close hug from Christian. I knew the hug wasn't going to make me feel any better about Nicolasha's disappearance, but I wanted one, just the same. My smile melted away in an instant. It was Felix.

There he was, still short, still cute, black hair going off in every direction, a face made to look happy but now wearing a mug that brought me back to the wake. He looked he had just gotten back from one. His father's Continental was parked and running on the street in front of our house. They wouldn't even pull into the driveway. "Hi." I nodded once, without moving aside to welcome him into the house. "I wanted to give you this." The young Cromwell held out a thick envelope.

"What's that?"

Felix shrugged. "I spent all afternoon writing it."

"I don't want it."

223

Felix reached forward with his free hand and touched my shirt sleeve. "What's happened with us? You were like my brother before we left for Florida. Mom and Dad are really upset." His voice broke in a sadly adorable way. I looked away for a moment. I missed Jason and Arlene, too. "Please take it."

"No."

I went to slam the door in Felix's face, but he sprang forward into the door jamb. I snarled like a werewolf, taking his parka in both hands and swinging him to the tile floor, knocking the breath out of him. I knelt over Felix and mashed my mouth over his, forcing his lips open, practically sucking his tongue down my throat. I didn't see or feel his legs flailing under mine, much less, his panicked arms trying to pry me off him. I only stopped when I tasted blood (which turned out to be his). The pause was long enough for me to hear him choking for air inside my mouth.

I rolled off Felix, who, rather than bolt back up and run or even scurry away on his knees, tried to fix his hair and re-arrange his layer of shirts with averted eyes. He stood up unsteadily and had trouble hitching his slacks back into place. He looked like he was going to try and say something, but left without a sound instead.

My heavy breathing stuttered with glee when I realized Felix couldn't get his britches righted because he had had a terrific hard-on from his first boy kiss.

*

Later, Christian didn't ask what was bothering me. He just saw the dead look on my face, sat us down next to the fireplace, and tried cuddling me. I stayed mute. We sat there for the rest of the night, silent together, until

224

we fell asleep, still in our clothes, still holding on to each other.

*

The following Monday morning, as I was going to my locker, Felix ran up and cut me off at the top of the staircase. He held me back with one hand and carried his letter in the other. "Please wait a minute. Please." He was out of breath. I glared at him, my teeth grinding. "Read my letter. It'll explain everything."

"Explain?"

He nodded like a drunken marionette. I lowered my head and took a step backwards. Felix relaxed a bit, which I took quick note of. I swung out the full length of my arm, throwing all my weight behind my fist as it smashed across and broke Felix's nose. Blood spurted out of his face as he screamed sharply and lost his footing. Felix tumbled down the iron stairs into a group of lower graders, knocking them over like they were bowling pins. I wheeled past Doctor Clive as he emerged from his homeroom, hearing Felix's loud, painful sobbing down the hall.

So, I got suspended. Not just the first in my class, but the first in the Pilot School for over 21 years. I was a scandal, a disgrace, and a champion, all in one. Uncle Alex cared less. I didn't say a word to Christian, because his 'why's' had a way of lasting hours, if not whole days. I caught up on my sleep instead.

*

In his first act as "head of the household", Uncle Alex turned our backyard into an ice skating rink. Instead of unpacking or buying a car or even cleaning out Dad's old bedroom, you know, something productive, he spent all week mounting and nailing the baseboards together, laying down and sealing the plastic tarpaulins he brought with him from Minnesota, and, to finish the job, filled the massive frame with hose water. It was below twenty-degrees the entire time he toiled away, and it still took two days for the water to freeze completely. My contribution to the project was to install an 8-track player (on loan from Christian's dad) into our barbecue shell, with speakers running along the back of the house. The stereo filled in the icy expanse of our back yard very nicely. Sound carries in a funny way during the winter. Unc proclaimed the rink suitable for use Thursday night. The first thing I did was to play the *Gloria all'Egitto* from Verdi's *Aida* rather loudly, shaking one of the speakers clear off of the house. Unc approved, and demanded I make tapes of every loud opera chorus and march I had in my collection.

I found being suspended from school vastly underrated.

*

Christian's dad, George, was the handy man's handy man, a first-rate landscaper as well as private cultivator of interesting equatorial plant species. Unc made a point of being too nice and over-paying him when he came over to install flood lights over the rink. Good handy men were worth their weight in gold, Unc believed. He didn't have go overboard, though. George was in on the secret about the nature of Christian's peculiar relationship with me, and seemed supportive of us in a quiet sort of way. We weren't sure about Doris, Christian's thirty-one-year-old mother, but, then again, nobody really was. I'd blanched when Christian revealed he had told his dad about us. It seemed important to Christian, so I didn't put up much of an argument, until he started pushing me to do the same with Uncle Alex. We agreed to disagree. Temporarily, Christian insisted.

*

During the weekend, Felix called twice. I hung up the moment I heard his voice the first time.

Christian and I were about to undress each other and do the fur-and-fireplace thing when Felix called for the second time. He sounded like he was crying, and said something I could barely understand, making me feel like I had been teleported into one of my bad dreams. I told him to go to hell, and slammed the phone down.

Christian sat down next to me on the couch and held one of my hands, waiting for me to start talking, but I didn't. I couldn't even begin to think about the betrayal I felt, the violence Felix used against Nicolasha to get to me, shattering the trust I between us. It was limitless. Much less, the pain and shame in my heart, knowing how Nicolasha must have felt about the trust and love he'd placed in me. It was inestimable.

I had years of familial inculcation to prevent me from spewing out what was raging inside of me. Christian didn't understand this, and took my not opening up to him as a deep and personal rejection. Our night together collapsed like a straw house in a gale. He didn't say a word to me and went home, leaving me alone to use Uncle Alex as a bad example and Wyborowa myself to sleep.

*

I became an odd sort of celebrity upon my return to school. In the bathroom, Zane whispered I was the first ever Pilot School student to be suspended for fighting. It wasn't a fight, I thought, it was an attack. Counterattack, really. I saw glimmers of respect in many eyes, especially the lower graders, as I stalked through the halls in my ticking time bomb style. I also picked up on the antagonism that Felix attracted wherever he went. The beloved Nicolasha was gone. Three students had been called down to the office over something to do with him. One was too quiet and unassuming to have said anything. Another got suspended for punching out the third, a new kid nobody had really gotten to know. And the new kid got blamed. Too bad for the little bastard.

*

I got off the train late that night. I decided I didn't want anything to do with the Pilot School coming into my house, at least for the time being, so I did all my homework at school. I was quietly stunned to see Christian waiting for me on the platform. It was already dark, and very cold. He had taken the night off from work and been waiting for me to get off a train for two hours. "What are you doing here? I thought you were mad at me."

The only friend I had left smiled weakly. "I still am." He took a step closer to me. "But I love you, and wanted to tell you that to your face, so you wouldn't forget."

"That would be pretty hard," I replied softly.

We hugged for so long out there in the cold, I wondered if any of the cars waiting for their commuting husbands and wives noticed, or made remarks about us.

*

Uncle Alex called for an outdoor party the following Saturday, and it was a gigantic success.

I invited Lawrence and his family (but they didn't come, as Unc predicted); Mister Granger, who couldn't go; Zane, who asked Farrah to be his date (and arranged for them to spend the night with us "since they lived so far away"!); and Doctor Clive, whose radio gal companion stunned us all by wearing a floor-length parka and a tight nylon skating dress, which showed off her sexy young body. Christian invited his parents and all our baseball friends, most of whom brought dates I didn't recognize. And Uncle Alex invited some tough-looking Israeli woman, who was his agent or something. She out-skated everyone, except Doctor C's radio gal. Unc found some caterers willing to do an outdoor spread prepared to withstand the winter elements, with cuisine featuring the very finest in ballpark eats: thick kosher hot dogs, beer-soaked bratwursts, giant pretzels, snow cones (with a number of tasty liqueurs on hand for flavoring with a kick), freshly-fried nachos, drumsticks, and, of course, a giant trail mix made up of Cracker Jack, unshelled peanuts, and over-salted cheese popcorn.

In little more than an hour, the food was cleaned out. Zane and Farrah stayed close to me, and were much more fun than I thought they'd be. The baseball gang hogged the well-lit end of the rink, playing a rough-and-tumble version of hockey without sticks or skates. Doctor C and the Radio Gal (how's that for a short story title?) carried on very romantically in our wrought-iron glider, watching the action on the ice, while the Israeli and George crossed swords over international politics. Doris and Uncle Alex were in some kind of drinking contest in the kitchen. I was afraid to see who was winning. Christian was happy to play bartender.

Everybody seemed to love the Viennese waltzes, polkas, and marches I taped for the party. I had thought about keeping a few good dance or sing-along songs handy, but there was such diversity in the age of our guests, I decided to keep it classical. The ambience of the Strauss family's compositions alone, combined with the ice rink, the Christmas lights in the trees, the baseball food (especially the snow cones), and the company created a wonderful atmosphere that left everybody giddy. And Uncle Alex had been here less than two weeks, I thought...!

Doctor C and his gorgeous date came up to me as I sat next to Christian at the rented bar. "Young man, we'd like to have a skate on that rink of yours. What do you suggest for a group round-a-bout?"

"I have just the song, ready to go."

We cleared the remainder of the baseball thugs off of the ice. Most of them had drifted off to their cars to light up or have sex with their dates. The others were too drunk to play on the ice with. I put in the new 8-track, and turned up the volume loud enough to convince the neighbors the Austrian Army was passing through. *The Radetsky March* trumpeted forward. Doctor C and the Radio Gal began waltzing around the ice holding each other close. Zane and Farrah skated up to Christian and I and took our hands. Neither of us was wearing skates, but it didn't matter. I couldn't skate, anyway. The four of us twirled around in a circle as we wound our way behind the romantics, pushing and pulling on each other's hands to keep us going, while Uncle Alex got everyone else to start clapping and stomping their feet in time with the Vienna Philharmonic, New Year's Eve Concert-style.

The march ended far too soon. Everyone demanded another. I waved them off and waited for the next song to start. My eyes fused with Christian's. Others saw this. Zane joked we should dance together. "Well," I said? Christian blushed as red as a Soviet ensign. Ozzie, our favorite catcher, echoed Zane. Christian gave him the finger as I saw a hint of tension in both George and Uncle Alex's eyes. Doctor C's date smiled at both of us and nodded for us to do so, the world be damned.

I grabbed Christian's hand and swung him out toward the middle of the ice as Lumbye's goofy *Champagne Galop* burst out of the speakers. We spun around dizzily, keeping the other one from falling, and began a playful half-chase, half-silly walk ballet around the rink to everyone's cheery encouragement, with either our hands or arms locked together the whole while. Chaplin would have been proud. Or embarrassed.

*

George took Doris home before she tried to start a fight. Doctor C and his companion retired to the broadcast booth of love. Uncle Alex and his agent went to her place to continue their negotiations. Christian waited for me in his half of my pajamas as I turned off the lights downstairs and locked up. Farrah and Zane emerged from Mom and Dad's master bathroom. They were still dripping wet from a shower, inside matching robes somebody had bought for Mom and Dad years ago, who had never wore them. Their faces were flushed and happy. Farrah's dainty features glowed in Zane's company. She thanked me for inviting them both, and kissed me softly in the center of my cheek. Zane waited for her to retire behind Mom's old bedroom door to give me a quick, self-conscious hug. "I'm glad we're friends, now, Hitman."

Was that the hundredth time he'd said that since New Year's? "Me, too, Zane."

*

I had scarcely closed my bedroom door when Christian, wearing my itchy pajama bottoms, put his arms around me and began one of our perfect hugs. We hugged our tartans off and were about to devour the other until I heard a related commotion come from Mom's room. "Listen," I whispered, pointing to my door. We knelt down and opened the door a crack. Zane had become possessed by his cowboy namesake's spirit as he and Farrah made noisy, almost hilarious whoopee.

"Man, is that rude! We should pound on their door and scare them. Maybe Zane would fire off, then!"

I groped Christian to the floor before lying down across his warm stomach. "I've got a better idea. Let's make more noise than they are."

Our bodies met and ran off together.

*

"I loved dancing with you earlier."

"I'd hardly call that dancing, Christian."

"What a great party. Thanks for inviting me." I exhaled melodramatically. Christian kissed my hand in reply. "Thanks for being my date." He sat up suddenly. "Hey! Let's go to the prom together!"

"No." I hoped that was a snow cone talking.

"I love you," he whispered.

"I still won't go, Christian."

"Okay." He lay back down and curled up in my arms. "We can argue about it later."

*

Winter hung on with bitter intransigence.

It was less than two weeks before Opening Day, and the temperature hadn't broken the forty-degree mark once that year. It rained or sleeted or snowed every other day, the wind never stopped, and I couldn't remember the last time I saw either the sun or the moon. Christian and I played catch in the middle of the muddy park field every afternoon. Ozzie, from the old team, sometimes joined us. He was the best catch out of us all. Christian had the best throw. Nobody wanted to pitch to me. They hated running to the end of the park to retrieve the balls I had hit.

The two of us were about to go back to my house for dinner with Uncle Alex when an early model T-Bird, the kind you could land a jet on the hood, cut us off. Felix parked badly against the curbside that lined our grassy knoll and hopped out of the pimp-mobile like he was somebody's boy wonder. What is it with short guys and their need to drive the biggest cars they can lay their hands on?

Christian stood beside me, instinctively showing his solidarity, and keeping close, in case I went to break something else on Felix's face. I kept my expression and tone plain, even though my stomach, already hungry for dinner, began to knot up as Felix approached us with his spiritual tail between his legs. "Hi, guys." We looked at him with indifference, feigned on my part. "You must be Christian. I'm Felix." He offered his hand. Christian waited a long time before taking it, and gave it back quickly. We never talked about the cold war that had set in between Felix and I, but I think it bothered Christian we didn't. He didn't believe there was a problem on earth that couldn't be solved by openly talking about it, and he certainly didn't believe the glacier of hurt and hate I had carved inside of myself over the whole thing was right, either, and he said so all the time. "Is it okay if we talk alone?" Felix's animated voice irritated me.

Christian shook his head. "I think I should stay here with my friend."

"I don't have anything to say to you." I began to walk away. Felix desperately grabbed my arm, but I shook it off with a violent tug. Christian stepped quickly in between us.

"Please!" Felix reached around Christian for one of my hands. I cried out and lunged forward yet again, this time trying to grab Felix's throat. Christian struggled to keep me in his arms and away from Felix, who, stupidly, kept coming closer. Christian yelled, "Get out of here, you idiot!" as I tried to break out of his grip.

Felix pointed at me and began to holler, too. "I'm leaving next week and you won't talk to me! You promised to spend my last weekend with me, like friends!"

"Damn you!" I screamed back, pulling the two of us a few inches closer to Felix and his shaking bottom lip.

"All I want to do is talk! You made me a promise!"

I swung Christian into a dirty snow pile near the curb and grabbed Felix by his sweater, throwing him against the side of his car. He hit the metal with a high-pitched cry before my fist struck him across the cheek and sent him to the pavement. Christian leapt back up to close his arms around my arms and chest, trying to pull me off Felix, who cried like a baby as I beat him against the side of his Godzilla-sized car. "Damn my promise and damn you!"

Suddenly, Felix stopped struggling. "Please don't," he begged. My mind flashed red, picturing us on the first night of our ruined friendship, twisted on the carpet outside of Felix's apartment. I flung him into his car's fender one more before Christian managed to pull me backwards onto the sidewalk. I stayed in Christian's arms, trying to catch my breath and wipe away the tears I didn't know I'd shed. Felix got to his feet, shaking like a leaf. "I kept my promise to you, Hitman," he sputtered.

Christian's arms braced themselves around me, but I didn't move. "You broke every promise. You broke our friendship, damn you," I hissed back. "Nicolasha...," who probably blamed me for the whole fucking mess.

"I didn't know what would happen," Felix wailed. "My God, I'm sorry!" Christian had another fight on his hands. I surged up and toward Felix again, who ran to the other side of his car as I exerted myself wildly against Christian's arms while he yelled repeatedly for me to stop. "I'm sorry for everything," Felix Cromwell heaved, scurrying back into his car and driving off recklessly.

Sorry? What the hell good was his sorrow to any of us, by then? Christian didn't relax his grip until the T-Bird was halfway down the block. We couldn't look at each other, trying to let the hysteria of the encounter seep out of us, me mostly, not giving it a chance to re-immolate. Christian walked me home and then left, without comment. I thought I would break down as soon as I closed the front door, and sure felt like doing it, too, but I didn't. I took a long, almost cold shower, and listened to an equally icy harpsichord sonata by Scarlatti over and over until I fell asleep on the couch, my own little overstuffed fortress of solitude in the family room that didn't have a family any more.

Much lonely and painful time would pass before I would learn it was Christian who, once we were apart, had burst into tears that violent afternoon, convinced I would eventually reject and hate him, too, after he'd read Felix's letter, which I'd beaten out of its author earlier that rotten day.

XXI

Such a man, so faint, so spiritless, so dead in look.
Henry IV

Our new apartment was a high-class dump.

It sat on the terminal corner of East 55th Street, overlooking South Shore Drive and Lake Michigan. It took up the entire sixth floor of the Depression-era building, and hadn't seen a lick of paint, soap, bleach, fresh air, and possibly daylight since. The cracked and dingy windows that flanked both the living room and dining room afforded us a nice east-southeast view, once you ignored the dead flies strewn along the sills. My bedroom looked straight out to the lake. It also had a small stone balcony that both Mom's old realtor friend and the building manager warned was just plain unsafe. Uncle Alex took the other two bedrooms that had the best part of their southern view blocked by the condominium high-rise across the street. You could fit them both into Dad's old suite. Unc chose the larger one for his painting studio.

We fled the boonies after Uncle Alex and I debated putting a pool in the backyard. The idea stalled when I concluded I would be swimming alone most of the time. Zane was spending the summer with his parents in their native Sweden, the rats, while the rest of the guys had joined their respective school's summer baseball programs. And the notion died a brutal death when, upon querying for an AWOL Lawrence the Laughing Lawyer, Unc found out I'd been Oliver Twisted by Simon, Frederika, and certain relatives which shall remain nameless (until I can get a suitcase bomb into the next Poiregaz Christmas, or I get to show up to their funerals in a red dress and black lace hose). Turned out, all the stocks that I had coming were basically worthless, the house was mortgaged past the firm's coverage, Dad had continually borrowed against his percentage of the firm, and the paperwork Mom left behind (or didn't) would require years of forensic accounting to make sense of.

So I was suddenly poor enough to belong in the poverty jet-set digs, as if it mattered to me. Unc took a one-year lease so I could finish school ("Now you don't have to spend all day on the train," he kept cheering to my repeated blank stares), paid the year in advance, most likely as a trade-out for some painting, and banked the modest leftover cash the Stingray netted from the local dealership, who came right out and said they were going to use it as a paper loss. The owner liked me. I was the lot's wash boy last summer. A friend of Unc's from Roseland secured this otherwise great address for us. I was almost sort of happy to be back in the city proper. The apartment might one day be awfully nice, a step up from our old Roseland bungalow, and the hell of an improvement over our shipwrecked suburban asylum, which turned out to be as bankrupt as it often felt.

Christian and I hadn't spoken since Felix's exodus. Team captain he was, Ozzie offered to mediate all the time, but neither 'best friend' would budge. Christian was mad at me for not, as he put it to our favorite catcher and only remaining link, "opening up my heart like a real friend is supposed to", while I was mad at him for being mad at me.

Ozzie had torn up his elbow early in the practice season, so he came up to Hyde Park to hang out on Mondays, when he didn't have to work at the local park. We usually caught a movie, brown-bagged lunch on the lake, and rode bikes through the neighborhood until dinner time. It became a routine for both of us, but one we liked. Oz and I got along pretty well, but were going in different personal directions: I spent a lot of the summer talking to colleges and reading up on the ones I thought might give me a ride, besides for filling up quite a few notebooks with my questionable poetry, not having much else to do at night; Ozzie, on the other hand, was bitter, unable to play ball, and had resigned himself to joining either the Navy or Coast Guard after graduating from one of the lower-tier state universities.

One evening, in the middle of another peace pitch, Ozzie told me Christian had made a clean breast of being gay to everyone, and was having a bad time on account of his big mouth. He got fired from the surplus store he worked at, and had been relegated as a little-used utility outfielder on his school baseball team, his one surefire ticket to college. He was also being verbally ostracized at school and throughout most of the subdivision neighborhood.

Warily, Ozzie asked if that was why the two of us were fighting. I was very matter-of-fact in replying that we'd been lovers more than once, but the fight was over something else. He dropped the subject after that. Oz seemed respectful afterwards, but my own 'fess up kept us at a polite distance. The phone calls became shorter and less frequent, and his visits noticeably briefer. I didn't care so much. Our friendship of convenience had already helped us both make it through that unhappy summer.

In due course, Poiregaz kept trying to have Uncle Alex and I come back out to the gulag for dinner. The unwelcome invites stopped almost as quickly as they came out of the woodwork. Neither of us went back to visit the cemetery, either.

*

The apartment was always quiet at night. There was always music playing, either my classical or Unc's jazz,

238

but we didn't talk much, and sometimes went days without seeing each other. Uncle Alex often didn't come home from his gallery do's until the following morning. I did a lot of reading and wasted a lot of time trying to complete some poems in Italian in between re-painting the entire place. We took in a few White Sox games with Zora, the Israeli woman had become Unc's prowling partner. She didn't understand our enduring interest in a team that never seemed to improve, and made much of the fact the team had been sold to a group of investors word had it were scheming to move the Sox to Florida. I was just happy for the diversion of the games we mostly lost. Every time I walked up from the concession area and filled my eyes with the bright green of the field, the seats, and the stands, the organist echoing through the pillars and concrete aisles, the hubbub of kids, families, and vendors, and the looming glory of our exploding scoreboard, it made me feel better about life, at least temporarily. It helped me to believe there were happy constants in everyone's life, which every winter would blossom into a summer of hope and glory. It would all fade by the time I got back to the scruffy eagle's nest.

I was lonely, tired, bored, and adrift, all at once. What made it hurt more was that I knew what was the matter, and didn't have the fortitude or the bravery to do anything about it. If it wasn't for my weekly visits with Ozzie, however abbreviated they became, I would have unhinged completely, not the least from all the paint fumes.

*

Uncle Alex scored a fairly nice job at the University, teaching applied art or something. Zora pretty much got him the gig. I doubted whether Unc would last until Christmas, the place was so hallowed and distinguished and...dull. The two of them were either in love, or Unc had his eye on her money (because there was no hiding the remaining Strasses were dead skint, flat on their uppers, and broke as hell). For some reason, Zora would never spend the night at the apartment. I don't know why. It might have been the dodgy ceilings. But we got along OK, even if she clearly wanted to slap me out of my general mood more than once. I'll say one thing, though: Unc had never finished or sold so many paintings in his career. Uncle Alex didn't start wearing a beanie, however.

*

I returned from an abortive lakefront writing session one morning to find a letter addressed to me in the mailbox. My heart stood still. I thought it was from Christian, but didn't recognize the handwriting on the envelope. I got excited all over again when I saw the postage stamp and postmark from **Suomi**.

Hyvaa paivaa, Hitman!

Sorry I haven't written sooner, but Pops keeps dragging us someplace different in Scandinavia every day. Don't worry. Got you a postcard from every place that had one. I'm saving them until I can give them to you in person. We're in Finland, now. Went to the sauna earlier tonight, and, <u>boy</u>*, was it embarrassing! Had to be a hundred people in there, guys and girls, and most of them were our age. Everyone was looking at me, I swear. Don't know why. I was too petrified to have a boner! I'll take the sauna over the Lab School, though. The only reasons I can think of to come back are to see you and Farrah again. I miss you both a lot. I'm hoping her parents will let us actually date, now that we're all gonna be seniors. Hope we're able to spend more time together, too. Thought about you every time I bought a postcard. Hope your summer is good and you're well. Tell Christian I said 'god dag', too.*

Love and hugs from the chilly land of naked white teenagers,

Zane

I sat on my bed and re-read Zane's letter until the dismal urge to cry passed.

*

I thought about Christian most every day and absolutely every night. I was ashamed about the perverse satisfaction I felt, learning about Christian's ostracism, but what mortified me most of all was the realization I could have used his (foolishly self-inflicted, I still believed) isolation to make peace between us. I wasn't strong enough to be susceptible to that.

*

My August birthday arrived, to a fanfare of silence. I had no reason to expect or even hope for a phone call from...well, anyone, but was miserable all the same when the morning went by without so much as a wrong number.

Uncle Alex took me to Old Town, a small enclave centered on Wells Street, just north of the Loop. When I was younger, the unkempt street was lined with dusty book stores and head shops, but now was re-gentrifying into an odd-ball collection of cafes and chic furniture stores. Ripley's Believe it or Not Museum somehow made it into the new decade. The candle shop, where you could buy scented bar soap or candles in such odd fragrances as Rain, Cloud, Narcissus, Venus, or Ocean, was shuttered. The triple-X movie theater was still there, too, but now was decorated with neon signs announcing films with all-male casts. I was too embarrassed to look at it twice.

We had lunch at the Steak Joynt, with its horrific, time-honored decor of velvet flock wallpaper and black leather. The food remained excellent, however, with a salad bar that included fresh Sevruga caviar and Nova Scotia smoked salmon that melted on your tongue. Unc insisted we order a bottle of Veuve Cliquot champaign. The wine steward, old waitress, maitre'd, and two Latino busboys presented the bottle with seventeen candles taped to the side of the wine bucket, and sang "Happy Birthday" to a blushing me.

We kind of indulgently took a cab up there, but rode the bus back. It let us off near a VW Bug convertible that looked as if it were being held together by the blotches of grey bondo liberally decorating the white bodywork. The top was down, which, pretty much anywhere in the city, might result in someone boosting the radio, the gear shift, the visors, the ash-tray, or the seats themselves, if they were relatively intact (which these were, surprisingly). But the interior was all there, actually almost new, if unattended. "Can you imagine how cold that thing gets in the winter?" Uncle Alex laughed. "A VW heater and a raggedy canvas top?"

"Slow enough to freeze right there on the road," I agreed, continuing to check out the car, which I'd never seen near the building before.

"Why don't you get in and see if it fits, nephew?"

"You're a bad role model, Unc."

Out of nowhere, I was goosed from behind. Zora appeared, grinning like a devil. She tossed me a set of car keys on a VW ring, and locked arms with Unc, enjoying the sight of my confusion. "Now that you've got your license, you need a car. Now you've got one."

I knew Uncle Alex brought new dimension to the phrase 'impulse buyer', but this was intense, even for him. I was afraid to touch the car, thinking it might disappear and I would wake up, alone in my bed, again. "Happy Birthday, brat." I threw my arms around my uncle and held him tight. I hadn't done that since I was much younger, when we used to sing along with the radio commercials while driving through snowy Saint Paul: "Thirst things first, get yourself a Grain Belt, get yourself a Grain Belt today..."

"Now you listen..." He pulled back a few inches, but kept his perpetually paint-stained hands on my face. "That's a fun car if you know how to drive it. You're new behind the wheel, so take it easy for a while. Don't start driving like Bond until there's a few thousand miles behind you."

Zora pulled us apart and led me like an Israeli Army officer might to the driver's door, which she opened for me. The freshly scrubbed black vinyl smelled and felt great as I slid behind the wheel and started the asthmatic engine. The glove compartment was filled to the brim with soul cassettes, still in their wrappers, obviously scored from the record store down the street. My words were stifled with disbelief and joy. "Where should I go for my first ride?"

"Anywhere you want. Here's some cash." Uncle Alex handed me a wad of mostly singles. "Buy some spray paint, maybe."

"Hey! Is this some of my tuition money?"

Unc blushed while Zora cackled wickedly. "No, bubbala. That's safely tucked away so neither of you can pilfer it on your own. This," she said, patting the Bug as if it were a thoroughbred Lipizzaner, "is paid for by the enduring appeal of avant-garde landscaping."

Unc cleared his throat. "I packed a bag for you, too. It's in the trunk, er, up front, with a couple of new notebooks."

"Are you throwing me out?"

"No. But a drive should do you some good. School doesn't start for another two weeks, right? Plenty of time to have an adventure someplace." We smiled at each other. It was the greatest birthday present anyone ever got. "Just don't get arrested, don't wreck the car, and don't be out driving past midnight."

Zora added, "Lock the doors and maybe put up the top until you get to the expressway." They walked arm-in-arm toward the apartment building and waited for me to putter around the corner before they waved goodbye. Just like that.

I figured on reaching the Canadian border in four hours or so. Pain? What pain?

*

The Interstate that connects Chicago to all points east passes through a particularly unimpressive stretch of northern Indiana, which, because of vast overuse and poor Federal upkeep, remains a fragile choke point to the constant stream of traffic that is forced to use the route. After I had sat in bumper-to-bumper gridlock for an hour, I threw the Bug into gear and wobbled down the grassy shoulder to the next exit. It took me another hour to side-street my way back into Illinois and to Chicago's far southern suburbs, where I hoped I could find someone to spend a few minutes of my birthday with. Nobody was home, not a one. I checked Christian's house twice. Even the DeVere's nursery was closed. And there I was, sitting in my first car, perfectly miserable and quite alone, having the uselessness of my birthday and the rest of my life stuffed down my throat.

Alone. Ah, *that* pain.

*

I had been hiding on my little unsafe balcony for over an hour. My legs and bare feet hung over the side of the concrete railing with my back pressed flat against the building. I glanced back and forth, watching the nighttime traffic motor along on South Shore Drive below. The air was warm, still, and muggy. The orange glow from the city's lights prevented me from seeing any stars. Uncle Alex stepped out from my bedroom and sat down on the single canvas director's chair I kept on the balcony. He had a large snifter of bloodcurdling Portuguese Marsala in his hand. I guess that meant Zora had gone back to her aircraft hangar of a house near Northwestern, of which, she quipped, "they call the Harvard of the Midwest, and I call the Harvard of Evanston."

"That wasn't a very long ride." As if side-streeting through northern Indiana wasn't a long ride through a suburb of Hell.

"I wanted to go to Canada, but a couple of trucks killed themselves on I-94. I couldn't get through."

"Canada, huh?"

"I figured I could maybe reach Kingston by sundown, and head to Quebec tomorrow." Despite Uncle Alex's paratrooper view of life, I decided against telling him I had intended to keep going east, far beyond Quebec, until I reached the ocean.

245

"Well, at least in Quebec, it feels like you're in a different country."

"That's what I hoped."

"Try again in the morning."

"I don't think so. It won't help."

"Help what?"

"I'll still be alone." My voice took a bitter edge. Happy Fucking Birthday.

"You're not alone." He waved me off and sipped his rot-gut.

The sound of the passing traffic below took over as I didn't say anything for a few minutes. "That's what everyone tells me, but I still feel that way. All the time, it seems like."

"Then stop being alone. You have a choice, you know."

Unc made it sound so damned easy. "I didn't have a choice about Mom and Dad."

"You can choose to stop hurting about it."

"Why? Have you?"

"No. I probably never will. But I'm trying to keep on going, to wherever I'm headed to. Whether I get there or not, well, I don't know. At least I'm trying, though."

"And I'm not..." His logic humiliated me into sullen and self-absorbed quiet.

"Oh, you're trying, all right, but not to figure out how not to hurt over people you can't have back. You're building some fortress around yourself, hiding behind all your music and your notebooks and all the being-a-teenager opera you take like a kind of drug. That's not the someplace you want to go, that's for sure."

Click.

I wasn't making a sound, but I was crying. Christian had made fun of me once, after I blurted out how much I hated crying, how badly I felt when I did, and how much I despised how often I did. "Crying is a sign of strength," he said. "You're someone who's strong enough to hurt, and strong enough to show that hurt by crying." I thought he was full of shit, Christian and his metaphysical quasi-spiritualism. Uncle Alex waited for me to stop the saltwater before he continued. "I should know. I've been there, more than once."

"How alone have you been, carrying on all these years?"

He chortled at me. "I'm alone every time I look at a blank canvas. I look in the mirror into my own eyes, remembering people and places that have gone away, all the hundreds of things I didn't do very well, or never did at all. Most people call it getting old."

"You're no old man, Uncle Alex."

"Okay, then, call it aging." We repeated one of his pet phrases together. "Everyone ages. Only old people get old." We laughed together, too. "I'm not pretending to know a lot about anything - "

"Unc, you're one of the smartest people I know."

"Three divorces and counting. Yep. I sure am smart."

"You're not any good at being married. So what?"

"Exactly! So fucking what? So what if the world isn't nice to you? It's not nice to anyone. So what if your wives turn out to be creatures from the Black Lagoon? Go out and get new ones."

"What are you, the Sultan of Constantinople? The guy who always tells me the only way to make something happen or keep anything worthwhile is through sustained effort?"

"And it is the only way," he said. "The bottom line is that, when something goes wrong, make it go right, and if you can't, not won't or don't, but can't, then hit the silk. Get on up and get away. Move the fuck on."

"I don't want to, alone." Did Nicolasha feel this alone, I wondered? Is this what I did to Felix, make him feel like he was the last man on Earth? Whether he deserved it or not, remorse blocked up my heart, tasting what I had so easily dished out to that absent friend. Was he sitting all alone, over a thousand miles away?

Uncle Alex stood up and put his hand over my eyes. "Sit back and take a deep breath." I did. "Clear your mind of everything." Sure. "Now, close your eyes and try to relax. Is your mind clear?" I lied with a nod. "Good. I'm going to ask you a question, and I want you to say the first thing that comes into your mind. Don't think about it, and don't try and come up with something you think I want to hear, or you ought to say. Answer immediately." I nodded again. "Fine. It's the day after your birthday. If you could have one wish, for anything in the world, what would you want?"

I took a deep breath and opened my eyes. "I want Mom and Dad back."

"You can't. God has them, now."

"Do you believe that?"

"It makes it easier when you try to. Next wish." He snapped his fingers, and I closed my eyes again.

"I don't want to be alone, anymore."

"Too vague. Be more specific." His fingers snapped once more.

"I want to be friends with Christian again." I opened my eyes and looked at the sky. I may not have been able to see them, but there were stars, somewhere up there. That was my wish, first star I see tonight.

"Out of all the things you could have in the world, that's all you want?"

That's all? Resentfully, I decided to jump into the far end of an ocean I suddenly wasn't afraid of. I didn't know how cold the water was, or care how deep the waves were (spoken like someone who grew up swimming in pools, not oceans). But I did know someone was already in that ocean, and was hopefully was still waiting there for me. "Yeah. I love him."

Uncle Alex's eyes lowered for a moment. He knocked back a gulp of his revolting red wine, swallowed loudly, and shot me an Oh, well, why not? look. "So, go find a star up there and make your wish."

XXII

If thou rememb'rest not the slightest folly
That ever love did make thee run into,
Thou hast not loved.
As You Like It

I always hated hospitals. Whether it was because Mom spent so much time in her damned emergency room, time we can never have back, or because of the deadening, antiseptic smell of fright I got when I walked into one, I don't know. But I hated them.

Christian's parents were hurrying out of their house when I drove up the next morning. I felt very self-conscious as they peered at me and came closer, as if to confirm it was actually me driving the VW Chitty Chitty Bang Bang. Doris' eyes filled as they met mine. George reached into the car to shake my hand, and asked me to follow them. I was mystified, but complied. A wave of despair and slow, creeping panic overcame me as their minibus turned into the parking lot of Mom's old hospital. It became unbearably worse as we passed through the place and stopped in a ward I could see held patients that were in a very bad way. Papu died in one of these...chambers. Was the fridge where Mom and Dad were kept downstairs somewhere? George and Doris DeVere gestured for me to enter a room without them.

God, how I hated hospitals.

*

Once I was in Christian's room, the rotting, lonely damp of my summer steeled me enough to open my eyes, but not enough to prepare me for what I saw.

Christian's body was a mass of bandages, tubes, and pain. His left arm, his throwing arm, was in a cast and suspended by a pulley. The cast went from his neck to his elbow. Both of his legs had bruises on them in different places, while his right foot was taped to a brace. His free hand rested sideways on his chest where the suction cups of the heart monitor were placed. There was a terrible, sewn-up gash across his wrist. Below that, he was hooked up to an IV. Christian's face was only slightly better. His long, blond hair was dirty and matted, pulled outside of the bandages that covered his forehead and the right side of his face. His right eye was surrounded by swollen and discolored flesh. Somehow, his thin, gentle lips were left intact, except that they were cracked from dryness. His breath sounded horrible through the oxygen tubes in his nose and a tube hooked over the corner of his mouth.

Had someone thrown him from an airplane without a parachute, for Christ's sake?

I was afraid to get close to the bed. A young Asian nurse came into the room as if I wasn't there, busily looking over the various checkpoints across my friend's body. She didn't appear very cheering. "He doesn't stay awake for very long, so don't you keep him up." I nodded before she left.

It took me a few minutes to be able to come up and stand beside Christian. I carefully touched his fingers. They moved slightly. I rubbed my hands over my face like I was trying to shake off some awful nightmare, but, no, it was still there when I opened my eyes and met Christian's, which had also opened a few centimeters. A sound croaked from his throat. He began moving his jaw even though I could see pain shoot through his face as he did. "Don't say anything, Christian." He kept doing it, and I began to panic. My eyes spun around the small and bright room until I saw a tray with a glass and pitcher of water.

I slid my hand under Christian's bandaged head to lift him up a few inches. His lips met the ice water with relief. He almost smiled at me. "I knew you'd come," he said, in a voice that left no doubts about how much pain he was in, just lying there, whatever doubts anyone but a blind man could have had. I put Christian back onto his rotten hospital pillow. I almost made him smile again as I brushed my hand over his soft cheek. I took an ice cube out of the glass and ran it over his lips until I couldn't hold it any longer. "That feels great."

"Don't waste your strength thanking me." I kept one hand on his face near his lips and the other flat on his stomach.

"Thank you for still being my friend."

"My God, Christian, be quiet." I was trying to be strong for him by not letting the tears in my eyes roll down my cheeks. I nearly started laughing, thinking about his theory about tears and being strong.

"It isn't as bad as it looks." Christian was such a bad liar. He looked like he was about to fall back into healing sleep. "I was going to visit you yesterday...you know, for your birthday." Christian drifted off just as my damned tears fell. His dad came in and walked me out of the room and the building with a rather fatherly arm over my shoulders as I smothered the remainder of my cry.

"We were so caught up with everything last night, nobody called you. I'm sorry."

"That's okay." I stared out across the hospital parking lot to the adjacent prairie. "I'm never around when someone I love gets hurt." I paused, trying to give my voice a transfusion. "I love him."

"He loves you," George DeVere replied, with an equanimity most fathers I knew would find impossible to match in a similar situation. The care and respect I saw in his tired grey eyes was not a by-product of too many drugs or a cool Woodstock way of life. It was much simpler than that. He was a father who loved his son, end of story. "It's that kind of love that put him in one of those beds in there." I couldn't tell if he was being accusatory. "He doesn't see why others hate him for his...your...love." I glanced up to the low and dark clouds covering the summer sky, wishing it would rain. "How no one seems to understand."

"Or won't," I added.

"Maybe in a different time and place," George said idly.

*

I spent the rest of the afternoon driving aimlessly through the smartly landscaped and mostly affluent streets of my old suburb. I passed our old house, and saw the new owners getting out of their car. They were black. I turned down four good offers before a non-white put one in. Uncle Alex thought my parting shot to the subdivision of ex-city dwellers was needlessly vindictive, and loved every bit of it.

It began to rain. I thought the canvas top was going to snap off its hinges as I tried to raise it back up before I was soaked through. I continued my cruise down bad memory lane before I spotted Ozzie running home through one of our old parks. He wore a short pair of cut-offs and a sleeveless t-shirt and had a towel rolled up in one of his hands. Probably coming back from the pool, I thought. "Hey, Kneecaps!" Ozzie skidded to a halt with a smile. "Get in." He stared at my Bug for an incredulous second before coming in from the cloudburst.

"I knew you'd start spending that money of yours before college, son of a bitch!" He playfully shoved me sideways with his elbow. Oz glanced down at his wet clothes. "Are you sure you want my wet body in your car?"

There was a time when I might have thought, no, I want your wet body someplace else. "Don't worry about it."

"Want to go to the show?" A movie or two sounded good to me. I gave him a thumbs-up and headed for the revival house. "Can we stop by my place to change my clothes?"

We looked at each other and smiled. "Only if I can watch."

"Hey, I'll let you watch me jack off if I can borrow your car Friday night!"

"Not just for watching, Kneecaps."

*

I waited inside of the large screened porch that took up most of Ozzie's backyard, enjoying the sound and smell of the falling rain as he got dressed. Oz emerged with two cans of Mexican beer in his hands. He tossed me one and sat down next to me on the wooden bench that faced the remainder of the yard. He was wearing an old red White Sox jersey. "I'm sorry I wasn't around on your birthday. We had to go to a barbecue at my Dad's house." Ozzie's Venezuelan parents had been divorced for years. He and his three little brothers lived in our old ritzy-titsy suburb with their mom, who spent most of her day at the health and country clubs before throwing in a few token hours at home with the boys. They ordered out, most of the time. The dad lived somewhere in the flatlands beyond Joliet, selling cars to pay for his ex's lifestyle. "Is it too late to get you a present?"

"That's okay. You've kept me company all summer. That's present enough. Besides, I made out pretty good this year."

"I'll say!" He took a long swig of the cheap beer. "You're so lucky."

My lips tightened. "That depends on how you look at it."

Ozzie put a hand on my arm. "You know what I mean." I nodded and finished my can. "I've always been kind of jealous of you. It seems like you've got so much more than I do, but I forget how you got a lot of it. Damn, I'm sorry."

"At least no one will throw cabbages and tomatoes at you and your date when you go to the prom." He put his hand on my arm again as we laughed quietly, hearing lightning in the distance.

"It must be hard on you, sometimes."

Did you say 'hard on', Kneecaps? "The loneliness is, I guess, but I'm not sure my being queer has anything to do with it."

Ozzie shook his head. "Don't call yourself that. If you didn't listen to all that old music so much, you wouldn't be so lonely all the time."

I sat back on the bench and finished the can of beer. "Have any of you gone to see Christian?"

"Huh. Most of them haven't talked to him since he...well, you know."

"No, in the hospital, I mean."

Ozzie looked at me. His eyes were wide and frightened. I could barely hear his voice. "Christian is in the hospital?" I nodded, watching him carefully. There was something I felt in Ozzie's measured, almost stiff reaction. "What happened?"

"I saw him earlier today. He was beaten within an inch of his life. His throwing arm was broken, too. I don't think one person did it, myself."

Ozzie looked away from me as he stood up, walking to the edge of the screened porch. He put one of his hands flat against the wire mesh, which was damp from the rain that gently hissed down around us. His head sunk to his shoulders. "I thought they were kidding." He began shaking his head in denial. "Christian..."

"Who?" My voice became level and cold, as cold as I felt my soul wax.

"I had no idea," Ozzie said, turning back to look at me. His brown curly hair and boyish looks were draped in regret. "My God..."

"Who was it, Oz?" He caught the hard and already vengeful glaze that had come over my dark eyes.

"Eric and Mickey..."

Eric Brazier was an effete toad from a stuck-up family of doctors just about all of us hated. Whatever was hip, he liked, and whoever wasn't popular, he didn't. He acted like a leader, but only after he knew what everyone else had in mind, so he could propose or promote an idea that he didn't have the imagination to come up with in the first place. There was always some rumor going around, about his father buying a grade for him here, or he buying one directly from a smarter student there. I didn't doubt any of it. His one redeeming quality was that he could move his wiry, sunlamp-tanned body like a pretzel, and was a great second baseman as a result.

Mickey Sreckov was a different story. His parents were second-generation white trash that maneuvered their way into what they fancied was 'class' through slum-lording and real estate graft. Like our suburb, a haven for whites of varying means who just didn't want to live with the blacks that had encroached into their old city neighborhoods, was classy, as if property tax had anything to do with class. Mickey was a soft-talking, hard-thinking mixer, handsome and well-built, but arrogant about it. He was the best center fielder I've ever played with, but a fink, all the same.

"...they were the ones who always talked about it...showing Christian 'how to be a man', they kept saying. The rest of us blew them off."

"You didn't do anything else?"

Ozzie's voice was almost hysterical. "We...I didn't take them seriously!" He sat down heavily next to me. "None of us could imagine what Christian told us. Here was our friend for, what, how many years? Then, one day, he's somebody else!"

I looked at Ozzie remotely. "You're right. He is somebody else." I stood up and dropped the empty beer can into Ozzie's lap. "He's a hospital patient now."

*

I called on Christian every evening until visiting hours were over. George spent the morning with him, and Doris covered the afternoon. As bad as he looked when I first saw him, Christian's health and fitness, not to mention glowing spirit, helped him recover quickly.

I got pretty silly about the whole visitation thing, bringing him a different gift each time I came to that damned hospital, which embarrassed him to no end and was part of the reason why I kept doing it. I especially liked bringing in forbidden food, like chocolates or pizza or bagels, because I'd always eat more than my half and knew perfectly well the nurse would be able to smell the goodies in the room after I left. Our conversations always remained light and cheery. We talked about the end of another remarkably undistinguished White Sox season, what we didn't do together over the summer, going back to school, nonsense like that. Christian was anxious to see the apartment in Hyde Park, to pitch in trying to get the place inspection-proof bribe-free, and couldn't wait to go for a spin in the Bug.

We spent one night going through the box of postcards Zane had brought me back from Scandinavia. An entire box! They ranged from glaciers in Norway and forests in Sweden to shots of naked skiers, dirty goings-on in Finnish saunas, and mysterious, spy story kind of frames of Helsinki, Oslo, and Stockholm. We excitedly agreed to try and follow Zane's footsteps the following summer, and to ask Zane to accompany us if we did.

On another night, Christian made me read him some of the poetry I had written in bad Italian. I read it badly, and Christian understood it badly. Just the same, we almost cried together, afterwards. That went badly, too. We both waited until I left before crying, making it that much worse.

*

August wound on slowly. I was glad Zane was back in town, since we talked on the phone every night, and school was finally about to resume. One night, in the middle of trying to write a poem about Christian, I decided to call up Ozzie. It was a short and unfeeling conversation. "I don't know if they'll tell me anything," he said. "They're afraid, you know."

Good, I thought. "Just find out for me, Kneecaps. Do yourself a favor and consider it my birthday present." I hung up and went back to my poem.

*

It was the night before Christian was to be released that we finally talked about something serious. I asked him, "So why did you go and tell everyone about yourself?"

Christian shrugged, as if the whole affair was nothing. "It's who I am. It's who we are."

"I know that. But does it matter if the world knows?"

"It's not the world I told, just our friends."

I tried not to laugh. "Oh, yeah, 'friends'. Sure."

"They're people we've played ball with, gotten drunk with, hell, we even went skinny-dipping with them those couple of times! Friends we've spent the night with, at their place and ours."

My God, he even sounded like he believed what he was saying! "Right, such good friends they attacked you like animals, because they didn't like the way you fuck." Christian was hurt. I leaned over and kissed his forehead. I think a passing nurse saw me. I wondered if she would get a few orderlies to beat me up. Let 'em try, I thought. I had Dad's old Beretta stuffed inside my belt, just over my crack.

I tried to change the subject. "By the way, Zane asked about you."

"Really?" I nodded. "That's cool. He's a pretty nice guy, you know?"

"If his father didn't control so much of his life, he'd be even nicer."

"Do you think he's cute?"

I was surprised by Christian's question. I'm sure the surprise showed. "I never thought about it. Now that you ask, well, yeah, I guess so. What about you?"

"It's hard to forget all the noises he made doing it with that girl at your old house. Talk about a party. What a turn-on!" Hm! "Do you think he's...you know?"

"Queer?" Christian winced. He hated the word. "No. His father wouldn't let him be, even if he was."

Christian gestured for me to sit next to him on his hospital bed. "I don't hurt so much anymore."

"It's the bagels and matzo ball soup. Zora says they're both medicinal."

"But physical hurt heals, eventually. That's not the worst way you can hurt someone. What if you crush their spirit? What do you think takes longer to heal, an elbow or a person's heart? Emotional and psychological hurt are just as bad as someone kicking you in the head."

He rubbed his cheek and shuddered. Christian's smile was feeble. I sighed. I knew he was talking about Felix.

Christian took my hand and held it between his. "What happened happened. It hurt a lot, sure. I wouldn't want it to happen again, but, as hurt goes," he shook his head as if it hadn't gone very far, "...it hurt a whole lot more not being friends with you."

He felt the flash in my hand and squeezed it. "We never stopped being friends, we just stopped talking." Ok, maybe not. "We're friends now, Christian."

"I want to be friends for longer than 'now'."

"I don't think anybody will let us get married."

He dismissed my witticism and stared hard at me. "Will you promise me something?"

My eyes wavered. "I'm not always so good at keeping promises."

"Make me one anyway." I nodded with hesitation. I think I knew what was coming. "I think strength is all about gentleness, in being able to cry or to forgive someone, forgiving your own self especially."

"And I don't?"

"No. You see strength like it's some kind of war you'd rather die fighting in than lose. To you, strength is any kind of scrap you can lay your hands on and win. Maybe that's why we love each other so much." He made himself blush. "At least, that's why I love you so much. You're what I'm not, and what I can't be. The same is true for you."

"What do you want me to promise, Christian, to love you?"

"No. You've done...you do that." We looked into each other's eyes and saw maybe the rest our lives might be there. The rest of the world didn't matter. Time didn't matter. All seventeen years each had wound down to that place that night, that room and that bed. "I don't want you to be a peacenik. It's not you. But if anyone offers you peace, then I want you to promise me, please, that you'll accept it. Okay? Do you promise?"

Take peace instead of making it, huh? I wasn't sure why peace between Felix and I was so important to Christian, not having read The McGuffin Letter and all. But I made the promise anyway. Maybe it would give Christian some kind of moral victory to help him heal faster. "OK, OK, I promise."

It was an easy promise to make. Indefatigably Felix had sent me a birthday card that had arrived a few days before. He invited the two of us to visit him and his family down in New Mexico. I'd decided to make the trip Christian's Christmas present.

*

Christian didn't make me promise to forgive anyone else, however.

Evidently, some local school board members received reports about grades being adjusted and test keys being sold and distributed. Much pressure was brought to bear on the teachers alleged to be involved. A bitter internal inquiry followed, and a senior, little Eric Brazier, it so happens, was implicated, and expelled. Daddy Doctor Brazier even lost the school's insurance account! Why, the mess was so bad, it scotched Eric's chances of getting into his dream school, the University of Illinois!

As if that weren't enough to keep the old burg buzzing, a big downtown modernization project being advanced by a local real estate investor just up and collapsed. The plan was scrapped and the properties rezoned, as were a few other holdings owned by this same investor. The foreclosures by a suddenly unfriendly local bank and the bankruptcy filing put a bit of a crimp in the Sreckov's rickety family finances, not to mention putting quite the torpedo in Mickey's college tuition fund, too. The last I heard, the Sreckov's even had to sell their house and "trade down" a few suburbs. Pity, that.

I never thought I'd reopen the guest register from Mom and Dad's wake, but I'm glad I did. They had many excellent friends that weren't blood relatives, and it was good to talk to them again.

XXIII

The quality of mercy is not strained;
It droppeth as the gentle rain from heaven
Upon the place beneath. It is twice blest;
It blesseth him that gives and him that takes.
The Merchant of Venice

The Land of Enchantment was exactly that.

On the day after Christmas, at around four o'clock in the afternoon, we crossed into what Christian referred to as sovereign New Mexico territory. You couldn't buy a cloud in the deepest blue sky either of us had ever seen. The sun, which was beginning to set as we arrived, painted a small collection of brilliant pictures athwart the vast and spectacular horizon. The air was crisp and clean, even when we stood beside the Welcome to New Mexico sign on exhaust-filled Interstate 40, where we took pictures of each other. I looked up and down the highway before stepping closer to Christian, who smiled and wrapped his arms around me as I placed my lips on his for the fourth time since we left Chicago late Christmas night. We decided to commemorate each new state by doing the perfect hug thing every time we crossed a border, or 'frontier', as Christian called them. That meant no hugs or kisses until we reached our next destination, which, to be frank, was difficult. Originally, we were going to do a lot more than hug and kiss at the "Welcome to..." state signs, but neither of us wanted to be arrested by a Deliveranceville sheriff or get run over; and the Bug, wonderfully eccentric car though it was, twasn't much good for misbehavin'. Besides, I had told Christian, if we were going to nakedly consummate our togetherness upon each frontier crossing, the first place we'd head to was New England, not the Southwest.

*

Even though we talked endlessly, sang along to Christian's glam rock and hair band cassettes, and simply enjoyed a few of mine - nothing like a couple of crashing overtures to keep you going through the night - it had been a long, exhausting overnight drive, and we were content to spend the night in Tucumcari, the first town we'd hit after crossing into New Mexico. There didn't seem to be much a town, per se, beyond the four or five mile strip of motels, gas stations, fast-food outlets, and antique stores that were once part of the fabled Route 66. It was the town that time forgot, in a state, we would soon discover, that was filled to the brim with such towns. I pulled into the last motel before the strip (and town) ended, a friendly enough looking place that had its own restaurant and bar. If you liked earth tones, died, and went to heaven, your resting place would look a lot like our hotel room did. The grizzled old man in the black cowboy hat and handlebar mustache grumbled an apology that all his rooms with double beds were being redone. After some shameless hemming and hawing, we took a room with a king-size bed big enough for an orgy.

We soaked the long drive out of our bodies in a bubble bath. I had packed a bottle of Mr. Bubble without Uncle Alex or Zora noticing. I fell asleep in Christian's arms twice.

*

The bar menu featured an item called Bucket of Beer. Was this a literal description, Christian wondered? A sweet old waitress named Sandy managed to forget asking us for any i.d. before serving us both a wine bucket filled with six bottles of Pacifico, a fine Mexican beer. Maybe we looked like good tippers (as opposed to under-age punks acting smart by ordering beer in the first place). The huge, stomach-busting delight of our dinner, which took over two hours to consume, consisted of a taco salad, bar-b-que filet quesadillas, chili rellenos, fried taco rolls, and the freshest, sweetest tortilla chips we had ever tasted. Then we sat and finished our beer buckets for the next hour.

Even though it was warm enough when we arrived in Tucumcari, the air was now almost frosty as we walked through a massive empty field beside the motel, which separated that end of town from the eerily deserted Interstate. The only thing we could hear was the whisper of the night breeze in our ears and the sound of our feet on the dry, wild grass. Above us, the moon was bright and brilliant across in the still-cloudless sky, giving us both a shadow as we walked beneath what looked to me like every star in the solar system.

Christian stopped and looked straight up. "Could you imagine every night being like this one?"

"Very easily," I answered quietly.

"Do you think it would get boring, like seeing the Eiffel Tower on the way to work every day?"

"I'd be willing to live in Paris for a year to find that out."

"This is so beautiful." Christian pulled one of my hands out of my jeans pocket and held it in his. "But I won't thank you for bringing me here." He stuck his tongue out at me.

I laughed. "Why not? You thank me for everything else."

"Because I'd rather thank you for being here with me, here or any place else. I'm not sure how to thank you for giving me a Christmas gift like this trip, though."

"Be my love slave until the sun comes up," I replied with a grin.

Christian ignored my defensive humor. "As long as you're with me, I'll be happy. It's the only gift I really wanted this year, anyway."

"I never know how to respond when you say things like that."

"That's why I say them."

We concluded the night with Christian giving me the massage of my life. I did most of the driving, so I got the rub-down, he reasoned. We took a quick shower and started to fall asleep in a tangle of freshly-scrubbed flesh. Before he begin his half-hour ritual of saying good night, I held his face in my fingertips and said, "I'm with you all the time. I'm with you even when I'm not. I'm with you wherever you go, no matter who else is there."

Christian peeped through the dark like a Cupie Doll. "How do you figure?"

"Because you're with *me* all the time, so it's only right."

*

Getting an early start, we swept south and west through the middle of the state. After successfully avoiding the state police near Ruidoso, we took a short detour through a tiny town called Cloudcroft. A friend of Uncle Alex's had sworn that the place looked like it belonged in the middle of Switzerland, rather than New Mexico, so I thought we'd have a look. He was right. The single, needle-thin road bisecting Cloudcroft wound like a rubber band through hills that were blanketed with coniferous, snow-covered trees and dotted with a few log cabins and A-frame houses. The outside temperature dropped to well below freezing for the few minutes it took to pass through. It was my kind of town.

We stopped at the White Sands National Monument to enjoy a pot luck picnic provided to us by a local 7-Eleven. I long ago bought into Dad's aversion to state and national 'points of interest', agreeing with his logic that, if the place in question had a crowd of ill-dressed tourists anywhere near it, it must not be all that special anymore. But I honored Christian's request to at least have a look, and was glad I did. I drove to the end of the Monument's curling path, into the spectral landscape of bleached sand dunes that the afternoon sun made dizzying to the eye. We wolfed down our sandwiches inside the car, took off our shoes and socks, and trudged even further into the rolling labyrinth of white silicon hills. Once we were surrounded by these geological anomalies and unable to see or hear anything else, we sat down on the sloping half of a sand formation. It looked like a huge, cresting wave about to envelop us.

"You should have brought your notebook. This is beyond cool, isn't it?" I nodded my head as I watched a pair of F-15s leave a vapor trail behind them as they raced upward to altitude. "It's a hell of a beach!"

"Superb beach," I agreed dryly, "but kind of bare coastline." The cool, powder-like sand felt like silk on my feet. I opened my dull white shirt, letting the sun keep my body warm.

Christian ran the flat of his hand over my chest before pulling off his sweatshirt and moving closer to me. "We haven't been in New Mexico for twenty-four hours, and I'm ready to stay here for the rest of my life."

I took off Dad's old Navy-issue sunglasses and looked at Christian. "The rest of your life is a long time."

"That's not what I meant." He bit his lip. "I mean, for us."

"The rest of *our* life together?"

"You're already rewriting my sentences. Some deal this is!" He laughed. I didn't. "Okay. I'll shut up."

Something was on Christian's mind. He didn't talk us to sleep the night before, like he always did, and said very little during the day's journey. It wasn't a hostile or selfish quiet, but, rather, a thoughtful one that just hadn't produced some epic exchange between us. Yet.

*

"Take off your clothes."

"What?"

"You heard me. Strip, right now."

Christian stood up, wide-eyed. He complied wordlessly. The wind threw his hair in every direction while he met my gaze head-on. The setting sun cast a warm orange glow across the creamy pastel of his body. The moment stretched out until it sounded as if we were inside of a sea shell. "Don't I get to look at you, too?"

Neither of us were hard (not fully, anyway) nor took a step closer, where either of our hands might reach for the other's body. We didn't speak; it didn't feel like we had to. We just looked and kept looking until we were shadows in the desert.

*

Morning done broke. For the first time in my life, jazz sounded good while the sun was still up. Uncle Alex scored another box of 8-tracks for our road trip: John

Coltrane, Dizzy Gillespie, and Charlie Parker; Art Blakey, Benny Goodman, Thelonious Monk, and Stan Getz, who I was especially excited to hear again; Billie Holiday, Dinah Washington, Miles Davis, and a generous serving of Duke Ellington, the master. And boy, did the first tape we listened to sound great as we drove the Bug the way its engineers likely didn't intend, breaking a land-speed Beetle record on our way through the splendid Black Range, in the southeastern corner of the Gila National Wilderness. It was a good thing there wasn't much traffic on the Range's mountainous roads that day.

*

We came to a fork in the road. If we turned right, we would head further into the forbidding Gila. If we turned left, we would straddle the southern edge of the Wilderness until reaching Piños Altos, an almost ancient dot on the map that served as the "gateway" to the Gila, and home to the Cromwell's humble ranch. Christian's eyes had a funny look in them when he asked if we could see more of the Gila, on our own. I shrugged and drove in. Felix had waited this long, I mused. Another hour or two would hardly change our lives, right?

Ho ho *ho.*

We stumbled upon a large shoulder off a wide curve in the road that also functioned as a scenic overlook. We sat on the rounded hood of the Bug, with our backs resting on the windshield. A seemingly endless and snow-covered valley lay below us. Once again, good fortune smiled on us; we were left without the interference of passing traffic, quite alone together on the cliff. Every place we had gone in New Mexico had some nearly chilling sense of silence about it, and not just because the place was gigantic and didn't have very many people in it, either. No, there was something more to it than that. If the smart one wasn't well into sensory overload, he would have tried to figure it out. It took his greatest friend's tears to unlock the secret. "Why are you crying," I asked?

"I don't know," he said, between sobs.

"Yes, you do." I put my arm around him and moved his body next to mine, keeping my hand on the side of his hip. Christian tried to smile through the tears that sounded like they had been building up for a while. "Tell me. After all, you're the honest one, right?"

He put an arm around my neck and pressed the side of our faces together. "I love you," he whispered. The tears began to peter out.

I kissed the top of his soft blond hair. "I hope that's not why you're crying."

"No." Christian wiped the tear stains from his face with the sleeve of my old pea coat. "Now I understand what you used to say about crying. I feel like a dick." He let out a long breath as he cuddled his face against mine. "You were right about something else."

"I'm almost always right. Can you be more specific?"

From behind my back, Christian snapped the elastic of my underwear. "One time, you said you wanted to leave, because you were in pain." I remembered. It seemed like a long time ago. "I said you'd take your pain with. Well, I was wrong." His voice sounded like he was going to cry again. "I've been in pain. But now that I'm away from home, I don't feel it, so much."

"Is it getting bad at school again?"

"No. I still get funny looks and smart-ass comments, people talking to me like I was from Uranus or something, ha, but nothing unusual. Ozzie almost tries to talk to me when no one else is around."

I was lucky. I had Zane and Farrah to stick by my side, in case I fell out of the closet or something. "Well, what is it, then? We're all alone, Christian, right here, in the middle of New Mexico. We could get buck naked again, for all anyone would know. If you can't tell me a secret here, you can't tell me one anywhere."

Christian pressed our lips together and held us still while our eyes opened and relented to the other. I felt his trust and love flood into me. He answered at once. It had to be the truth. "This is the most beautiful place on earth. I feel so free here, and I don't want to leave. I want to stay here forever, with you."

Flash.

My voice was quelled with fearful excitement. "Do you want to get married, or something?"

"I don't think we can," he joked quietly, "at least, not in the old-fashioned way."

"Christian," I said, sitting us both up on the trunk, "do you know what you're saying?"

"You don't believe me?"

"You're the worst liar I know. Yes, I believe you, but what you're saying is - "

"Till death do us part, OK? That's what I'm saying." I closed my eyes. I had no reference point to this. Who would, in our shoes? There wasn't anyone nearby I could ask for advice. Maybe the trees or the sky had some views? "I didn't think I could say that, before now. That's the hurt I was moaning about."

"We still have a lot of life...left to live." My alliteration made Christian smile. "Forever is a long time."

"Forever and a day." Christian scowled as I laughed defensively. "Well?"

I got off the hood and took Christian by his hands with me. We stood at the edge of the overlook, encompassed by the majesty of the Gila and the hushed wonderment we felt being there together. Uncle Alex and Zora, the clever swine, they saw this coming. I heard his subtle little hints about a bunch of colleges out west. And her, starting mile-long conversations over dinner about happiness, companionship, being married, and love, real love. "Before I give you an answer, will you hear me out?"

"I always listen to whatever you have to say. You know that."

"Fine." I took a deep breath and gathered my thoughts as best I could. "I'm assuming you've thought about what you're asking."

"Since we left home - no, wait, that's not true. When you came to the hospital to see me? I've thought about it since then."

"Christian, we've never gone steady with anyone else, boy or girl. You're only the third guy I ever touched, and I'm your first. We've only met two other people like us. Who knows how many others we'll both meet or where we'll meet them? College, travel, or whatever, there must be a million others out there."

His eyes didn't waver. "I don't think I care."

"For God's sake, listen to yourself, Christian!" My voice raised, but so did the breeze of the early dusk. "Think about it! Out of everything in the world you like in people, out of all the things you want in someone, whether they're a friend or a lover, and what you know you need, deep down, can you tell me with a straight face that I'm that person?"

"Yes." He closed his eyes for a moment. Hah! He looked away first! "I'd call the person you just described perfect, but I don't think love is perfect, any more so than me or you are. Happiness and friendship aren't perfect, either."

"We're talking about the rest of our lives, Christian."

"Which may end tomorrow, for all we know. Look what happened to your folks!" I looked away. Christian held my shoulders in place, in case the rest of me tried to make off. "Look what we let happen between us. Hell, look what happened to me, because of my big mouth! Before those kids found me, I thought I was going to die. It felt like I was going to." I saw tears begin to fill up in his eyes, but they didn't fall. "I thought I was going to die alone, sprawled out in my own blood in that alley." Alone. My God, I dreaded to myself, alone. Christian touched my face with his lips for a moment. "But I didn't, and we're here, now, together."

"There'll be a lot more tomorrows before either of us die, Christian."

"You don't know that, any more than you know how to ice skate."

"Nope," I admitted, "I sure don't."

Christian's soft hands touched my face again. The tips of his fingers followed the lines of my cheeks, my nose, my chin, and my lips. It made me tremble. Everything was making me tremble, either from fear or excitement, I couldn't tell which. "I'll tell you what I do know."

"What's that?"

"I know I like you. I like you as a friend, and I like you as a lover." He smiled shyly. "I desire you, too. But most of all, I need you." Christian nodded his head with confidence. "I know I need you. It took being apart to realize how badly." We stared at each other the same way we did on my porch almost a year ago, seeing and feeling the other through our eyes, as if for the first time. "I need you to love me."

"I do, bro."

Snap! He broke the spell. Christian broke the fucking spell by pointing at me with a shit-eating grin on his face. "Ah ha, you said 'I do'!" My eyes narrowed with slight stage anger. He folded his hands together and put on a good look of contrition. I let him continue. "I need you to let me love you."

"I will."

"Then marry me."

My head shook involuntarily. "Marry you...here and now," I mumbled. "You have a priest in your duffel bag?" OK, don't laugh. "We're not even eighteen."

"Hey, it's a tradition, south of the Mason-Dixon Line."

"Forever," I said, continuing to mumble.

"Right here. Together. Till death do us part."

I scarcely believed we had come to this point. I struggled to understand what I was hearing and feeling. There wasn't much consolation in knowing I couldn't be alone, drunk from head to soul in some incarnate daze. I looked out across the valley and pictured the entire world turning upside down. What would we grab on to, one of the piñon? Or would we be swept into the stratosphere, clinging to the Bug's dented bumper? Maybe this was what heroin is like, I thought. I kept shaking my head, but finally smiled. The epic exchange was every bit the ringing equal of even the mightiest Shostakovich symphony:

"I, Christian Andrew DeVere, in good health, clear mind, and pure heart, do solemnly swear, in plain sight of God, to take you, my most treasured friend and lover, into my hands forever, as one...married, married as the rest of all the jerks out there who don't have half the love we do." Out of the blue, a pick-up clattered down from the deeper interior of the Gila. Christian glanced at it anxiously as he waited for me to say my bit, which was hard, because my half-opened lips were frozen, just like my heartbeat. "If I can say it, so can you," Christian stated quietly.

I privately appealed for sweet baby Jesus to give me the right words. "I, Miles Frederick Strasse...call the gods to witness...one feast, one house, one mutual happiness...with Christian, my friend and lover, my heart and soul, who I will love, cherish, and hold, *le jour le plus long*, forever and a day, till death do us part."

A single tear rolled down Christian's cheek. Hah! Game, set, and match. I may have said 'I do' first, but he not only blinked but cried first! "Yours sounds better."

"I'm the smart one."

"Good. Then you can think of what to tell Felix when he asks what we did up here."

Our arms brought our bodies together, for the first time, again, forever. Epic, indeed.

XXIV

*In dreaming, the clouds methought would open
and show riches, ready to drop upon me,
that, when I waked, I cried to dream again.*
The Tempest

The naked olive-skinned teenager sighed. "Epic..."

Shant Nakhararian folded the portfolio against his chest with arms that were crossed as much in misery as controlled anger. He heard the echo in the humble attic room, of Miles' soft voice reading his own handwritten manuscript, every page, every word, while an unseen city rattled away outside the church-shaped window. Shant could hear the longed-for voice whispering in his ear, close enough that he might feel Miles' lips once more, for only the third time.

It had been just about a year since Miles had wheedled Shant off of a dingy nearby street corner, away from the alley adjacent where Shant often slept and sometimes ate after plying his meager trade. Miles led him off the familiar over-lit boulevard into a strange leafy neighborhood that made Shant sullen and suspicious. He half expected the fine-looking guy in the Chicago White Sox jersey to turn on him with a blade or gun, or, worst of all, a needle. But all he got for his qualms was a wing-backed chair at a dinner table with fancy carvings on its corners at the center of a vast candlelit dining room inside what looked to Shant to be a haunted mansion. He was served a heaping bowl of spicy hot goulash with a straw basket of fresh baked rolls by a second pretty guy with crazy long hair who fussed over him throughout the unexpected meal. Both hosts seemed kind, though in Shant's bitter experience that often spelled trouble. He then figured some three-way action was coming but didn't have the strength to care; he was too hungry. So he just kept eating, inaudibly walling himself off from his surroundings, his company, and his own body to face whatever lay ahead.

"So, are you guys together, or what?"

Miles and Christian looked at Shant in curious amusement. "As in a tag-team," Miles quipped.

"No, I mean, like boyfriends."

"Yes, we're a couple," Christian answered quickly. "We've been, since high school."

Shant stared back at them until his eyes watered. "That's...cool."

Ignoring the awkwardness of the moment, Miles gave Shant the dime tour of his and Christian's romance. Christian took over after he reached their fateful trip into the Gila: "We went to Felix's, who started bawling just seeing us. We were his surprise Christmas present. The Cromwells welcomed us like we were long-lost sons. You should see their house. It looks like a ski-lodge. Jason built it right in the middle of a pine tree thicket, next to a little stream where they let their horses roam freely. What a place, so full of love."

Shant recalled not thinking he knew what *any* such place could be like. "And we lived happily ever after," Miles giggled.

"Continuing thusly, with occasional unexpected dinner guests such as yourself," Christian added, serving Shant a fancy parfait of fruit, custard, cake, and thickly whipped cream. "We rented a room from some elderly folks with a beautiful old house in Silver City, further down the road from Piños Altos and the Gila. It was built up on a hill. You could see the whole town and all the surrounding mountains from the living room window."

"It sounds nice," Shant mumbled through a mouthful of the best dessert he'd ever had, still trying to get past the couple thing.

"The codgers only ever rented to college students, so the room was like a small dorm, two beds, two desks, and two dressers. We only used the one bed but messed up the other every morning so our landlady's arteries wouldn't harden from suspecting untoward carnal knowledge had been gained after class," Miles intoned with a laugh.

That night, Shant slept on a lumpy sofa out on the porch that wrapped around two sides of the mansion. It took a few more nights before Shant decided he wasn't going to wake up tied to a chair or hooked on some bad shit or be starved into making videos until his body gave out (which another hustler he knew claimed happened to him). With a smile Shant would later say changed his life, Miles led him up to what was once the cobwebbed attic but was now four small but spotless bedrooms, private places, with doors that locked from the inside, not out. The hallway between the rooms was crowded with piles of neatly folded clothes any teenager or college student might wear even if they weren't penniless or plucked fresh off the street. The room Shant was given had a spotless rollaway bed with a set of snow white towels at its foot, and a small nightstand with a very old-fashioned table lamp and a stack of paperbacks with orange spines on it. "The water closet is down a floor," Miles said.

"Huh?"

"The bathroom."

"Oh." Shant blushed under the weight of Miles' latest smile. "I don't have to go."

Miles saw a wounded animal inside Shant's eyes, wide black pools that fascinated as well as unsettled him. "You look like you could use a nice bubble bath."

"Do I smell?" Shant asked in a choked voice.

Miles carefully drew up and touched the tip of Shant's nose with his. "No," he whispered slowly. It was the first time anyone had undressed Shant as if there were a human being under his worn-out jeans and colorful but faded print shirt. It was also the first in a very long time Shant's skin didn't crawl as it occurred. "Christian, Felix, and I all went to college together," Miles told him, sponging him down as if the gesture might erase the various now exposed signs of abuse strewn across Shant's body. "There was a small state university there in Silver. It was just an OK school, but at least we were together. I was a lit geek and Felix did math. Christian never had a major. Felix and Christian became close friends in their own right. Christian always thought Felix secretly wanted to have a ménage-a-twat with us. I couldn't tell."

Shant stared at the bubbles wafting under him, the bright morning sun reflecting off the foam like diamonds. Miles might as well have told him a science fiction story. Suddenly, he couldn't catch his breath, or something was caught in his throat. Had Miles sucker-punched him? Was he slipping below the bubbles, into the steaming bath water? Shant's body shook like a ragged leaf, despite Miles' grip on his forearms. Then he screamed out, once, against his will, making the awfulness trying to claw its way out of his gullet that much more wicked. A sirocco of tears and tiny shrieks followed until Shant all but fell unconscious.

281

He came to later that afternoon, tucked into the rollaway's cool itchy sheets. He found Christian and another young stray planting a pineapple-shaped palm tree next to the front porch. Shant was mightily reassured by his cheery grin. "Saltwater! How about giving us a hand or two here?"

*

The century-old manor became the first proper 'home' Shant Nakhararian had ever known, what with his first being dumped on an itinerant father then fobbed off on a disinclined and eventually violent half uncle before being cast off altogether nearly the minute he was of age. At first the streets were a perverse respite from his grisly blood family, a big terrifying adventure that fast became simply terrifying. The crash downhill came on the third night, the first time he would take money to suck a stranger's cock just to buy food. How he made it to what he thought was possibly his sixteenth birthday, Shant didn't know. But now he had a home. Where others had come and gone, hardly any staying a week, most only a day or two, and some for as long as it took to eat and wash up for another night wandering between corners streetlights and closed storefronts, Shant hung on. Had he asked to? Not verbally. He scarcely spoke; he mostly communicated with his wide, expressive dark eyes. Neither Miles nor Christian ever asked when he might leave, so he just stayed. It was no secret he had no place else to go.

But he earned his keep, helping with the never-ending maintenance of the dilapidated Victorian Miles had been the sole bidder for, at an auction of properties on the verge of being condemned, a quixotic move that would've made his late uncle proud. Christian had learned most of the trades from his ex-hippie dad, so he and Shant set about to repairing the intricate parquet floors, renovating the sculpted ceilings and walls, refurbishing the wiring and the plumbing, and restoring the bathrooms to proper working order. The musty stacks of highly wrought furniture that came with the house were all in various states of disorder and tackled one piece at a time. The weedy backyard had an odd mix of trees to which Christian and Shant added any plant and flower they could lay their hands on, turning it into a verdant if rather mad garden.

To pay for it all, Miles used the remainder of Uncle Alex's estate, the lion's share of his graduate school stipend awarded for as he put it 'doing a whole lot of nothing very impressively', and for good measure took out a student loan he didn't need. Christian meanwhile became the indispensable weekend help at a nearby hardware store, who also gave him priceless discounts on materials. Every penny they had was inhaled by the mansion. The weird little safe haven they ran out of it was the least of their perpetual money problems.

All Shant had to give was his meager savings and his willing, if extremely quiet, labor, which Christian happily accepted. Almost overnight Christian became very fond (and not a little shielding) of Shant, though he couldn't say why him particularly and not the various others who came and went from the grand old house on Emiliani Street. Shant once overheard Miles tease Christian that Shant had become as much a project for him as the house. Shant wasn't hurt or offended, more bewildered rather, at having spent his life being unwanted and suddenly finding himself the object of so much unsolicited and otherwise inexplicable attention that had as yet no strings attached. Plus, Shant was quite content to use his helpful toil to beat back the voluble assortment of ghosts and demons still careening inside him. It never occurred to him either Miles or Christian would know from a few of those, or care enough to try and help him silence the infernal racket.

Shant took Christian's good-natured mothering as a domesticated form of flirting that never crossed any lines (which for Shant had long since become twisted beyond recognition, anyway), a kindly sort of older brother he'd never had. Miles was another matter entirely. Shant was painfully attracted to him, becoming ham-fisted and doubly tongue-tied whenever all three of them ate together. Miles thought it was funny, but didn't let on. Christian took it in stride. He was just as deeply attracted to Miles, still.

Shant became dumbfounded at the skill and complexity of both his guardian angels' ability to keep secrets and lies from each other that even more bizarrely were eventually confided to him. Shant found most of it funny if not silly, stuff not worth lying about, except for Christian's tremors. Christian was very slowly developing tiny motor and memory problems which Shant observed from all their time spent in close quarters. Miles' studies and university gig and long commute allowed Christian to hide the worst of it. But it soon got to the point Shant had to take over Christian's household duties. Only after they'd visited a nearby clinic for the umpteenth time did the male nurse take Shant aside and explain Christian's condition: the concussions he had gotten in the attack years prior were lingering with a vengeance. The specialist Christian finally got in to see confirmed there were severe internal bleeding issues in his brain that only a chancy surgery could fix, as if there was that kind of money for it in the first place.

The tremors began once more while they waited for an overdue bus home. "Is it OK if we hoof it, instead?" Shant nodded, knowing a long walk would help. "Will you hold my hand?" Shant was startled by Christian's simple request. He bravely ignored the few hostile looks they got on the way back to the Victorian. "Let's go to your room." Shant didn't know whether he was turned on or scared stiff. On impulse he began to undress once the door was locked behind them. Christian stopped him with a sad smile. "No. Just hold me a while." Shant complied awkwardly. "Will you take a nap with me?" They wrapped themselves into a shared fetal position on the rollaway, where over and over Christian whispered, "I can't tell him," until his voice faded away. Shant felt a surge within him, to comfort and somehow guard Christian, the same as he and Miles had done for him. Shant was unable to fall asleep.

*

Shant hadn't been to church, any church, in his life, but he began attending the odd weekday morning Mass with Christian, at a tiny but beautiful old Catholic place not too far from the house. Christian participated; Shant did not, though he listened intently to the goings-on. They sat a pew away from the few other mostly older attendees so they could hold hands unseen. They held hands when they walked home, too. Christian told Shant he believed in the intercession of saints and tried to explain it to him over their many strolls, something *else* Shant had trouble getting his head around. But, as their visits went on, Shant tried to talk to a saint, any of them, maybe all of them, not knowing exactly how many of them there were or were not, or which one he should try and call on. He did once light a candle and felt good about being able to put a few dollars in the collection box. True, he was weirded out by the holy water, but crossed his wet fingertips nevertheless, just in case, just to make sure. He found he couldn't wait to tell Miles about what he'd done, but suddenly felt trapped by the inevitable 'Why? What were you doing there?' that would follow. He would keep Christian's secret. That was more important than anything he felt.

It was a warm and beautiful dusk when Christian was firing up the brick barbecue pit he and Shant had built.

He looked like he was about to tell another funny, flirty story when his mouth froze and his dreamy guileless eyes cried out to Shant in silence. Shant caught him before he collapsed to the grass and cradled him closely until the ambulance arrived. The others, two girls and one guy, watched helplessly from the mansion's wraparound porch. Nobody could reach Miles at the university. The cerebral hemorrhaging killed Christian before they reached the hospital. The paramedics were shaken by the chillingly silent ferocity of Shant's breakdown; it was all they could do to pry their hands apart.

Worse than living with his birth father, worse than being forsaken by him, worse even than ending up with the worst uncle on Earth and the final heave-ho, Shant was there when Miles at last arrived. His uncontrolled sobs and near convulsions made Shant feel like a waxwork figure. Shant had to hold Miles upright throughout. Back home, the pre-dawn phone call to Felix was just as terrible. But somehow the younger man took matters in hand and made what arrangements he could, just as Christian had entrusted him to. It was the one combative conversation Shant and Christian ever had, as Shant fought accepting Christian was on borrowed time.

Miles and Shant took part of Christian's remains to an obscure beach hours north of Los Angeles. The smell of the ocean, the feel of its spray, the warmth of the sun and its brightness on the water, the sound and power of the waves became deafening as they deposited the heavy grained ashes into the crashing surf. Shant pictured Miles and Christian swimming naked on this very seashore. Christian had told him all about it. Felix had come to foist money on them for the house but wanted to go skinny-dipping in the ocean with them for his trouble. The three of them lasted only a few seconds before the cold of the Pacific got the better of them and they ran back out, Christian laughed.

When Shant woke up the next morning, he found Miles had gone. His 'Dear Shant' note read like a cold set of instructions, what to do, who to call, who to trust, where to send the one last 'part' of Christian, and when Felix would pick up the rest to bring back to the Gila. Shant did as he was told, and then scrambled too many eggs and made too much toast for the others, as if he'd been doing it all along. Later that day, Shant found the manuscript, along with Miles' dog-earned and nearly unbound Complete Shakespeare after all the stomach-churning rigmarole was at last behind him. Inside was the personal note from Miles that Shant had longed for. On pure animal instinct Shant had learnt out on the street how to hide and safeguard the little boy cowering deep inside him. And, if not cleverly but at least instinctively, Shant realized Miles had been doing the same thing: Playing hide-and-seek, even recoiling, not from an unkind world or rotten people but from something deep inside, something Miles himself didn't know from any of the saints, but something he undeniably felt, germinating within. The note confirmed it, making Shant weep, which he rarely did and only with great difficulty and utmost unwillingness.

Shant slid on one of Christian's jock straps (Shant stopped wearing underwear after a john once tried to strangle him with his) the new pair of designer jeans Miles bought him the previous Christmas and one of Miles' White Sox jerseys before heading downstairs to deal with whatever was causing a lot of racket. It was nothing, just squabbling over one of Miles' innumerable books. Shant sat down on the great wraparound front porch, right where he had slept the first few days at the house, unwilling and afraid to go in, huddled in the thick wool quilt Christian treated like a magic carpet. The immediate block was always quiet, but the nearby rest of the city was remarkably still. He could even make out a few far-flung stars beyond the cul-de-sac's one pale streetlamp.

Shant was certain Miles wasn't going off to kill himself, even to be with Christian in the next place. Shant smiled, still a slightly unnatural reflex for him. Miles might go off and kill somebody else, him and that little Beretta of his (which, to Shant's delight, Miles had once ground into the cheekbone of a rat-like Korean pimp who tried to stop him from taking a boy Shant had known out of his grips). No. Shant let out a long, audible breath. Miles may have disappeared, but he wasn't gone. Like he'd read (and re-read almost every night thereafter) in the manuscript, Shant didn't know if what he felt, could still feel, was love, but he knew he wanted it to be. Not just to prove he actually could love someone or long for something other than the next meal, but to try and catch up to where Christian and Miles had been, so inexplicably early, so breathtakingly much, and so wonderfully shared with the most desperate and truly alone.

Shant knew that terrible *alone* Miles had written about, he knew it agonizingly well. But for the first time in as far as he could remember, perhaps most queerly - or least so - in light of Miles' vanishing, Shant Nakhararian did not feel alone. That wall had fallen. His love for both Christian and Miles filled him that hushed night. It stayed with him at the slightly less scruffy manor long after, like a lowered rifle that turned out to be empty in the first place. "Please, Saint Christopher, watch over Miles. Please, Saint Joseph, help me show Christian's love to the folks here now, to anyone else that might come..."

*

A small dog scurried out of the leafy neighborhood's darkness right up to the porch, his wide black eyes boring into Shant's. For weeks, Shant has seen the dog darting in and out of the yards all along the block, but had no idea who if anyone it belonged to. He had no collar or tags and looked hungry, his coat was a wreck, and he smelled a bit. Wow, Shant thought, just like I'm sure I had. "Come on, you." The dog's dark eyes floated around him, not quite sure if the warm house was a trap or Heaven. Shant laughed to himself and thought, I know how you feel, little guy. The dog eventually followed Shant into the house. "Thanks, Saint Francis," Shant murmured.

~ F i n ~

Adam Henry Carrière is an online habitué specializing in letters, publishing design, and instruction. A former NPR broadcaster, he holds a BA in Film & Video from Columbia College and an MA in Professional Writing from the University of Southern California. He has taught writing at both his alma mater and for the United States Navy across the Pacific. Born on the South Side of Chicago, Adam resides in Las Vegas, where he has won the Nevada Arts Council Fellowship in Poetry. He is Editor-in-Chief and Publisher of Nevada's first online literary magazine, **Danse Macabre** and its daily gazette **DM du Jour**. He is the author of the poetry collection **Faschingslieder** (2014).

Shant by Adam Henry Carrière, will be published in 2017 by Hammer & Anvil Books.

Last Chapter review to adam!

Made in the USA
Middletown, DE
27 December 2016